MAYAN BLOOD

Book One of the Stone Legacy Series

Theresa DaLayne

Limitless Publishing, LLC
Kailua, HI 96734
www.limitlesspublishing.com

Formatting: Limitless Publishing

ISBN-13: 978-1-68058-429-5
ISBN-10: 1-68058-429-4

DEDICATION

The Stone Legacy Series is written in loving memory of my late stepfather, Walter E. Donat. With unconditional love and patience, he taught me how to be strong, caring, and most importantly, he never let me forget where the Tigris and Euphrates rivers are. ;) Love you and miss you every day, Walt.

CHAPTER ONE

Zanya

"Let's get the formalities over with before we begin." Dean Nelson shifted through paperwork scattered across the table. "Patient identification number A692. Age, seventeen. Mother, unknown. Father, unknown. No living relatives." He rubbed his bearded chin. "Hmm, that's unfortunate. Name, Zzz…" He flipped back through the case file.

Zanya watched everything from her special spot—center stage in the nearly vacant evaluation room, in a single wooden chair—as he butchered her name, yet again. She should have been used to it, considering every dean who had come and gone did exactly the same thing. "Zan-yuh," she said, "with a short a."

"Ah." He nodded. "Right. Well, now that we've been introduced, let's continue. Nice to meet you, Zanya. I'm Dean Nelson." He smiled, though the deepening creases in his forehead made it seem painful. "How are you feeling today?"

She glanced at him between layers of chestnut brown hair draped along her high-set cheekbones. Squinting, she and blinked under the burning lights, then turned her gaze to the floor. "I'm okay."

"Just okay?"

She shrugged. Why the hell was he acting like he cared, anyway? He was just one in a long line of interim administrators. The stress of working with a school full of insane teenagers every day ran most of them off pretty quick. This one had that eager zeal—all too happy to pick her brain—and he probably wouldn't last long either.

Dean Nelson set down the papers. "I know I'm new here, but in order to conduct your evaluation, you need to answer my questions."

The two board members flanking him shifted in their seats. Zanya's breath sped up. Damn it. If she didn't want to be sedated again, she'd have to keep the panic attack at bay.

She shut her eyes and played a classical melody in her mind. Ludwig van Beethoven's violin concert in D major, *Op. 61—Larghetto*. That piece always slowed her heart rate. She imagined the sounds pouring out of her violin as she caressed imaginary strings.

Dean Nelson cleared his throat, jarring her out of the moment. Annoyance tugged at her, but at least she could breathe again.

She lifted her chin. "I said I'm fine."

"How are you managing the panic attacks? Have you had any recently?"

"Yeah. I had one last night…and the night before."

"They're becoming more frequent?"

If he had bothered to actually read her case file instead of just skimming through it, he'd already know the answer. "Not really. Pretty much the same."

"And how are you sleeping?"

"Like usual."

"It says in your case file you suffer from night terrors. Are you still experiencing them?"

Zanya shrugged.

Dean Nelson frowned. "Okay. Let's talk a little about The Man. Is he still hurting you?"

The mention of him made the hairs on Zanya's arms twitch. She pulled her sleeve over the blue and yellow bruise that encompassed her wrist. This team of board-certified, renowned medical professionals didn't know the first thing about what could be found in her dreams.

They claimed she suffered from severe anxiety and night terrors. They had no idea. The knots in her stomach tightened. She balled her fists, but stayed quiet.

After all, what could she say? If she told them the man in her dreams hurt her almost every night, they would continue to believe she was delusional. If she lied and told them she hurt herself, it would only confirm their misdiagnosis. She'd just tell the truth and prove both theories correct.

"He's always in my dreams." Bits and pieces of her nightmares reeled in her head. "He's always waiting for me."

"But you do understand that a dream cannot hurt you? Dreams are simply images, feelings, and sensations that collect and pool involuntarily in your mind during sleep. They can seem very real, but once you wake up, they're gone. A simple figment of your imagination."

Zanya fidgeted nervously with the sleeve of her uniform, twisting a seam that had come undone.

"And dreams certainly don't leave bruises or any of the other alarming wounds Nurse Faber has found on you over the years." He flashed photos taken during Zanya's countless visits to the hospital.

"I guess." She tucked a lock of hair behind her ear, forgetting about the fresh gash on the back of her hand—evidence of last night's brawl with a demon of some sort.

Nurse Faber leaned forward in her seat and peered at the swollen wound. "Where did you get that cut? I haven't seen that, and it needs to be treated—maybe with stitches."

Dean Nelson scribbled a note on her evaluation paper. "Perhaps we should continue this patient's assessment once we get an updated report of her physical condition."

The nurse stood and waved Zanya to her feet. "Come on, honey. Let's get that taken care of."

***

The stone sat high on the altar's peak, as it always did, glowing like a beacon in the darkness. Its whispers echoed in Zanya's mind, guiding her blind footsteps. It drew her in with some invisible tether—a connection she couldn't explain.

She never understood why she searched for it.

Longed for it.

Needed it.

With each careful step, her bare feet padded up the cool, smooth steps. Then another source of light flickered on, casting a soft glow around her.

The light churned out from her chest, pulsing with hues of blue and white—colors of recognition. The stone and the illumination in her chest seemed to be connected; only flickering to life when they were close.

At the temple's base, she steadily ascended the narrow steps until she reached the peak. Zanya cupped the stone in both hands and lifted it from its perch. Orbs of light twinkled over its smooth surface.

Searing pain tore through her belly. She gasped and jolted forward, then wrapped shaky fingers around a blade protruding from her gut. Scarlet liquid slowly seeped through her shirt. The stone dropped from her hand and thudded to the altar, rolling down one step at a time until it reached the bottom. The blade was yanked out of her, though she couldn't see by whom. No matter. It was always the same person who watched her die.

Zanya stumbled down the steps while gripping her belly. When she reached the bottom of the temple, she fell to her knees and curled into a fetal position, the pain more than she could bear. The edges of her vision became fuzzy. Darkness closed in while she stared helplessly at the stone lying just feet away.

Warmth cradled her body. Death was warm. She'd always heard passing would be peaceful, like slipping into a pool of serenity. With her cheek rested against the cold ground, hot liquid saturated the dry, cracked dirt.

A slithering creature slinked toward her, its eyes as black as onyx. Thousands of legs stuck into the hard soil, pushing its armored body forward.

It was not a creature Zanya would soon forget, as the last time she encountered it, it had killed her—again.

The Man had to be lingering somewhere nearby. His bitter scent whirled through the air. His footsteps grew louder as he approached.

Not again. She lay like a suffocating fish, gulping in her final breaths.

Zanya jerked awake and shot up in bed, gasping for air. She clawed at her chest where a thin mark etched her skin. It burned, as if someone had pressed a cattle brand to the delicate curve between her breasts. She moaned, willing away the pain. It never took longer than a half hour, but it hurt, and this time, it nearly made her cry.

Zanya glanced at a clock mounted on the far wall. It read three thirty. She wouldn't be able to sleep for the rest of the night. She lay back down in bed and rolled onto her side, searching for a hint that Tara was awake. Only a few feet separated their beds. Tara was the only person in the world who understood her.

Tara shifted under the covers, and Zanya caught a glimpse of her face—her angelic, freckled cheeks, rosy and flawless, under dark auburn lashes. Tara yanked the thin blanket over her shoulders and under her chin.

Zanya whispered, "Are you awake?" After a moment of silence, she sighed and exercised her only option—to stare at the ceiling and wait for the morning community alarm.

At six o'clock sharp, the bell sounded. Tara blinked open her eyes. With a sleepy stare, her lips tightened and she let out a deep sigh. "Another nightmare?"

"What else is new? That's the third one this week." Zanya rolled on her side to face her. "At least it wasn't accompanied by a midnight panic attack this time." Zanya touched the now faded mark on her chest. "They're getting worse."

"Any real-life damage?"

Zanya shook her head. "Not this time."

The day unwound as usual. Secular studies followed by a mid-day group therapy session, journal entry writing, and their afternoon dose of medications.

Zanya found her last class of the day and ascended to the fourth row in the music room. Miss Lippard must have been sick. A sub had written his name on the stand-alone chalkboard in the front of the class: Dr. Fitzgerald.

Zanya slouched in her chair, pinching her violin case between her feet.

Great, another doctor. He'd be watching the students during class, assessing, and trying to pick out which students needed more psych work. "Patient B843 has the beginning symptoms of early onset Diogenes Syndrome, and patient A119 seems to be suffering from clinical depression, brought on by early childhood trauma, abuse, or neglect." Blah,

blah, blah. Ugh, she hated doctors.

Tara skipped in, holding her clarinet; an instrument she wasn't particularly good at. All students were required to take up an instrument. Apparently, music helped to express emotion and heal physiological damage.

Tara sat beside her. "Hey." She tucked a curl behind her ear. "New teacher?"

"Just a sub. Miss Lippard is out sick. I needed to ask her a question about our sheet music." Zanya leaned forward and propped her elbows on her knees. "I guess I'll have to wait."

"Yeah. The sub probably doesn't know a thing about music, anyway."

"Well, just try not to be," she waved her hand in the air, "yourself. I don't want him picking your brain."

Tara grinned. "Afraid he'll discover what a genius I am?"

"More like what a—"

"Don't you dare finish that sentence." Tara puckered her lips, then smiled.

When the bell rang, Dr. Fitzgerald made his way to the center of the room. A tailed sports coat hugged his tall, lean frame. His skin—like toasted caramel—complemented his dark brown eyes. He was handsome for a middle-aged man, and she tried to imagine what he might have looked like twenty years ago.

He locked his hands behind his back and cleared his throat. Zanya sat up straight as the room fell silent.

"Good morning." He had a charming Spanish

accent. "As I'm sure you have already noticed, your teacher is out for the day. Everyone please get your books and arrange into groups." He pointed to several areas of the large music room as he spoke. "Strings in the upper right corner, percussion in the lower left, and winds in the center. I understand from Miss Lippard's instructions the advanced strings students are working on a piece, *Canon Pachelbel in D Major*. Those students, please break off to the lower right corner. Everyone else, practice your sheet music."

Violin in hand, Zanya descended the stairs, the soles of her shoes catching on the Berber carpet along the way. *Canon.* She rolled her eyes. If the other advanced students practiced more often, they'd be on to something more challenging by now.

She reached the right corner of the room and took her place at first chair. With the rest of her group ready, she tucked the chinrest in place.

Her fingers relaxed, and she held the bow with balance rather than tension. Her pinkie pinched against the frog, loosely cradling it in her hand, her index finger draped over the top.

Just holding the sleek wooden tool made her breath rhythmic. It was a rare feeling—peace. But with her violin cradled against her and the familiar strings calling out, all her fears melted away.

She drew in a cleansing breath and began to play. The notes pulsed through her body, feeding life to parts of her soul that lay dormant, hiding from the realities of life.

She became lost in the melody while each note

stirred her heart and awoke her senses. The darkness, the pain, it all stepped back, overpowered by the light and energy of the notes. Music was always there to fill the space in her heart that she had locked away.

With one final pass over the strings, the vibrato left her with a feeling of drunken satisfaction. Her muscles relaxed as she exhaled and opened her eyes, then lowered her bow to her lap.

Dr. Fitzgerald watched her intently. His gaze did not waver as she sat motionless, returning his stare. He peered into her. Through her.

The bell rang, and she slinked out of the room, avoiding eye contact with the sub.

***

Weekends weren't much fun at the institution. To kill time, Zanya sometimes listened to Tara's stories about what normal kids did on Friday nights. Parties, bonfires, sleepovers. Teenage girls painting each other's toenails, their polished feet later dressed in fuzzy slippers, and blushed cheeks that accompanied stories about a boy and a kiss.

None of that happened here. And although religion was only taught for educational purposes in their institution, Zanya often felt like she was stuck in purgatory. Long, terrifying nights. Tedious, drawn-out days that always ended in the same way with lights-out in her assigned bed.

Someday it would be different. Someday, things would change.

"Lights out in fifteen minutes," the dorm mother

announced, shuffling through the sleeping quarters. Her shoes squeaked against the tile with every step. "Let's go, ladies." She clapped to gain everyone's attention. "Get changed and into bed."

Zanya snatched her pajamas and slipped into the bathroom. When she came out, all but the backlights were switched off. The soft glow cast over the room painted tall shadows of headboards on the walls.

After settling in bed, she braced herself on the edge and leaned over to inspect the dark space beneath her mattress.

"There's nothing under there," Tara whispered.

Zanya glanced up. "I know."

"No, you don't, or you wouldn't be checking."

Zanya's attention returned to the dark space. If Tara only knew what could be hiding in the darkness, though it was best she didn't. Zanya was glad her friend wasn't taunted by the same horrifying images she was every night. It gave her someone to talk to—someone who wasn't equally paranoid, and who made her feel normal.

A shudder crawled up her arms and down her spine. "There's no harm in checking."

"There's plenty of harm, Zanya." Tara played with the corner of her pillow. "The board will never place you with a foster family if you don't show them you're getting better."

"Who said I want a foster family? Besides, I have you. You're all the family I need." Zanya slipped under the over-starched sheets.

The lights shut off and the room fell silent. Zanya closed her eyes, wishing, praying, that just for one night she would sleep peacefully.

The fire alarm sounded. Bright red-and-white emergency lights cast color over the room. The screaming sirens sent every student shooting out of bed. Staff members flooded the sleeping quarters. They rounded up the children and shouted instructions to form a line and exit the building.

Zanya jumped up and followed Tara to the back door and down a ramp, which lead them outside into the bitterly cold night. She hugged herself as breath flowed from her lips in clouds of white.

Emergency vehicles sped down the gravel driveway. They skidded to a halt, and a team of firemen loaded with gear poured out of the trucks.

While Zanya watched the men in uniform, a strange sensation tugged at the back of her mind. Her eyes narrowed. Shivers quaked her muscles. She blinked and huddled against Tara as a stretcher was unfolded from an ambulance.

"Oh, crap!" Tara's eyes grew wide. "Do you think someone got hurt? I hope it's not another suicide attempt. I swear to God…"

As Tara rambled on, Zanya couldn't shake the feeling someone was watching her. She glanced over her shoulder at the tree line of the forest— aspen and beech trees sprinkled between a thick blanket of fallen leaves. But there was nothing. No one.

She turned back around, the freezing temperatures biting at her toes. She hadn't thought to put on her slippers, and the soles of her feet were paying a heavy price. She balanced on one foot, then the other.

"I mean, if every kid here who hated their lives tried to kill themselves, we'd have nobody left," Tara continued to rant. "Just two more years and I'm so outta here."

A whisper, from what seemed like far away, caressed Zanya's ears. She glanced over her shoulder at the tops of frail trees swaying under the moonlight. Leaves danced across the soggy ground, blown by gusts of chilled wind. She rubbed her arms.

Maybe it was just the breeze. Through the branches, it could sound like a whisper. Just as she prepared to chalk it up to fatigue and chaos, she spotted a tiny shadow lurking between the trees.

Zanya gripped her arms tighter. She blinked once, twice…Her eyes watered from the cold. When she blinked again, the shadow was gone. She spun back around, determined to ignore any more noises.

The image of the tiny shadow pulsed in her mind. Another whisper. Zanya's heart raced. The urge to look again grew stronger, and when she finally collected the nerve, she turned around one last time.

The figure stood motionless just beyond the first row of trees.

Not just a figure—a girl in a thin, white nightgown with her hands hanging at her sides.

Zanya tugged on Tara's sleeve. "Turn around."

Tara's attention was solely focused on the broad-chested firemen. Zanya tugged harder. "Turn around and look at this."

Tara finally obeyed and followed Zanya's

attention toward the trees. She gasped. "What the hell is she doing out there?"

Zanya shook her head. Without saying another word, Tara stalked toward the woods.

"Wha…Where are you going?" Zanya's voice cracked, her gaze flickering between Tara and the child.

"To get her." When Zanya didn't reply, Tara stopped and spun to face her. "Well? Are you coming?"

"Am I coming?" The eerie night suddenly consumed her. "I can't. You know I hate the dark. And there could be…" She frantically searched her mind for some epic excuse to keep Tara from trekking forward. "Wolves."

Wolves? That was the best she could come up with?

Tara snorted. "It's fine, Zanya. I'll go alone. It'll only take a sec."

Zanya shifted her weight as Tara walked toward the shadowed figure standing unnervingly motionless in the woods.

"I…I…" Zanya forced her feet to uproot from the ground and rushed to catch up. "I'll come with you."

Tara grinned. "You have to admit, being eaten by a hungry pack of wolves is still better than being stuck in this loony bin by yourself."

Zanya's eyes widened. She'd made the wolf thing up, but what if…

Tara rested her hand on her hip and cocked her head. "Oh, come on. I'm just kidding."

"Definitely not funny."

"Sorry." She grabbed Zanya's hand. "Now come on. The longer we wait, the more likely it is she'll catch frostbite. Poor thing is out here in nothing but that dress."

Zanya walked over the damp leaves, pushing muddy water through the moss, between the cracks of her toes.

Now just yards away, Tara reached out to the young girl. "Hey. Come here. We'll take you back."

A gust of wind blew, carrying the child's blonde waves off her shoulders. Her bright green eyes seemed to glow in the silky moonlight.

Tara dropped her arms and sighed. "I guess she *likes* freezing her ass off in the middle of the night." When Tara stepped closer, the child darted into the woods. Tara scoffed. "I never want to have kids."

Zanya blinked at the maze of shuddering trees. "Let's get out of here." She stepped back. "Now."

"We have to get that girl. If she stays out here overnight, she'll freeze to death."

Zanya couldn't feel the cold anymore. Whether that was good or bad, she wasn't sure.

The little girl carved a deeper path into the forest.

Tara shook her head. "Something's not right. It's like she's running away from us."

"Maybe she's one of the more critical psych patients."

"I don't know, maybe." Tara cupped her fingers over her nose and mouth to keep them warm while she searched their surroundings. "You're right. We shouldn't have come out here alone. Let's go back."

A tiny girl, no older than eight or nine years old,

stepped into sight. Her nightgown was damp and smeared with mud.

Tara's eyebrows crooked downward. "There you are. Now we can get out of here." Tara held out her hand to the child, who only stared at her reaching fingers.

The child stepped to the side and slid her small hand into Zanya's. The little girl's bare feet was covered in pine needles.

"Come on," Zanya said. "I'll carry you back. You must be freezing out here with no shoes." She would know, being in the exact same situation. She lifted the small-framed child to her hip, and the girl wound her legs around Zanya's body. "What's your name, sweetie?"

She didn't reply.

"She's probably too freaked out to talk," Tara said. "Let's just get back."

Zanya did her best to shield the child from the wind as she followed Tara back toward the orphanage. She hummed the tune to *Romance* softly in the little girl's ear. The melody had always calmed her. Maybe it would do the same for the kid.

The girl's cheek pressed against hers. "Thank you for rescuing me," she whispered in a tiny, angelic voice.

Her humming must have worked. "You're welcome, sweetie."

The girl's blonde hair bobbed up and down with a subtle nod. "Everything will be fine, Zanya. Do not be afraid."

Zanya smiled softly. "I'm not scared. Are you?"

"No." The little girl hugged her tighter. The stars

twinkled above them blurred into streaks. Her head spun and her knees buckled. She collapsed onto the damp forest floor.

Trapped in a thick mental fog, she fought to break through. Her eyes fluttered open and closed. Snapshots of what was happening around her filtered through the cerebral haze.

The girl stood over her, staring down with a sweet face and bright eyes. A tiny smile curled the corners of her delicate lips.

Another voice. It was stronger. Deeper. Who... God, she was so tired. She would give anything to be able to just relax her mind and drift off.

A mixture of voices and a shout from Tara sprouted a renewed resolve, and Zanya pushed against the desire to sleep with all her might. When she managed to force open her eyes, a dark-haired man leaned over her. Tara crept toward him with a small log clenched in her hand.

Heavy lids drew over her eyes.

A loud thud followed by scrambling movements forced Zanya's eyes open one last time.

The man struggled to hold a flailing Tara under his arm like a bag of potatoes while rubbing the back of his head. Was he talking to himself? The child seemed to be paying attention, but didn't reply. Still, while Tara kicked and punched, he continued to hold what seemed like a one-sided conversation.

A second later he dropped Tara to the ground with a shout, and lifted his shirt to find a crescent bite wound over his ribs.

The young girl loomed over Tara; then, silence.

CHAPTER TWO

Arwan

Arwan knelt beside his mother's grave, empty handed. Since he was a young boy, every time he visited he had brought an offering. Something small, to mark that he had been there—that someone had been there.

This year was different. He hadn't stood in front of her grave for three season cycles. Three long years.

"She is back wit' t'e earth." The priestess' thick accent weighed down her words. "It is where she belongs." She rested her wrinkled hand on his shoulder.

"She doesn't belong here."

"One cannot undo what has been done."

"Yeah. I think about that every day." He clenched his jaw.

Drina sighed. "You were only a boy."

A helpless boy.

He examined the new headstone that marked her

grave. Renato would be satisfied his gift fit perfectly.

The old man meant well.

"Can you sense her soul?" Arwan asked.

Drina's hand slipped from his shoulder, leaving it cold. A breeze swept past them, carrying the scent of mountain flowers and crisp water pooled in the valley below.

"Your mot'ers spirit has passed beyond." Drina said the same thing every year; every time he asked. "I cannot see her."

"Do you think she's happy?"

"Happy?" There was a long, silent pause. It was a question he'd never asked her. One that seemed to catch her off guard. "I believe she is proud."

"Of what?"

Deep creases reached from the corners of her dark eyes. "Of her legacy."

He fisted his hands. "You know better."

"She did love you, boy."

He pushed to his feet. "Because she didn't know. She didn't know who..." He turned his face from her grave. "What I am."

Drina pushed him out of the way and shifted to the foot of his mother's grave. Piles of dried corn, jade, pouches of cinnabar, and a whistle carved from stone sat near her headstone. "Your mot'er ascended, yet you mope as if her soul was damned to the underworld." She set another bag of cinnabar over the mounded earth. "You must move on." She turned to face him. "You must not disappoint her."

He scowled. "You say that as if I have an option."

"You do." She smiled softly, something she didn't do often. "Everyt'ing is balanced. The sun wit' t'e moon. Cold wit' heat. Mountain wit' valley."

"Not everything."

"Yes. Everyt'ing." She jabbed her finger at his chest. "But you are too stubborn to remember where you come from. Who you come from." She grabbed a stick from the ground. "Even a mighty tree dies and goes back to the earth." She smacked him in the arm with the stick. "Stupid boy."

He rubbed the spot she'd hit, if for no other reason than to amuse her. The old woman showed love in strange ways. "Thanks, Drina." He placed a kiss on her forehead.

Arwan walked past her, admiring the rolling hills of plush rainforest below. The echoes of monkeys and birds carried through the air. "We should get back. I have to meet with the seeker before returning home. Renato may need me. My phone doesn't work up here, and I haven't heard anything from Marzena."

"Always in a rush. For what? To see the guardian, perhaps?"

Arwan looked at her. "Is she there?"

Drina shrugged. "Perhaps." She waddled past him, toward their Jeep.

"Wait." He caught up with her. She was surprisingly fast for an old woman. "Have *you* heard from Marzena?"

She shrugged again and tugged open the car door, then climbed inside. "Perhaps."

Arwan shut the door and leaned in close through

the open window. "You're a cruel, agonizing woman, you know that?"

She pursed her lips, clearly suppressing a smile. "Perhaps."

Arwan hopped in the driver's seat and started the Jeep. The engine roared to life. He watched Drina, who didn't say a word. "Are you going to tell me what's on your mind?" The woman was never quiet. Not unless she was worried.

She gave a long exhale, her ghostly eyes trained on the mountains below. "I have spent many years wit' you, boy. Good years. Bad years." She met his gaze. "T'ere is a balance, even for you. Everyt'ing has balance."

He shifted the car into drive. "*Tia*…"

She turned away, staring back out at the jungle. "Until you believe you can find balance, you will never find peace."

He shifted the car into drive. At least her intentions were in the right place, even if she could never understand. He would never find peace.

***

Arwan reached the Punta Gorda Airport just as the sun vanished behind the horizon. The car horns, neon lights, and scent of burnt motor oil in the air all reminded him of why he hated the city. It was too busy, too chaotic, and all of the sights, sounds, and smells assaulted his senses.

He pulled up to the passenger pick up/drop off area, where he scanned the crowd of people gathered under the tin roof. With only a brief description from Renato, it would be easy to miss the seeker. The people were mostly women of various ages, some with children tugging on their coats. Elderly men, and middle-aged men dressed in business suits. Some teenagers, though they all seemed like locals.

A guy stepped toward the curb with only a duffle bag hung over his shoulder. His cutoff sleeves showed both of his arms, covered in bold, black tattoos.

Arwan slowed to a stop, peering out the window at the stranger. "Hey." Arwan blasted the horn in two short beeps. The guy bobbed his head, staring down at his phone. Arwan honked again, this time leaning on the horn. The stranger lifted his head and met Arwan's gaze. He stepped forward and flung open the door. "What's up? Are you my ride?"

"Depends. How good are you at hide and seek?"

The stranger grinned. "Pretty damn good." He tossed his duffle bag in the back and sat and slammed the door behind him.

Even seated, Arwan was an inch or so taller than the seeker. He extended his hand. "I'm Arwan."

The seeker ignored his gesture and kicked his feet up on the dash. "Well, I'm starving. Any chance at getting something to eat around here?"

Arwan slowly retracted his hand and rested it on the steering wheel. "What's your name?" He pulled away from the curb.

"Jayden. Where can we grab some grub? Is there a McDonalds around here?" He snorted. "Maybe a Taco Bell."

Arwan worked his jaw. "It's a long drive. Any

stops will slow us down."

"That's why they call it fast food." He plugged one earbud into his ear and bobbed his head. "Any word from Renato? Did he get Zanya?"

"Who?" He glanced at the seeker, who stilled from his question.

"You don't even know her name?"

He did now. Arwan veered right, onto the main road through Toledo City. "How do you know her?"

"I'm a seeker, remember?" He reached in his back pocket and pulled out a beaten, leather wallet. "I can pay for my own food, but seriously, I'm starving." He opened his wallet and pulled out a twenty-dollar bill. Arwan spied a picture tucked behind the clear, plastic window. A picture of a girl with long, brown hair and wolf-gray eyes. The seeker snapped his wallet shut and shoved it back in his pocket, then held up the bill.

"You can't use that here." Arwan turned left, taking them deeper into the city.

"What, you guys don't use dollars?"

"We use the Belize Dollar. You'll have to go to a currency exchange."

"And where the fuck is that?"

Arwan ground his teeth. "That would be at your hotel." He slammed on the brakes, throwing the seeker against the dashboard.

Jayden pushed away, his features tight.

"We'll contact you once Renato decides it's safe," Arwan said. The seeker inspected the hotel with stucco walls painted in sky blue and toucans painted on either side of the entrance. "Or you can find a *peseros* to exchange your money. They'll do it without a lot of paperwork."

"I thought we were going to Renato's house." He turned to face Arwan. "I have to see Zanya. Tonight."

Arwan tightened his grip on the wheel. "Sorry. There must have been *la falta de comunicación.*"

"I speak English."

"*Sí. Inglés.*"

"No," the seeker said, louder now. "E.N.G.L.I.S.H."

What he wouldn't give to punch this ass in the throat. "Get out, seeker."

"I'm not going anywhere until I see Zanya."

Arwan tilted his head and cracked his neck in an effort to release some tension. There was obviously no way to get rid of this idiot without someone getting hurt. He wouldn't bring him to the guardian. Not until he spoke with Renato—until he saw the guardian himself. It was all still so unreal. They'd finally found her, and there was finally hope to put this battle to an end. "She isn't here yet. When she is, we'll send for you. Now get out."

The seeker huffed and kicked open the door. "Fine. But—" Arwan reached in the back seat, grabbed the seeker's duffle bag, and threw it at him. It slammed into his chest. He stumbled back, clenching the bag in his arms. "Hey, asshole. What the—"

Arwan stomped on the gas, peeling away from the curb. The door slammed shut as he shifted gears.

He watched the seeker in his rearview mirror for a moment, then grabbed his cell phone from the cup holder and dialed Renato's number.

It rang only a few times before he picked up. "It's good to hear from you."

"I picked up the seeker."

"Good. Will you be home tonight?"

"Tomorrow, most likely." He paused, pressing the phone tighter to his ear. "I left the seeker in Toledo City."

"You left him?"

"Who is he? Can we trust him?"

"Arwan, he has done everything we have asked, and more. He is the sole reason we found the guardian."

"Zanya."

Renato paused. "Yes. That is her name."

"Why didn't you tell me?"

"Her name?"

"Anything." Arwan's tone was sharp. "You didn't give me any word that she'd arrived. No information about the seeker, that he knew her already. You didn't even tell me her name."

Renato exhaled into the phone. "I wanted to give you time."

"I've had enough time." He turned onto an isolated road, leading into the jungle. "I thought you of all people would not just want to wait around—"

"Let's take this one step at a time. Allow the guardian to find her bearings. She will be frightened when she awakens. She'll have questions that need to be answered. She needs guidance, not pressure."

"Marzena hasn't woken her up yet?"

"We thought it best to allow her to sleep through the night. Tomorrow will be a grueling day, and I hope you have the patience and maturity to stay calm while we work out the details."

Patience was one of his mentor's best, and worst qualities. "We don't have time to waste. We have to find Sarian."

"Our first priority, young man, is to find the stone. If that leads to Sarian, so be it. Either way, we must not push her. The guardian must fulfill her roll on her own terms. In her own time. Until then, you will have to put aside your personal vendetta. That, or do not come home."

CHAPTER THREE

Zanya

Zanya rolled over in bed and pulled the plush feather comforter over her shoulders. The luxurious, satin sheets brushed against her skin.

But the sheets at her orphanage were over-starched and stiff.

Her eyes flew open and she sprang off the pillow-top mattress, landing on the wooden floors of a large bedroom with muted, canary-yellow wallpaper and powder blue accents. It was beautiful. Too beautiful. The perfect stage for yet another death.

She could either sit and cower, or fight. As many times as she'd been through this in her dreams, she always chose the latter.

There had to be something she could use to wake herself. She scanned the room and viewed a shiny object sitting on an antique vanity. She rushed toward it and snatched up the silver letter opener.

The Man could barge in at any second with a

countless number of creatures at his command. If she were going to jar herself awake, she'd have to do something drastic.

Holding her breath, she gripped the handle and drove the sharp, metal tip deep into her forearm. Pain shot up her arm in one swift spike of adrenaline.

Zanya clenched her jaw as blood slid down to her elbow, splattering scarlet drops on the wood floor.

In her dreams, self-inflicted pain was the only way to wake up. To escape. Her eyes widened when she realized—this wasn't a dream.

With a firm grip on the weapon, she silently walked across the room and pushed the door ajar. All was quiet. She slipped through the hall and descended a grand staircase with old wooden handrails. One last step put her in the foyer of a large Victorian-style home.

Voices murmured softly from a room beyond an open entryway. Casually placed footsteps grew closer. She spun and pressed her back against the wall, hoping whoever it was wouldn't notice her as they passed.

A tall, lean man crossed the threshold and into the kitchen without so much as a glance in her direction. Cupboards opened and closed, followed by the clattering of dishes. "Would you like a cup of coffee, Zanya?" His voice curled with a charming accent.

Cautious steps led her toward the kitchen. There was no way of telling if she would have to use her weapon. She swallowed. Please, God, don't make her have to stab someone. She slowly approached the kitchen and spied around the corner at the man pouring coffee. She had seen that tall, lean frame before, with skin the color of toasted caramel, that complemented his dark eyes.

The grip on her weapon relaxed slightly as her lips parted. "Dr. Fitzgerald?"

He held out a steaming mug of coffee. "Yes, that was my name, wasn't it?"

Zanya pushed away the raw fear clawing up her spine.

He peered at the weapon in her hand and frowned. "There is no need for that."

She glared. "So says the creepy kidnapper."

His gentle laugh caressed the air. "I suppose that's true." He noticed her bloodstained pajamas and frowned. "You're wounded. How did that happen?"

Classic pretend-to-care-so-she'll-let-down-her-guard act. Not happening. "Who are you?"

"My name is Renato Coreandero. You may call me Renato. Please, allow me to get you some bandages—"

"Who. Are. You."

He examined her for a moment, then gestured toward the French doors. "Have some coffee with me on the veranda."

Her gaze flickered to the exit. Once she was outside, she'd make a run for it—or at least try.

She cautiously took the mug from the counter. The brew smelled heavenly, but she'd been drugged once already, maybe, and wouldn't take a chance of it happening again.

When she stepped outside, hot, humid air smacked her in the face. The veranda was spacious, made of white, glittering stone and alabaster pillar railings.

"Where are we?" She sat on a wicker chair and set down the coffee on a round stone table. The guardrail was at least twenty feet away. She slid to the edge of her chair, ready to sprint into action, her heels pressed firmly against the cool stone.

He lunged toward her. Zanya jerked away and pushed back on instinct, skidding her chair across the veranda floor. He froze, watching her with parted lips and raised eyebrows. She aimed the letter opener at him, her hand quivering. "Back off."

"I'm sorry." He sat back, taking a moment to collect his composure. "It will be much safer if neither of us has a weapon. I won't hurt you."

Her wound throbbed. She stole another glance at the railing. It was tall and far away, a long chance, but still possible.

"Perhaps if I told you a little about my home, you would feel inclined to put that away."

Irritation plucked her nerves. He must have thought she was stupid. "Not happening."

He crossed his ankle over his knee and sipped his mug of coffee. "Then I suppose I'll just do my best to explain."

"Damn straight. Why did you bring me here?"

"We brought you here after rescuing you from the orphanage."

"Rescuing me?" She froze. Panic flooded her mind. "Tara—where's Tara?" She shot out of her chair. "Is she here?" The idea of leaving her behind was almost more terrifying than being here with this stranger.

"Please, there is no need for concern. My niece, Hawa, took her by horseback to tour the property."

"I want to see her." She aimed the letter opener at him. "I want to see her now."

"I'm afraid you will have to wait until they return. Perhaps you would be satisfied with having some breakfast and freshening up? I'm sure she will return by the time you're finished." He stood and extended his hand toward the doors leading into the kitchen.

She gripped the letter opener tighter.

"Please, Zanya. I don't want to force you into compliance, but I can, and I will if you make it necessary."

Her stomach churned with nausea, and she glared defiantly at him. She could still run, but if she did, it would mean leaving Tara behind—if she were really there. She couldn't take that chance. Worse, he knew it. "I don't have much of a choice, do I?"

Zanya stormed back into the house, through the kitchen, and back up toward the bedroom she awoke in. It wasn't ideal, but there was nowhere else for her to go. Half way up the stairs she came to a realization that stopped her mid-stride. "I uh...I don't have any clothes to change into."

"Of course. Wear whatever you like out of the closet in your bedroom. Some of the clothes are vintage, but I believe you will take a liking to them. You should fit into her clothes quite nicely."

Zanya's peered at him. "Whose clothes?"

Renato mumbled something in Spanish, and then walked away without offering a reply.

***

After giving some much-needed attention to her arm, Zanya set off in search for Tara. The long-sleeved cardigan and jeans she'd found while fingering through the closet fit her fine. Even though she wasn't used to picking her own clothes, she was used to wearing things that covered most of her skin. It had its advantages—like hiding injuries. Today was no exception.

As Zanya wandered barefoot through the house, the wood floors were warm and natural, unlike the cold, sterile tile that covered the orphanage floors. She poked her head into several large rooms. One was a conservatory, with a dark wood desk and a quill pen beside a bottle of ink. The other was what she could only guess to be a greeting room, with plush upholstered sofas and a fully stocked bar.

Zanya finally located Renato in a study at the back of the house. In fact, the room took up almost half the wing. The home was huge, and the fact she was allowed to roam free was unnerving. If she were a prisoner, she would undoubtedly be locked up somewhere. Perhaps it was a false ploy to make her feel comfortable, which didn't make sense either since she had nothing to offer and nothing they'd want. Nothing about this situation made sense.

The bookcases lining the walls towered to the ceilings, making it necessary to have a rolling ladder to reach the upper shelves.

Zanya approached Renato's desk, where he sat puffing on a stone pipe.

"Where's Tara?" Her icy tone didn't seem to faze him.

"I hope your room is satisfactory." When she didn't offer a reply, he continued. "The ladies arrived back a few moments ago. They are in the kitchen having—"

Zanya rushed out before he could finish his sentence. She needed to see Tara, to make sure she was all right. Through the foyer and around a corner to the kitchen, she found her friend sitting at the eat-in table, chatting with a girl of similar age.

"There you are!" Zanya threw her arms around her neck, inhaling the salt and fresh air in Tara's red curls.

"Zanya," she croaked. "You're choking me."

"Oh, sorry." Zanya let go and stepped back. A wave of comfort washed over her as she examined Tara's familiar face. Now that she and Tara were reunited, it was time to concentrate on the next important issue—escaping.

A girl beside Tara, with jet-black hair that fell straight and sleek down her back, cleared her throat.

Zanya wasn't good at meeting new people. She hadn't had much practice, but under the circumstances, she'd have to give it a shot. "Hi." The girl silently inspected her with narrowed, chestnut-brown eyes. "Thanks for taking care of Tara."

"You took long enough to wake up. I couldn't leave her wandering around the house by herself, now could I?"

Zanya turned to Tara. "How long was I asleep?"

"Longer than the rest of us." The girl gestured at Tara with a nod. "Your friend was actually *almost* keeping up with me." She slid off the barstool. Now standing, Zanya could tell she was a few inches shorter than their new best friend. "Speaking of—I have to go brush and feed the horses." The girl glanced at Tara. "Stay out of trouble, would you?"

Tara nodded, and the girl left without another word.

Zanya slowly sat beside Tara. "Who was that?"

"That's Hawa. She's Mr. Renato's niece."

"Oh, right." Zanya paused. "Wait, you've met Renato?"

"Yeah. I had breakfast with him and Hawa this morning. He's a really nice guy."

"Nice? Tara, we don't know these people. We were drugged...or something, and kidnapped, and then brought here against our will. We need to get home."

"Home?" Tara snorted. "Earth to Zanya. We don't have a home, remember? And Mr. Renato said we can stay as long as we want." Tara crossed her legs and relaxed in her chair, bobbing her foot. "I don't know about you, but I'm in no rush to go back."

This was some kind of trap. It had to be. Their lives weren't straight out of a fairy tale. Real people didn't just wake up one day and find themselves in a mansion with rich strangers willing to take them in. Not without paying a terrible price. "This isn't right."

Tara pushed to her feet. "Of course it is. Don't you see? This is our ticket out of that shithole. No more medications. No more isolation. We can finally start our lives. I mean, come on. This place is amazing. Just look at the view. You can't tell me you don't want to wake up to that every day."

Zanya's entire body tensed. Staring at the French doors, she came to a sickening realization. She hurled herself through French doors, onto the patio. Her fingers tightened over the cool, stone railing. As far as the eye could see was unoccupied, pristine beach and aqua blue waves. A gentle breeze caressed her cheek, tickling her nose with salty air. The screaming seagulls snapped her back to reality.

She turned toward Tara, who stood in the doorway with her hand on her hip and an ear-to-ear grin. Tara drummed her long fingers smugly on her waistline. "Welcome to paradise."

Zanya's stomach bubbled and pitched. She pursed her lips and drew in a deep breath through her nose. "I have to sit down. I think I'm gonna throw up." She walked to a chair in the kitchen and sat. "Where exactly are we?"

"Belize. Can you believe it?" Tara's voice was hysterical with excitement. "Where exactly in Belize, I'm not sure. Honestly, I don't really care, as long as we get to stay." She inspected Zanya. "Do you want some water or something?"

Zanya raked her fingers through her hair and pulled it back as she mumbled to herself. "Okay, we're in Belize. How did we get here? I don't have a passport and neither do you. Neither of us has ever traveled outside the U.S." She gasped and stared up at Tara with wide eyes. "What if this is one of those human trafficking things, where we'll be sold to some local drug lord?" Zanya's skin iced over and her feet turned as heavy as ten-pound weights. Her chest constricted until she couldn't breathe.

Tara stooped beside her, gliding her hand over Zanya's back in soothing circles. "Deep breaths. Try to calm down."

Zanya did the only thing that would calm her down. She covered her ears and hummed a melody—*River Flows In You*, composed by Yiruma. Covering her ears isolated the sweet, slowing melody. The tune filled her mind and gave her back the ability to breathe.

A few more breaths and she lowered her hands from her ears. "Once we get some answers from Renato, we'll figure out how to get out of here."

"You have to be conscious to talk to him." Tara vanished for a moment and came back with a glass of water. "Here. Drink this. It'll help."

Zanya sipped the cool liquid, restoring moisture to her throat. "Thanks."

Tara sat down, propping her elbows on her knees and her chin in the palm of her hand. She examined the room with a warm smile. "This place is…It's nice—and, I don't know—" she shrugged, "—homey. I like it here. I like most everything about it, actually." She sat up. "Especially the incredibly good-looking company."

Zanya arched an eyebrow. "Come again?"

Tara grinned. "You'll see."

***

"Ah, you found your friend." Renato stood from behind his desk as Zanya and Tara entered the study.

Renato invited her and Tara to the sitting area with a few sofas in dark leather and an oval coffee table in the center. She was determined to stay close to her friend, but as usual, Tara didn't seem concerned. Tara waved at Renato and then hunkered down on the leather love seat. Zanya sat beside her.

A boy with shaggy brown hair walked toward them. His radiant skin and soft smile seemed to entrance Tara, putting Zanya more on edge. She reached in her pocket and ran her fingers over the sharp edges of the letter opener. It was the only weapon she could find, and one she wouldn't give up.

Tara leaned in close to Zanya. "And—cue incredibly good-looking company," she whispered, studying the blue-eyed boy. He winked. Tara's cheeks flushed so red, they nearly matched the color of her shimmering hair.

Typical. A cute face and Tara goes weak at the knees.

"This is Peter." Renato laid his hand on the guy's shoulder. "Peter, this is Zanya. I believe you have already met Tara."

"It's really nice to meet you. An honor." Peter shoved his hands in his front pockets and leaned in close to Renato. "Where's Arwan? I'm pretty sure he didn't want to miss this."

"I spoke with him last night. He's on his way.

With or without him, we need to focus on the task at hand." He directed Peter's attention to Zanya's arm. "If you don't mind, can you please tend to our guest's wound?"

Tara shifted back and scanned Zanya. "Wound? What happened?"

"It's not a big deal. I've had worse." It wasn't a lie, but the puncture mark still hurt like hell. She'd gotten used to managing pain through ignoring it, pushing it to the back of her mind. The nurse at her school wasn't keen on prescribing anything to dull the discomfort.

Peter knelt beside her and gently rolled up her sleeve.

"Really." Zanya coiled back. "I'm fine."

Peter unveiled brown, clotted blood that had formed a thick scab. He sucked a breath in through his teeth. "Ouch. How'd that happen?"

"It was an accident," she mumbled.

"Some accident."

"What are you, some kind of doctor?" The swollen, red skin throbbed and itched. Her pride was strong, but the fear of infection in a third-world country was stronger.

"I guess you could call me that." He gently laid his hand over the torn skin. Nervous bubbles built in Zanya's stomach while warmth from the guy's touch radiated up her arm. She was used to people touching her, but always on their terms. Here, there were no restraints or drugs to force her cooperation. Zanya shoved Peter back and cradled her limb close to her chest. "I don't like to be touched."

"Well, unless you want an infection, which is a

lot harder to heal, you'll have to let me help you."

"I don't see how touching it with dirty hands is going to prevent infection." She worked her sleeve back over the scab.

Renato cleared his throat. "Then, shall we begin?" He spoke as if he'd said those words a thousand times.

Zanya would match Renato's calm demeanor, for now, though she'd be a liar if she denied the raw panic bubbling just under the surface. She'd have to seem calm, strong. At least until she figured out what the hell was going on. "Tara said we're in Belize."

"Yes. Our home is located in a southern district called Toledo. I have lived here for many years."

"The last thing I remember was walking in the woods with Tara and that little girl. Did you drug us?"

"Certainly not." He seemed horrified at the suggestion. "You were merely sleeping. Marzena assisted us in relocating you." He packed his pipe with loose tobacco and struck a thick wooden match against a sandpaper strip. It popped and hissed with smoke and fire. "I assure you, you were both given the utmost respect during the commute."

The idea of people touching her while she slept made her cringe.

"I'm sure it is a lot to take in," Renato continued. "Marzena is a close friend of mine. In fact, she wanted to formally introduce herself, if you wouldn't mind. I believe she can provide answers to many of your questions."

"Um..." Her gaze flickered from him to Peter,

and back to the stately man. She slipped her hand back into her pocket, curling her fingers around the letter opener. "I guess."

The sound of brushing fabric alerted Zanya someone was behind her, though she hadn't noticed anyone walk into the room.

Her stomach cramped, remembering the quiet approach of the nurses holding loaded syringes and the mental blackout that always followed.

She quickly spun in her seat to see Hawa, leaning against a marble pillar, her arms crossed and her lips curved in an arrogant grin.

"You can't honestly believe she'll be convinced just by meeting Marzena, do you, Uncle?" She lingered for a moment, then vanished.

Zanya blinked, searching the space where the girl had stood.

"Over here, pumpkin."

Zanya spun back to Hawa, now sitting in a chair opposite her with a magazine propped in her lap.

"How..." Zanya glanced over her shoulder again, then back to Hawa. "You..."

"You'll get used to it." She flipped through the pages of her magazine, seemingly bored.

"My niece is quite nimble," Renato said, "though I did hope to ease you into these details." His eyes narrowed, focused on the girl. "Hawa, would you be so kind as to fetch Marzena?"

Her jaw dropped. "I just got here. Marzena's all the way in the north wing."

"Since you are so keen on exercising your talent, at least you can put it to good use."

Hawa rolled her eyes and tossed her magazine on

the table. "Fine," she mumbled, and then vanished in a streak of color.

Zanya buried her fingers in her hair. Had she finally lost it? "What the hell is going on here?" She looked up at the others, their faces now blurry from the spinning in her head. "How did she—"

"So. Cool." Tara beamed with a smile, staring after Hawa.

"Please excuse my niece. She hasn't had female company for quite some time and has forgotten her social graces. I'm sure once she warms up to you, you will become good friends." He shifted in his seat. "While Hawa is fetching Marzena, perhaps you can tell me a bit about yourselves."

What was there to tell, really? She'd been stuck in an institution her entire life. But if she was going to get to the bottom of this insane situation, she'd have to give a little. Tactfully, she sat back and allowed her rigid muscles to relax. "Tara and I live in an orphanage in Ohio. I've been there all my life, and Tara, for almost six years."

"So, neither of you have any family?"

"No." Zanya laid her fingers gently over Tara's wrist. Talking about their lives was hard for Zanya, but it was always much more difficult for her friend.

Renato turned his attention to Tara. "Do you mind if I ask why you were sent to that particular orphanage?"

She bit her lip, and her fingers tightened over the fabric of her shirt. For the first time, she tore her gaze from Peter. "I, uh…my dad has never been around, and my mom…well, she wasn't around much either."

41

"Who took care of you?"

She shrugged. "I kinda took care of myself. My mom was…neglectful, as they called it. If she was home, it was because she brought back a new boyfriend and was busy entertaining him. I was put in that particular orphanage because…" She swallowed and rubbed her palms along her jeans. "Sometimes my mom would leave me home alone with one of her boyfriends, and…uh, well, they usually didn't care who was entertaining them."

There was a long, silent pause. Zanya tightened her fingers around Tara's wrist. "But that doesn't matter anymore. As long as we're together, we have family. Tara's my sister, and the closest thing to family I've ever had."

Peter's eyes had saddened; he focused intently on the floor.

"So, no." Zanya smiled softly at Tara. "We don't have parents, but we have each other."

Renato removed the bone pipe from his mouth and leaned forward in his chair. "Yes. You have each other. Very good."

Hawa returned to the room in a streak of color, followed by a young, blonde girl at normal pace. "We're back," Hawa stepped aside, allowing Marzena to pass.

"Zanya, this is my dear friend Marzena— Marzena, this is Zanya and her friend Tara." Renato gestured through the introductions.

The girl slightly bowed her head in response.

"You're the little girl from the woods."

The child simply stood there, still and brilliant, with blonde waves cascading over her frail shoulders and tiny bronze freckles dotting her milky skin.

"Marzena is very gifted. She is our group's dream-walker and plays a vital role in our endeavors. She has assisted in influencing and infiltrating the human mind in ways we are normally not capable of."

Influencing the mind. Like a shrink? Obviously not, considering her age. But at least Zanya would know how to deal with that. She'd had more psych evaluations than she could count, and had more or less figured out how to manipulate the outcome.

There was something peculiar about the girl. Zanya hadn't noticed it in the woods, but she carried herself in a way unlike a child. The kids in her institution couldn't hold still for more than ten seconds at a time—if that.

The hairs on her arms stood straight up and a wave of goose bumps traveled over her skin. She turned to Renato, who clearly had manipulation talents of his own. The guy didn't seem the least bit concerned over the fact he'd smuggled two girls out of the country. "You need to start talking. Like, now."

"She's not ready," Peter said.

Renato raised his hand and silenced Peter, who blew out a puff of air in compliance.

Okay, so this Renato guy was the clear leader. He was the one everyone else answered to and obeyed.

Zanya shifted to the edge of the couch. "Not ready for what?"

Renato examined her for a moment before he

spoke. "We brought you here to recover the stone of Muuk'Ich, the only surviving legacy of the Maya. The stone was blessed by the gods and given to a guardian to protect. The last guardian was killed, and the stone was taken. You are the only one who can locate, retrieve, and protect it from underworld forces. This is your destiny."

Zanya's eyebrows shot up.

Hawa snorted. "That was laying it on a little thick, don't you think?"

Renato simply waited for a reply.

"My destiny? You want to help me fulfill my destiny…with a rock?"

"The *stone* has existed since the days of the early Maya civilization; the civilization of our creation—of your people."

"Of my people," she said, more as a statement than a question.

"You are a natural-born leader, Zanya. You have a great responsibility, one that you must first understand, and then accept."

Zanya laughed, mostly from nerves. Renato's expression didn't waver. She blinked and her smile vanished. "Oh, you're serious."

Renato retrieved a leather-bound book from the table beside him and handed it to her. It was open to a page with strange symbols. He pointed to a drawing of a stone altar. "The first record of our people dates back to 1800 B.C. in the Formative Period. The earliest texts of the enchanted ones were found in the Temple of Inscriptions, carved into the stone walls. They named our kind Riyata, meaning ones with inner strength. Men capable of carrying tremendous weight, such as myself. Healers. Sprinters, like my niece. Even those who can manipulate elements."

Zanya tore her attention away from the pages. "What, like superheroes?"

"Where do you think the idea came from?" He sat back in his chair. "Comic book characters, children's fairy tales. Every myth has some truth in it, Zanya. We were given a great responsibility—to protect humans from the forces of the underworld." His open hands teetered side to side like a balance scale working to even out. "Thus, the age-old battle of good versus evil."

Her back fell against the cool surface of the leather love seat.

They had been taken from one madhouse and thrown into another. The only difference was these people didn't know they were crazy.

CHAPTER FOUR

Zanya leaned over the bathroom sink and splashed cool water onto her face. She stared into the mirror. All the color drained from her cheeks. "Get it together." If she didn't want to wake up facedown on the bathroom floor, she'd have to calm down.

The toilet was the only available seat, so she rested onto the lid and cradled her head in her hands, drawing in deep breaths. *The Gadfly Suite* by Shostakovich was her saving grace. The sweet melody eased her anxiety until the spinning in her head eventually stopped.

She blinked open her eyes to a reddish-brown stain on her sleeve. With the gauze removed, blood had seeped through the fabric, leaving a tarnished stain.

She walked to the sink and turned on the water, snatching an embroidered hand towel off the rack. She damped the rag with warm water and wiped the clotted blood from her skin. Every gentle stroke sent flakes of scab swirling down the drain.

Zanya's breath hitched when the dry blood wiped away. The wound was still there. It had to be. Injuries like that didn't just vanish.

Her skin burned from her scrubbing with the texture of the towel. She stopped, staring down at supple, irrefutably flawless skin. The cloth slipped from her fingers to the floor.

"What the hell..." She recalled Peter's warm hands pressed over her wound. She flung open the bathroom door and crossed the study, her hands balled into fists. Peter glanced from Renato to Zanya, pushing back in his seat as if bracing himself for impact. She stopped right in front of him. "What did you do to me?" She glared at Renato. "Who the hell are you people?"

"If you would calm down for a moment—"

"To hell with this." Zanya pulled the letter opener from her pocket. She pinned her knee to Peter's chest and pressed the blade to his throat.

Tara shouted.

Hawa shot to her feet, shifting her weight and pumping her hands.

Renato extended his hand to Hawa.

Peter swallowed against the metal edge. "I...I was just trying to help."

"You." She leaned into him. "What did you do to me?"

"I'm so going to kick your ass," Hawa said from where she stood.

Zanya scoffed. "You're like him. Who are you? *What* are you?"

"Why aren't you doing anything?" Hawa scowled at Renato.

Renato stepped forward, his fingers curled around his jacket lapel. "I certainly could, if I wished. Any of us could. The important thing is that Zanya makes the decision on her own. That she learns to accept who she really is. Who we all are."

"I disagree." Peter pushed his back against the couch.

"People don't heal that fast," Zanya said. "It's just not possible. Now you tell me what's going on, or I swear—"

"You'll what?" Hawa shifted her weight, her hands balled into fists. "You'll have no one to protect you if you so much as give him a shaving nick."

"Zanya." Tara's voice caught her attention. Her friend slowly pushed out of her seat and extended her hand. "I know you. You aren't a..." Her gaze flickered to the letter opener. "You're not this person."

The savage heat pulsing inside her was cooled by the tears welled in Tara's eyes.

"Please, Zanya." Renato slowly sat and relaxed into his char. "I'll do my best to tell you exactly who we are and, more importantly, who you are."

"'We're ancient superheroes' is not an explanation." She glanced at Tara, who had tears streaking down her face. Even though they didn't know much about Renato or these people, Tara wanted to be here. She wanted to be anywhere but back at the orphanage. Zanya looked back to Renato.

She could either kill this Peter guy and make a valiant effort to run for it, or back off and hear the madman's story. The latter seemed more realistic, considering the black-haired, snarky one was some kind of track star on crack. Plus, it wasn't likely Tara was as willing to fight her way out, which would most likely mean leaving her behind. That was not an option.

Zanya tightened her grip on the letter opener and ground her teeth. "You're not leaving me much of a choice."

He smiled softly—a reassuring kind of smile. "We all have a choice, my dear Zanya."

When she pushed off of Peter, he sucked in a breath and touched his throat where the blade had left a thin, red line.

"Oops." She glared at Hawa. "I wouldn't call that a shaving nick, wouldn't you?"

Everyone watched in silence as Zanya moved to her friend's side. They sat, and she took Tara's hand. Zanya drew in a deep breath, working to recollect her composure.

A flash of color followed Hawa, who landed beside her in the blink of an eye. Then another streak cued her sprint back to her chair across the room.

It happened so fast, Zanya didn't have time to react. She looked down at her hand, which was now empty.

"I'll be hanging onto this." Hawa sat, her legs crossed, playing with the letter opener between her fingers. "Sharp things are dangerous when they're handled by idiots."

"You should be extra careful then," Peter mumbled.

Hawa's eyes darkened. "Jerk."

Renato leaned forward. "Let us not forget our history. We have had quite enough blood shed of our kind."

"Our kind?" Zanya suppressed the urge to roll her eyes. But the fact she had no weapon was a game changer. She'd have to shift gears. Play nice. Seeing she had plenty of experience with her psychiatrist, it was a role she'd become skilled at. "Go ahead." She withdrew her focus from Hawa and trained it on Renato. "Tell me. Tell me who you think I am."

Renato crossed his ankle over his knee. "What do you know about heaven and hell?"

She shrugged. "Whatever we learned in world religion and history classes."

"Did you learn about the history of the Mayan civilization?"

"Just that they were famous for measuring time, medical treatments, and knowing a lot about astronomy. They were also barbaric. Practiced human sacrifices. Bloodletting. That sort of thing."

"And what are their religious practices?"

"I really don't remember. Can you get to the point?"

He leaned forward in his chair, his eyes gleaming with whimsical anticipation. "Allow me to fill you in on the true history of the Maya. The history you won't find in books." He drew another long puff from his pipe. Fear slithered inside her, mirrored by the smoke seeping from Renato's lips.

"Many millennia ago, the gods feared for mankind. They knew humanity was no match for the underworlders, who strove to control every realm in their quest for power. As a result, the middleworld gods, who have limited abilities, pleaded with the deities of heaven to help protect mankind. Seeing the poor chances the humans stood to defend themselves, they gave the people a tool; a stone from the earth, blessed with the ability to transform human into Riyata. A guardian was chosen to protect the stone, and for generations, did. That is, until she was captured, slaughtered, and the stone was taken from her possession."

A migraine throbbed through Zanya's temples. She massaged the ache, only spreading it behind her eyes. She sighed and squinted at Renato. This guy must have thought she was a total idiot. "Tell me, Renato, if that's even your real name. How do you know all of this? Did someone tell you this ridiculous story, just like you're telling me now?" The migraine surged with her aggravation. "How gullible do you think I am? You really expect me to believe all this? Underworlders? An ancient super-race of enlightened people transformed by a magic stone? Where are the vampires and werewolves? Oh, and the giants? You forgot the giants." She crossed her arms, tapping her fingers over her biceps. "I'm sure they wouldn't appreciate that very much."

Renato's gaze intensified. "I know because I was one of the first volunteers to be changed by the stone."

A tiny wave of relief washed over her. The story had taken a turn for the ridiculous. "Oh, come on. That's not even possible." She leaned forward with a smug purse of her lips. "You forgot to do your math. That would mean you've been alive—"

"Longer than I can keep track of. I have witnessed man discover the earth is round, the creation of penicillin, and the birth of electricity. However long it has been exactly, I couldn't say."

Zanya sat back, her lips parted. "You can't be serious."

"Riyata generally stop aging between sixteen and forty years old, unless you are a dreamwalker." He gestured to Marzena. "We may stop aging, but that does not mean we cannot die. Countless have fallen while protecting the stone. Life can be prolonged, but it can never be ensured."

Renato extended a book. Zanya slinked back. Maybe he didn't mean any harm, or maybe he did. She still couldn't tell. Either way, old habits die hard. She examined it for a moment before taking it from his grasp.

On the aged paper was a drawing of a woman who stood with her arms outstretched and her face tilted toward the sky. An illuminated orb of light glowed from under her skin. Threads of recollection tugged at her. She pushed them away, refusing to fall into his black hole of madness.

Tara tilted the book toward her for a better view. "Wow."

It was time to put an end to this. "If I am who you say I am, why haven't I ever felt different? I mean, consider the facts." Renato listened, puffing his pipe with no particular expression. In fact, he seemed completely convinced of his own story. Convinced this fantasy world he lived in was real.

"You know, facts? They're those little tidbits of information that make things real. Scientific documentation, studies, and observations of things you can see, taste, touch, and smell."

"Such as the wound on your wrist being miraculously healed by the touch of a healer's hand."

She ran her fingers across the area where it had been, the skin supple and flawless. Her stomach fluttered and tightened. She still hadn't figured out how she healed so quickly, but there had to be an explanation.

"Zanya, I know this is difficult to understand," Renato continued. "But please trust me. We have been searching for you for a very long time. Searching for the Stone Guardian who would save us from the dark powers of the underworld. With our people so scarce, in hiding, and afraid to expose their abilities, we are very limited on resources. You are truly our only hope."

"How are you sure? There's never been so much as a hint that I was anything more than just a girl. Super strength, healing, and whatever the hell she does." She gestured to Hawa. "How can I be capable of any of that?" She held up the book. "I'm sorry, but I'm not the one you're looking for." She searched Renato's face for an expression other than certainty, but found none.

"You are the Stone Guardian. The responsibility was handed down to you by your mother, as it was handed down to her."

Zanya widened her eyes, and a wave of heat rushed over her skin. She gripped Tara's hand.

53

"Wait…" She swallowed against a dry throat. "You…you know my mother?"

"I knew her, yes." Renato stood and walked to his desk, where he picked up a picture frame that faced away from the sitting area. He stared into the photo, lost in thought. "She and I were very close." He ran his fingers over the black velvet backing. "Her name was Eleuia. I called her Ellie. She was an honorable woman who loved your father. She loved you too, very much, Zanya." He crossed the room and handed her the frame.

Zanya snatched it and peered at the black-and-white photo of a beautiful woman with long dark hair and light eyes. She stood on a stone path wearing a summer dress, her hands gently resting on her pregnant belly.

"Is this really her?" Suddenly, she desperately wanted it to be true. She wanted to believe the woman in the photo was the person she had longed to know all her life.

"Yes, that is the last photo I took of her before—"

Zanya raised her gaze to Renato, and then Marzena. The girl tilted her head and spoke, though no words passed through her lips. Instead, her voice echoed in Zanya's mind. Zanya dropped the frame into her lap and clasped her hands over her ears, clinching her eyes shut. "You are capable of doing this, Zanya. We cannot succeed without you." When Marzena's voice faded into the recesses of her mind, Zanya forced her eyes open.

"I hope you will consider staying," Renato added. "I know I am asking you to trust a group of complete strangers, but I assure you that you and Tara are safe here. You will come to understand the importance of the stone and your responsibility toward it."

Zanya's focus never wavered from Marzena's angelic face. The silence was taunting, something she should be used to after spending endless nights listening to only her heartbeat, lying alone in her orphanage bed.

Zanya pulled her knees to her chest and buried her face between the humps of her knees. No amount of music could settle the unraveling of her mind.

The Man who haunted her had always been a mere figment of her imagination. He had always been in her head—a twisted reminder of her supposed mental instability.

The wounds acquired in her lucid dreams were painful reminders that The Man was waiting for her. He lurked in the empty space of her subconscious, looming in the shadows, disguised as insanity.

He'd lived there his entire life.

Believing these people's impossible stories would mean the monster with dark hair, empty eyes, and an inauspicious grin, was real. That she was never crazy, and all of the medications and nights spent in hospitals were a lost cause. Worse, it meant the one who cloaked his desire with torture, his motives with greed, and his power with the service of horrifying creatures, was coming for her.

If she believed them, it would mean there was no limit. The door between dream and reality would be flung open. Anything could cross between them.

And there was no doubt it would.

Her friend's gentle touch reminded Zanya to breathe. Tara rested her head on Zanya's shoulder, spilling curls over her chest. "Even if it's all a lie," Tara whispered, "it's a beautiful lie."

Zanya searched her memory, riddled with images of the stone. "W-what does the stone look like?"

Renato stood, grabbed another book from a shelf, and handed it to her. She opened it and scanned the pages until she came found a drawing of the stone, roughly the size of a mango. Light shined from its core, illuminating its walls.

Zanya's lips parted. "I've seen this before." She glanced around the room. "I, uh, I have nightmares. I've seen the stone in my dreams."

"I have no doubt your true abilities have made themselves known to you, even if only in your subconscious. There are still many things you do not know. Please understand that I would not have brought you here if I was not one hundred percent sure of your identity."

Zanya picked up the photo in the silver frame.

"You look exactly like her." The tender edge to his voice caught her off guard.

"You have to at least try," Hawa said. "What do you have to lose? No one will miss you at your school, and your friend is here with you. If you don't try, you'll grow up wondering what you could have been other than some pathetic orphan."

Zanya sucked in a breath.

"Hawa," Peter scolded. "How can you say something like that? What's wrong with you?"

"I don't know, Peter. But I bet you have a long

list written up to share with everyone. Why don't you start with—" As if she had suddenly become aware she had an audience, Hawa crossed her arms over her chest and sat back in silence.

Zanya turned to Tara. "You've already made up your mind, haven't you?"

Tara shrugged. "I'll go wherever you go, but..." Tara's eye swelled with more tears. "I can't go back."

The sadness in Tara's voice tore at her. Every day they woke in the community sleeping room, a tiny piece of her best friend died. Tara wanted the life that had always been just out of her reach. She didn't want to go back to the probing and monthly strip searches for hidden wounds they both endured. Tara couldn't return, and Zanya wasn't going to make her.

She stood and offered the book back to Renato. "For the record, I don't trust you."

"You will learn to, in time."

"And we don't owe you anything."

"Understood."

Zanya shifted her weight. "And I'm not agreeing to this because I need you, got it? Because I don't. We don't."

A smile curled the edges of Renato's lips. "Are you agreeing to stay?"

She tightened her jaw, holding Renato's gaze. "Under one condition. You have to tell me everything you know about my mother."

His smile widened. "Of course."

"So, are you going to tell her the rest?" Hawa arched a brow.

Zanya's shifted back. "Tell me what? There's more?"

Renato put out his pipe and set it down on his desk behind him. "We can start with the day your parents told me they were expecting. Ellie couldn't stop giggling, and your father was beaming with pride." Zanya's jaw dropped open. "I, of course, was equally thrilled I would soon have a niece."

Zanya's fingers went numb and her breath stalled. Renato stood, grinning like a madman. He burst into laughter and threw his arms around her. "I'm sorry, Zanya. I desperately wanted to tell you earlier. This house is the house your mother lived in many years ago. You are staying in your parents' bedroom." He braced his hands on Zanya's shoulders, his arms outstretched. He admired her as if in that very moment he were seeing her for the first time. "Ellie would be happy to know you're back home."

Zanya's throat tightened and she peered at Hawa. "If he's my uncle, does that mean…"

Hawa smirked. "You're not that lucky. I'm not your sister. I'm your cousin."

"Good God," Zanya whispered. "How much family do I have?"

His expression became solemn. "We are the only ones left." The warmth slowly drained from his eyes, and was replaced with what she could only identify as pride. "Everyone here has come from different places for various reasons, all for a mutual goal. Those of us standing here are the few who are brave enough to fight for what is rightfully ours."

"So…what now?" Tara asked.

Renato handed Zanya a small stack of books. "Here is some literature for you to read. Please don't skip any of them, as all of them hold pertinent information that will be useful to you."

"And will these books tell me how to, you know, do whatever I'm supposed to do?"

"You need to protect the stone, but first, we must locate it so there can be a bond. You cannot do that alone. Not yet. I've called in reinforcements to help."

"Really?" She gripped the books tighter against her chest. "Who?"

After a slight shake of Hawa's head, Renato sighed. "This cause is of the utmost importance. Sometimes we must do things in order to ensure that our plans move ahead without delay or errors. The person who is coming to help—please, just promise you will try to be patient."

"What?" She glanced between Hawa and Renato. "You won't tell me who it is?"

Marzena's voice echoed in her mind. "One step at a time, Zanya. You have been through quite a lot today. Take some time to explore."

Renato nodded. "Yes. I believe some rest and relaxation would be good for you before things get…eventful."

Hawa stood and strutted past her, pausing just long enough to let out a fleeting comment. "Better get ready. I hear he's excited to see you."

CHAPTER FIVE

Arwan

Arwan walked through the open entryway of the front of the house. "*Hola.*" He closed the door, listening for a response. "Renato, I'm home."

"In here." Peter's voice came from the kitchen. Arwan walked through the hall, turned the corner, and stopped short. A fair-skinned girl with red hair sat at the kitchen bar, giggling as she picked at a burnt pancake.

She didn't look anything like Renato, or Eleuia from what he'd seen of her in the photo on Renato's desk. Perhaps her father had red hair. Arwan stepped forward and gave a formal bow while holding her gaze. "It's an honor to meet you."

The redhead's expression wiped blank, and Peter chuckled. "Arwan, this is Tara. Zanya's friend. Tara, meet Arwan. The local trainer and general badass of the town."

Arwan stood, examining her. "You're not the guardian."

"Nope." Her eyebrows bounced. "But I think she'll be mighty happy to see you." She winked.

Arwan shifted his weight. Was she hitting on him? Though she seemed nice enough, he wasn't interested. He turned to Peter. "Where's Renato? I need to speak with him."

"He ran into town to grab some supplies, but he'll be back soon." Peter pushed a plated pancake across the counter. "Hungry?"

There was no time to eat. Not when the guardian was there, and he hadn't laid eyes on her. "Did he take the guardian with him?"

"No. She's on the beach. Renato said he wanted you to wait to talk to her." He shrugged.

Arwan checked his watch. It was only nine-thirty. "*Bien*. Then we have time to train. Get geared up." He had to see her, just for a second, to know she was really there.

Peter's shoulders slouched forward. "But I haven't eaten—"

"Then you should have woken up earlier." He gestured to the veranda that lead to the beach. "Five minutes." He looked at Tara. "Nice to meet you."

"Yeah." She swallowed a mouthful of pancake. "You too."

He walked through the double doors, onto the veranda. The guardian was nowhere in sight. He yanked off his shoes and socks, then stripped off his shirt. The warm breeze wove through the tall, alabaster pillars. He jumped the railing and landed in the hot sand.

Arwan drew in a deep breath, balling his hands into fists.

"Ready." Peter followed him over the railing.

"That's what you said last week." Arwan pulled the drawstring to his sweatpants tight. "Have you been practicing while I was gone?"

Peter stretched one leg out in front of him, then the other. "On and off. I've been kind of busy—"

Arwan threw a low kick and swept him off his feet. Peter hit the sand—hard—and sucked in a labored breath. He coughed and rolled to his side.

"I thought you said you're ready."

Peter nodded, pushing himself to his feet. "You caught me off guard."

"Do you think your enemy is going to give you a heads up every time he attacks?"

"No." Peter swept grains of sand off his shorts. "I guess—"

Arwan threw a left hook. It landed on Peter's chest, throwing him back. Peter narrowed his eyes. "Come on, man."

"Your lack of preparation is disappointing. You said you would train every day while I was gone." He readied into a fighting stance. "Every. Day."

Peter shifted his foot back and lifted his fists. "Things got crazy while you were out." He tightened his fists. "Warm up?"

Arwan grinned "Warm up."

Peter sprinted down the beach. Arwan chased, staying on Peter's heels as they raced over grains of sand. "Faster."

Peter puffed out his chest and picked up the pace. Good, but not good enough. Arwan leaped ahead and threw a roundhouse kick at his head. Peter skidded to a stop and arched his back, barely dodging the attack before he rolled forward and landed on his feet. Peter struck a few punches, all of them too slow and not strong enough.

"You're not focused." Arwan tested his theory with a solid punch to Peter's jaw, followed by a front kick to his chest.

Peter landed in the sand and spit out a mouthful blood. "Just because I can heal fast doesn't mean I enjoy getting my ass kicked."

"Then stand up and show me what you got." Arwan extended his hand. Peter took it, and Arwan pulled him to his feet. The blemished skin on Peter's face had already begun to heal.

Peter punched Arwan in the gut. Arwan let out a muffled grunt and raised his brow. "Not bad." He slashed Peter in the face with an elbow strike, cutting deep into his cheek. The clash of bone on bone vibrated up Arwan's arm. Peter doubled over and cradled his face, mumbling a string of curse words as blood seeped through is fingers. A moment later the wound had healed, and Peter fisted his hands even tighter.

"Healing is your one advantage. But you can still be killed. Never forget that."

A flash of blue caught Arwan's eye. He peered over Peter's shoulder.

Peter glanced back, and returned his gaze to Arwan. "Before you go doing something crazy—"

Arwan stepped around him and to get a better look at the guardian. Long, brown hair brushed over her narrow shudders, with olive skin. Every muscle in his body tensed. There was an aura about her— the way the sun reflected off of her petite silhouette.

"Hey." Peter stepped in his line of sight. "Renato said to wait."

Arwan clenched his jaw. "Did he say why, exactly?"

"I don't know. Ask him." Peter gestured to the house. "He just got home."

Arwan turned to see Renato's SUV pull into the covered garage. "*lo haré*." He walked toward the house.

"Um…" Peter jogged to catch up with him. "Are we done with training?"

"No. Meet me at the cliffs in one hour. I have to talk to Renato."

Peter slowed his pace. "I guess I'll just…hang out." He huffed.

Arwan reached the veranda and hopped back over the railing. He grabbed his shirt and slipped it on, then continued inside. "Renato."

"*Sí*. In the welcoming room." Arwan followed his mentor's voice through a pair of open double doors, into a small room with a bay window. He shook Renato's hand firmly.

"It's nice to have you back," Renato said. "I hope your trip went well."

"I'm sorry if I was gone too long. I hope you didn't need me." Arwan withdrew his hand, glad to see Renato smoking the familiar bone pipe—the same pipe Renato had smoked since Arwan was a boy. Renato was most likely worrying about him, as he often did. Even at Arwan's lowest times, Renato was always there.

Renato slid his hand down the lapel of his gentleman's vest and braced his pipe in his mouth with the other. "We can survive without you for a short while. Besides, what you were doing was equally as important." Sadness flooded his gaze. "I hope you gave your mother my regards."

Arwan's chest tightened. It was still difficult to talk about, even though he'd done his mourning years ago. "I did."

"And the headstone?"

"It was a fine replacement. Thank you." He leaned against an alabaster pillar supporting the Victorian style fireplace. "It's been too long since I went to see her." He perched an elbow on the stone mantel, admiring the night sky through windows.

"Your mother would have understood."

"Maybe." She would have, but there was no excuse that would make him forgive himself.

An electronic ring came from Renato's pocket. He pulled the phone and promptly answered the call. "Yes?" His expression stayed passive. "You're where?" He looked at Arwan. "Did he?" Renato pinched the bride of his nose. "Yes. Stay where you are. I will contact you when it's time." He held up his finger for another moment of patience. "I'll wire the money right over." Renato flipped the phone shut and tucked it back into his pocket. "That was the seeker. He requested funds for food and hotel stay. Did you not assist him before you left?"

Arwan scowled. "How much can we trust him?"

"As much as we can trust any of our people."

"How much does he know?"

Renato waved his hand in the air. "He seems to know little of our ancestry—typical for the younger generation of descendants."

"It's not my ancestry. Not anymore."

"One cannot run from their bloodline."

Arwan scoffed. "I've been doing a decent job so far."

"Indeed." That one word, spoken in that accusatory tone, was enough to reel back Arwan's annoyance. "How is Peter's training going?"

Arwan examined his mentor. Anger morphed to impatience, plucking his nerves. "Why don't you want me to meet the guardian?"

"We both know why."

Arwan ground his teeth. "Sarian has eluded us for long enough, and she's the only one who can help us find him."

"There are more important things than revenge, young man."

"*Like what*?"

"Like recovering the stone. She may be the only hope we have of finding the general who killed your mother, but we must not forget—she knows very little about the stone. Nearly nothing."

"That'll make finding it more difficult."

"That's precisely why I have called in the seeker."

Arwan turned away. "I don't think it's safe to bring him around the guardian. He seems reckless."

"He is the only one who is willing to help. We have little choice but to trust him."

Arwan examined his mentor. "I thought you said we always have a choice."

Renato rested his hand on Arwan's shoulder. "Do not rush her. This mission is more sacred than revenge. The fate of the world is in our hands."

His mentor was usually right, and had the patience Arwan had yet to learn. Arwan planted a firm hand on Renato's opposite shoulder, engaging in a more traditional embrace. Warriors greeted each other with hands braced on alternate shoulders, such as they had done for centuries. "I'll do my best."

There was a knock on the door.

"Um…hello?" An unfamiliar voice called from the hall. "Renato?"

His mentor stepped away. "Well. It seems as though the gods have fated you two to meet sooner than I intended."

Arwan leaned against the bookshelves in the corner of the room while Renato answered the door. The same soft voice came from the hall. He leaned slightly to the side, catching a glimpse of the girl he'd seen on the beach.

She curled her arms around herself, still wearing the blue dress. She drew strands of wild hair over her shoulder. "I almost got lost trying to find my way around your house."

"Our house," Renato replied. "You must remember, this is your home now too."

"I don't have a home." Her hands dropped to her sides and she tugged on the ends of her sleeves. "It's better it stays that way."

"Perhaps you'll learn to like it here if you're given a tour. It can be quite overwhelming if you're left to explore on your own."

Arwan tilted his head as he observed her carefully. There was something familiar about her, as if he'd caught a glimpse of her in another life.

"Yeah, I guess that'd be good," she said. "I should know where everything is if we're staying here for a while."

"Fantastic." Renato stepped aside and waved Arwan toward them. "I have just the guide. Arwan, this is Zanya. Zanya, meet Arwan, a young man who has been a part of our rather unique family for many years." Renato gestured him forward. "Please show Zanya around the house. She hasn't had a proper tour. You might like to be a decent host and take some time to get to know our new guest."

When her gaze met his, her chest jumped with a tiny gasp. Arwan squared his shoulders and gave a slight bow. "*Absolutamente.*"

A blush spread over her cheeks.

When he walked toward her, she backed toward the open door. He couldn't be sure, but she seemed scared. She watched him with no particular expression. Just like on the beach, she was hard to read. Perhaps he would find out more about her while showing her around.

He extended his hand toward the hall. "Shall we?"

Her wolf-gray eyes examined him through a curtain of dark eyelashes. She gave a single nod. "Thanks." She crossed her arms and stepped aside. "You first."

He led her through the hall to a curved archway with two letters engraved in the center of a large, wooden door: E.W.

"This is the east wing." He opened the door to another foyer, smaller than the one in the main wing.

Cement floors covered the space, giving it a medieval feel. Arwan had walked barefoot on these cold floors countless times. "This is Renato's wing."

Zanya ran her fingers along an alabaster statue of an Egyptian pharaoh. A large painting of a man with dark eyes and dark, wavy hair hung on the wall.

She stopped to examine the portrait. "Is that Renato?"

Arwan nodded and laughed quietly to himself. He'd always thought that painting was overdone. But the old man didn't look half bad. His features were proud and patriarchal, posing with his hands rested on the hilt of a sword.

When she was ready to move on, Arwan pulled open another door and stepped aside. "Ladies first." He had a thousand questions, all of them pertaining to her knowledge of the stone and her readiness to find it.

Zanya passed him, into the hall. Her hair flowed behind her, leaving the air infused with the scent of vanilla and lavender. He followed her with his attention trained on the subtle, almost unnoticeable glow radiating from her skin. If his senses weren't so keen—if he didn't have such heightened perception—he may not have noticed it. But he had, and his curiosity wouldn't allow him to rest until he understood exactly what it meant.

CHAPTER SIX

Zanya

Zanya's eyes widened at the sight of the north wing, beautiful and brilliant, with mostly white, silver, and splashes of teal and burnt orange as the color palette. Shaggy throw rugs lay over the shiny marble floor, which sparkled with flecks of silver.

Her stomach hadn't settled since the tour began. Usually she was gifted at hiding her nerves or any sign of stress. She had to do it almost every day at the orphanage. But something about this guy threw all of that off.

A glass coffee table sat in the center of the living room with an entire ocean habitat of exotic fish and brightly colored coral, providing a temporary distraction. She crouched beside it and admired the two sea horses, a clown fish, and several other colorful creatures she couldn't identify. She'd only seen fish like these in textbooks. Everything in the institution was drab and dull. Saltwater fish were anything but. "They're beautiful." She turned toward Arwan. "Who stays here?"

"This is Marzena's wing. Hawa has a room here, too. If you prefer to stay here, I'm sure it wouldn't be a problem."

She admired the sea creatures a moment longer, then stood and smoothed out her dress. She would give her right arm to go upstairs and change. Dresses weren't her thing, but either were bathing suits. This seemed like the lesser of the two evils. "No, I like it where I am. It was my mother's room. I couldn't leave it. Plus, I don't want to intrude on Marzena. She seems to enjoy her privacy."

"Most dreamwalkers do. They are quiet, solitary people. Don't take it personally if she's not around often."

She appreciated her own privacy too, not that she'd ever had any. But the few times she was allowed a drawer for her things or a cubby to keep her toiletries, they belonged to her, and that was something.

They continued into a hallway lined with candles, guiding the way in a soft luminescence. The shadows from the flames danced across the sharp angle of his jawline.

"Zanya, can I ask you a question?"

"Um..." There were no promises she'd be truthful, but... "Sure."

"How long have you known about the stone?"

She snorted. "Five minutes." A bit exaggerated, but mostly the truth.

His rubbed the back of his neck. "It doesn't make sense."

"You're telling me. None of this makes sense."

71

"No. It doesn't make sense you don't know anything—that you haven't known anything all this time. How is that possible?" His words quickened, becoming more intense as he spoke.

"I don't know. I mean…" Why did he care so much, anyway? "It's complicated I guess. I'm still wrapping my mind around it all, so I'm probably not the best person to answer that."

He tightened his jaw. "So much time has been wasted."

She stopped. "You think I don't know about wasted time?" She pursed her lips into a tight line. "You're talking to the queen of lost time."

He hung his head balled his hands into fists. "I'm sorry. I shouldn't have asked."

"There's a difference between asking and probing," she muttered. Something told her he had a motive other than the kindness in his heart. "Especially when it comes to my destiny." She quoted the last two words with her fingers.

"A great destiny is never an easy one." He walked ahead, leaving her in the hall.

"Some tour." She followed him through another door with a W.W. engraved in it.

It had a more relaxed feel than the others. In the center of the living room were two dark leather couches and an oval coffee table showing obvious signs of wear. A plasma television was mounted to the wall with gaming systems and a DVD player below.

It screamed bachelor pad.

"Is this your wing?" Zanya noticed the stack of UFC magazines lying on a side table. Built-in shelves housed DVDs and books.

"Yes, Peter and I live here."

"It's nice." She fingered through the small library of books. "Renato's study doesn't have enough books to read?" It was straight out of a scene from Beauty and the Beast.

"I like to read."

"Are all of these yours?"

"Most. Some are Peter's."

She huffed. "He probably hasn't had much time to read lately, with him getting along with Tara so well."

"He's been slacking off on his training. That's for certain. But it seems like he's fond of her."

Zanya rolled her eyes. Of course he would take Peter's side. What guy wouldn't play wingman and try to score brownie points with the best friend? "Yeah, well, I hope he *stays* fond of her. Tara's...naive."

He cocked his head. "She means a lot to you."

"She does, and I won't see her get hurt just so some guy can get in her pants. I mean, he may act like he adores her, but boys are really good at acting, and even when they're not, they change their minds—a lot." She wasn't about to forget that, not even over a pair of dazzling eyes and Spanish accent.

"Do they?"

"Yes, they do." She turned her back to him and pulled in a quiet breath. She had fallen for a guy's charm before, and all it got her was a shattered heart. She wasn't about to make the same mistake again.

"It sounds as if you're speaking from experience."

And we have a mind reader.

Zanya scoffed, and then froze.

What if he really was a mind reader? It wouldn't be the only unexplainable thing she'd seen. "All I'm saying is that Peter seems nice enough and charming enough, but Tara is reckless in the world of love. She falls too easily, and it would be simple for some guy to see that and take full advantage of it."

Arwan uncrossed his arms and walked toward her. His lime green shirt complemented his olive skin so stunningly, she almost forgot to breathe. "You think he's charming?"

"Not my kind of charming. *Tara* thinks he's charming. But he's..." She fingered through the DVDs absentmindedly. "He's not my type." Flashes of dirty blond hair and crystal blue eyes reeled through her mind.

Yep, there it was—the searing pain in her chest reminding her why she could never be that vulnerable again.

Her fingers rested on a DVD, not like the rest. She slid it out and examined the cover. It was a CD. "Eleuia." She turned to Arwan. "That's—"

"Your mother." He stepped toward her. "She was a musician, so Renato has told me."

Her fingers shook. "A musician?"

"I believe he said she played the cello."

She couldn't hold back a beaming smile. "Can I borrow this?"

"You can have it." He eyed the case in her

74

hands. "Do you play?"

"The violin." She tucked the CD in her back pocket.

"Then there's a room you'll want to see, just past that doorway." He walked to the far end of the den and pulled open a heavy wooden door.

Zanya walked through the threshold into a small auditorium stocked with instruments. A tiny thrill ran through her. "A music room!"

It looked like they'd collected every instrument in existence. She caressed shiny finish of an acoustic guitar. Moving along, shiny flutes sat beside a wall of drums. She bounced her palm off the surface of one, then spotted a long, wooden pipe leaning against the far wall. "You're kidding. Is that a didgeridoo?"

"Is that what it's called?" He held up a violin—a piece of musical art made of exquisite red wood. He handed it to her.

She traced her fingers over its curves and then cradled it under her chin. He held out a bow made of matching red wood, with a silk grip and a leather thumb cushion. "Gold mountings? You don't see that anymore. This thing must have cost a fortune." Zanya dragged the white horsehair ribbon across the strings. Each note was smooth and flavorful. She played a few bars of a favorite tune. A satisfied grin stretched her lips. She lowered the bow and opened her eyes. "Can I come here to play sometime?"

"Whenever you want."

Her heart ached to hear music again. "This has got to be the best room in the entire house."

"You may think so, but there's another room I

like more." Arwan escorted her through another hallway that led to a martial arts dojo. International flags and medals hung proudly displayed on the walls.

He circled a black mat that blanketed the floor. "I spend a lot of time in here practicing capoeira and with my glaive." He gestured to a long staff with a curved blade at the end. "I'm sure Renato will want you to learn at least the basics now that you've found your way home."

"I wouldn't say I found my way, exactly." She followed him around the corner of the room. "More like I was brought…by force."

"You're very important." He held her gaze. "To all of us."

***

That night Zanya slipped the CD of her mother's cello recital into the disk player in her bedroom. She pressed play and slipped under her cool sheets. The room was dark and she was exhausted, but hearing her mother's music was the closest she'd get to knowing her.

The rich, robust tone of the cello filled the room. Zanya closed her eyes and rested into the mattress. The tempo of the notes was slow and heavy, carrying an undertone of sadness. It was one reason Zanya loved music. Emotion flowed through it like a direct link to her soul.

Her muscles relaxed while she absorbed every note. She could almost picture her mother, sitting with an arched back in a chair, straddling the cello, playing with her eyes closed. Zanya mind drifted into a sleepy fog.

It seemed like moments later when she blinked open her eyes to her dark room.

Except there was no furniture and no walls. Nothing but endless black. Zanya still wore the pajamas she'd changed into before bed. She peered into the distance. "Hello?"

Something wasn't right. She had been stuck in countless scenarios in her dreams, all of them fearfully lovely or dreadfully gruesome. But this time was different. This time it was vacant and somehow endless.

Zanya turned in a circle, searching above her, below her, and in every possible direction.

A soft glow slowly illuminated the space. She searched for the source, and after a moment, realized it was not coming from a lantern, flashlight, or even a candle. The warm light came from the center of her chest in an oval, pulsing orb.

She ran her fingertips over her chest and settled the palm of her hand over the ice-cold light. To her surprise, it didn't hurt.

The light grew brighter, allowing her to see farther into the space.

A man's silhouette appeared in the distance. Fear thrashed through her. It was The Man. The one who haunted her. Who hurt her.

His bitter stench filled the space as he limped closer. Zanya stumbled back and reached for a wall to lean on, but there was none. She fell to the ground—or what seemed to be the ground.

His face was framed with dark black hair, and

even blacker eyes that peered down at her. "Ah, there you are, young guardian." He walked forward, using his cane for support. The brass handle had a dull shine, worn from years of use. "I heard they had recovered you, but I had to see it for myself."

Zanya coiled back her legs in preparation to kick if he got any closer. "Get away from me," she screamed, her voice cracked with panic.

His lip curled in disgust. "Have some dignity and stand." He stretched out his hand to help her up. "If you can stand, please, I only wish to talk."

Zanya scooted back and forced herself to her feet, leaving his gesture untouched. Her body trembled, and she twisted her hands together to ease the shaking.

"Much better." He squared his shoulders. "Thank you." He stepped forward. "Please forgive me. You see, meeting you here, in your mind, is much easier than the efforts I would be forced to endure in order to speak to you in person—though we haven't had that pleasure just yet."

She didn't know what to say or do. He had never spoken to her like this before. Like she was a real person. It didn't take long to decide she wouldn't stick around to find out why.

As he stood waiting for a reply, she calculated her escape. What horrors the darkness held were unknown, but what The Man might do to her would be much worse.

She sprinted into action. The darkness was consuming and frightening, but the possibility of a successful escape spiked her adrenaline. Each frantic step put space between her and The Man, until she slammed face-first into some kind of invisible barrier. Her body ricocheted off the unseen wall and collapsed to the ground. Nearly slipping into unconsciousness, she coughed and gasped for air, her ribs aching from the impact.

A pair of black dress shoes with silver buckles stepped into view beside her head. The brass foot of his cane slammed audibly on the floor. "I had to stop you somehow." His tone turned harsh. She'd angered him. In her experience, that was never good.

Zanya swallowed down a sob, refusing to give him the satisfaction. "Get away from me." She pushed up on her forearms, and with wobbly legs, managed to stand. Her vision was still blurred from the impact. She swallowed and sucked in another breath, swaying on her feet. "You…"

His gaze dragged down the length of her body. "It has been quite fun stepping into your dreams, watching you squirm under your sheets."

Zanya held her ribs, hunched over with pain. "What do you want?"

"Now, that is an interesting question. What do I want?" He stepped toward her. His eyes churned with magic and something else she couldn't identify. Something that made her stomach turn.

The space around them shook, rippling like the surface of a disturbed pool of water. The sensation of her subconscious being torn open nearly made her drop to her knees. Before either of them could react, it was gone.

The atmosphere was different. Zanya's skin tingled and the hair on her arms twitched. They weren't alone anymore. What creature had he called this time? Not that it mattered. There was nowhere to run.

Small fingers wrapped around Zanya's wrist. She jumped and looked down at Marzena, who now stood beside her. Her blonde hair was weightless, drifting away from her body as if gravity no longer existed.

A wave of relief washed over her, cooling the raw fear scalding her veins. Marzena's angelic face was shadowed with skill and timeless knowledge. Power churned in her emerald eyes.

"Sarian, why have you come?" The projection of Marzena's voice was enormous, it echoed through the empty space.

"What did you just call him?" Zanya said. "You…you know him?"

Both of them ignored her question.

"I was merely paying a visit to our young guardian. I hadn't formally introduced myself, although we've been acquaintances for many years. Perhaps I should thank you for doing the honors."

Marzena was clearly not amused. She let go of Zanya's hand, her eyes now completely black like drops of onyx. "Do not jest with me." The raw fury in her tone shook the space.

Sarian winced, but quickly reassumed perfect composure.

"Where is the stone?" Marzena's lips never moved as she spoke with her mind. "Give it back to its people. It does not belong to you—nor has it ever."

Sarian tightened his grip on his cane. "I will

follow through with my plans, dreamwalker. If you and your kind wish to live through my reign, I suggest you stop your foolishness and turn the guardian over to me. I have her stone. We both know she is worthless without it."

Marzena's hair whipped wildly around her, slashing at the air. Wind conjured from the stillness, pressing Marzena's thin nightgown flush to her frail form. The space around them trembled a second tie. Crawling fault lines spread through the darkness like a glass dome bearing too much weight.

"We will never surrender the guardian. We will never stop fighting." Marzena thrust her hands forward. Light burst in from every direction, collapsing the space on top of them.

Zanya's eyes flew open and she shot up in bed. Unable to control the urge, she threw her head over the mattress and vomited on the floor.

CHAPTER SEVEN

Arwan

Arwan pushed through the French doors, onto the veranda. Stars dotted the sky, accompanied by the moon hung over the ocean in a perfect crescent. Marzena had woken him up and told him what happened, and about Zanya's healing session with Peter.

Everyone was huddled on the marble patio overlooking the beach. Cups of steaming tea sat in the center of the coffee table. The scent of clove and honey mixed with the salty air.

"His name is Sarian," Renato said. Zanya was curled up beside Tara on the wicker love seat. She looked pale and clammy. Arwan removed a woven blanket from the storage ottoman and draped it over her. Even with Peter there, they couldn't afford the time it'd take for her to recover from getting sick. Every day mattered.

She gathered the blanket in her fingers. "Thank you," she said softly, her gaze following him as he walked across the space. The irises of Zanya's eyes seemed to swirl like storm clouds. Arwan blinked, refocused, and the swirling had stopped.

Perhaps he was more sleep deprived than he thought.

Zanya draped half of the blanket over Tara's lap and turned her attention back to Renato.

"We feared he may have the stone," Renato continued. "We were hoping otherwise."

Zanya cradled her head in her hands. "He's made my life hell."

Renato frowned. "I am truly sorry for your suffering. But the fact that he has been able to tap into your subconscious is only further proof he has the stone in his possession. The guardian is linked with the stone. He is using the connection to infiltrate your mind."

She picked her head up. "He said something about how I was useless without it. What does that mean?"

"You must formally bond with the stone in order to have full access to the abilities it provides."

"Wait, what?" She lowered her legs and sat up straight. "What abilities?"

"The abilities that lay dormant within you, Zanya. Haven't you sensed them? When you're angry, or passionate, or scared?"

She shook her head. "Not that I can remember. But…something really strange happened to me right before The Man…Sarian…showed up. There was this light—"

"Ah. The light is within every guardian. Ellie carried her light in the palm of her hand."

"Mine was in my chest." Zanya tucked her hair behind her ear. Arwan tried not to notice how softly her fingers brushed against the curve of her neck. How was it the most powerful of all Riyata came in the form of such a delicate woman?

He walked to the farthest side of the room to create some space between them. The scent of her hair carried in the wind, quickening his heartbeat. He turned his head away from the aroma of vanilla and lavender. Heightened senses were sometimes more of a curse than a tool. Especially when his instincts drew him towards her.

"I've seen it before," Zanya said. "Except only in my dreams. I never thought it was real."

"The guardian's light is nothing short of miraculous. It is the link between you and the stone."

"I'm sorry. I'm just a little confused." Tara sat forward. "So, who is this guy exactly?"

Everyone's attention shifted to Arwan as he leaned against the railing. While the group waited for a reply, he debated the outcome of what he had to share. How Zanya would react to the news was anyone's guess. Unfortunately, there was no way to say it delicately. "He's the general of the underworld forces."

Tara threw her hands into the air. "Well that's fan-freaking-tastic."

"It's both very good and very bad," Arwan said. "Now that Zanya knows who she is, Sarian has come out of hiding. The bad news is, now he'll be even more motivated to break the obedience spell."

Zanya sank into her chair. "I'm guessing I

should know what that is."

"I'm guessing you haven't picked up any of the books I gave you," Renato said.

She bit her bottom lip. "Uh...not yet." Renato scolded her with a stern glance. She drew the blanket tighter around herself. "I'll start on them. I promise."

Renato pinched the bridge of his nose. "The obedience spell is what keeps the stone loyal to the guardian. It was placed on the stone by the heaven deities, when the stone was first bestowed on our people. Without it, the stone will follow the orders of whoever possesses it."

Zanya's throat tightened. "And if Sarian has it..."

"So, now that we know where the stone is," Hawa said, "we can get it back, right?"

"The stone is with Sarian, but we have not been able to locate him for almost two decades. He vanished just months after Zanya was born." Renato paused. "After he located Ellie and took the stone."

"What do you mean, he found her?" Zanya sat up straight. The blanket dropped from her lap to the marble floor. "Did he..." The color drained from Zanya's face. "Oh my God." She cupped her hand over her mouth.

"As I told you, Sarian has killed many. He has no boundaries, no—"

"But my mother?" Her voice cracked.

The room fell silent.

Arwan's chest grew heavy. When he visited his mother's grave, it was as if the hole in his heart had been torn open again. Zanya was likely experiencing the same thing.

"Sarian will do whatever he must on his quest for power," Renato said. "He shares bloodlines with both the underworld and the middleworld, and if he is able, he will take this realm as his own kingdom."

"We'll find him before that happens," Arwan said, in an effort to soothe Zanya's obvious heartache.

She looked at him. "And if we don't?"

He offered the only truthful answer he could. "We have to."

"I think we should get back to this later," Tara said, resting her hand on Zanya's arm. "This is some next level shit, and I think Zanya needs some time to process it all."

Zanya nodded. "That'd be good, if you all don't mind." She curled up and drew the blanket under her chin.

"Very well." Renato gestured to the group. "Everyone should get some rest."

Most of the group stood and walked back inside. Tara looked up at Renato. "I'm going to sleep in Zanya's room tonight, just in case she needs anything."

Renato nodded. "Very well."

The guardian and her friend followed Renato inside, leaving Arwan alone on the veranda. He pulled back his hair and turned to the beach, scanning the jungle.

The fight had begun.

Sarian had made himself known. They would soon begin the hunt for his location, if only the guardian could locate the stone.

His gaze drifted over the treetops to blue and green lights wavering in the distance. He narrowed his eyes. It wasn't the right time of year for the borealis lights—unless someone else had summoned the lights. Someone with the necessary power.

Drina.

He returned to his wing and gathered his things, then took the Jeep on the long drive to the priestess's village. The old priestess was up to something.

Once he reached the outskirts of the jungle, he parked and shoved the keys in his pocket before hiking into the trees.

Though the moon and stars provided soft light, the darkness was never an issue for him. His vision was enhanced, his senses heightened. It was one of the only perks to being what he was.

The sounds of the jungle were deafening. Insects were the loudest at night, only second to the sound of rustling branches in the treetops. When he reached the top of the hill, Drina's modest hut appeared in the distance.

He walked toward the campfire, burning brightly with newly placed logs to keep it alive. "*Tia* Drina?" He checked the sky. The borealis lights were nowhere to be seen. "Drina?" He smelled her musky scent. She'd always reeked of herbs and nectars from flowers, which she used to mix her various elixirs for the village people. The ones who still believed.

"T'ere you are, boy." Drina wobbled from her house. "Where have you been?"

"I saw the lights and—"

"Is about time." She struggled to balance a stone bowl in her hands.

The pungent stink hit him in the face, making him crinkle his nose. "What is that?"

"Stop asking questions and sit." She jabbed her finger at a log positioned near the fire pit.

Over the years he'd learned not to question her. Arwan sat, embracing the warmth of the fire as it reached out to his skin.

"Tell me." Drina groaned as she sat across from him. "What of the guardian?"

"We've found her. But you already knew that. She doesn't have much knowledge about—"

"No." Drina scowled. "Tell me what you see."

Arwan drew his brows together. "What do you mean?"

"When you look at her, boy. Do you see somet'ing others do not?"

"What am I supposed to see?"

She peered at him from across the fire, her irises reflecting the red and orange flames. "Everyt'ing has a balance." She pressed her fingers into the stone bowl and scooped out some of the runny mixture. "Breathe deep, boy. Breathe deep, and do not fight the journey." She flicked the mixture into the fire. It sizzled against the glowing embers. Smoke rose with the flames and mixed with the wind.

Arwan closed his eyes and took in the scent of burnt herbs and ground flowers. With every deep inhale, his mind wandered into a neutral space, as if he were falling into a deep sleep. He hadn't meditated for a very long time.

His mother's voice echoed in the distance. She hummed a tune, then stopped and let out a soft laugh. "The world is a mysterious place, my beautiful boy." His chest tightened and his heart tore open with new, scalding pain. He had spent countless nights trying to remember her voice.

He blinked open his eyes to see her sitting across from him, where Drina sat just moments ago. She was exactly as she appeared in the sketches hung on his bedroom wall—the only clear memory of her had to keep her from slipping away completely.

"Listen to Drina, would you, son?" She tilted her head, a soft smile playing over her lips. "She was a dear friend to me. Even if she is a bit…" She crinkled her nose. "Difficult."

"Mother?" The word came out in a whisper. He hardly recognized his own voice. He stood and walked toward her. When he reached the other side of the fire, she was gone.

"And stop punishing yourself." He turned. She stood on the other side of the flames. "You don't deserve to live in such agony."

The sharp reminder of what he was pushed to the surface. "You don't know who I am. Not really."

"A mother knows her son better than he knows himself." Her voice was right behind him. He spun around, meeting her face to face. "And you, my dear boy…" She gently ran her fingers through his hair. "The guardian is the answer to my prayers for you. Embrace her. Protect her at all costs. Keep her close, and most importantly, do not fight your destiny."

He lifted his hand to touch her cheek, only for his fingers to pass through her. A texture like cobwebs broke against his skin as he dropped his hand to his side. "I don't understand."

"You will. In time." She smiled, which sucked the breath straight from his lungs. He had forgotten how beautiful she was when she smiled.

His hands shook. "How will I know what's right and good when…" He balled his fists. "When something dark lingers inside me."

"With darkness comes light." She stepped back, creating distance between them.

He reached out to her. "Wait."

She smiled. "With darkness comes light," she said again.

"I don't know what that means." He stepped toward her, but she vanished into the darkness.

His vision blurred and his head spun. His knees buckled, and he fell to the damp, jungle ground. He grabbed handfuls of soil and twigs, crushing them in his fists.

"I said, do not fight it." Drina's familiar voice said from behind him.

Arwan's breath was ragged. "How long have you been able to contact her?"

Drina paused before she answered. "Many years."

He ground his teeth, fighting the darkness that clawed through him like a sickness. It swirled in his head and wove through his veins. He tightened his fist and pounded them into the ground. He jumped up and turned to Drina. "How could you?"

"It was not my decision to make. Your mot'er

felt you were not ready."

"And I am now? Why now?" He scowled. "I want it out of me." He clenched his chest. "I can't live like this anymore."

"If you do not trust me, trust your mot'er. You have great purpose, boy, if you only believe."

Arwan paused and dropped his hands to his sides. "With darkness comes light. What does that mean?"

Drina nodded. "*T'at* is the right question."

"Just tell me. I need answers!"

"And they will come. In time."

He exhaled, his shoulders slumped forward. "In time."

Drina's gaze lifted to the horizon. Streaks of yellow, orange and red streaked the sky. "The light has arrived, boy. It will guide you home. Follow it."

CHAPTER EIGHT

Zanya

With everyone asleep, Zanya sat in her room, sorting through the massive stack of books Renato had given her. She promised she'd read them—anything to avoid that 'straighten up' glare he'd given her on the veranda.

She picked up a hand written journal and scanned the pages. A translation, from the look of it. The first half was written in a language she didn't recognize. She skipped to the second half that was written in English, with what seemed to be an ink quill pen.

Entry 14: Sarian Pech, exact date of birth is unknown.

His mother, Aditya, birthed Sarian in her home with two midwives, who were later found dead. One had thrown herself from a cliff, the other had hanged herself near her home. Black magic is suspected to have influenced their suicides.

Sarian and his mother are unusually close. Aditya mentors him in the ways of dark magic, and he is growing in wizardly strength much quicker than we expected.

Entry 15: Several more villagers have vanished over the last month. The elders issued search parties, who returned with reports of Aditya walking alongside a beast in the jungle.

Entry 16: Our shaman received a vision during his worship. The gods are angry for allowing a witch to practice underworld magic in our village and have cursed us as punishment. They have ordered Atlacoya, the goddess of drought and barren land, to roam our village. As a greater punishment, they have exiled the goddess Chiconahui, who grants fertility and protects our families.

Entry 17: To my utmost despair, the last scribe has been found dead; her body was tied to a tree, disemboweled and decapitated. We will remember her bravery always.

It has been six months since rain last touched our soil. Our crops are dead, and our people are starving with no harvest. Most of our livestock have perished from dehydration as the lakes and rivers have dried up, leaving no oasis for them to quench their thirst.

Entry 18: A much worse curse has befallen our people. Without Chiconahui to bless our women, eight children have been stillborn. Our village grows angry. The people are becoming more fearful of the gods' wrath than Aditya's magic.

Entry 19: Our village has turned on Aditya. But the uprising was not without bloodshed. We knew Sarian was dark, but the cruelty of a boy should only extend to the limits of man.

What we witnessed today was far beyond that of man.

The boy is not human. Before our eyes his skin changed. His body changed. Splintered bones and a frail frame morphed into that of a beast, only thought to exist in Xibalba. And when the dark transformation was complete, he fed.

Now the bodies of our people are scattered through the village like ornaments. Their blood stains the earth red. Their terrified expressions are frozen in time. There is no returning from the hell we are living. There is no coming back.

Entry 20: We have successfully exiled Aditya and her demon son. It seems to be an effective victory. Banished for the remainder of their lives, the head shaman now prays through the night for forgiveness for our initial disobedience.

Entry 21: It has been three months since Aditya and Sarian have fled. The bodies of our fallen warriors have been laid to rest with the highest honors, maize wedged in their mouths and jade placed on their graves for the journey to their next lives. The tomb for the martyrs is now full. Since the burial, Atlacoya has returned with the rains and several of our women have conceived. The elders declared that we have regained the gods' favor by casting the witch and her forsaken *offspring from our village.*

Zanya lowered the book to her lap. There was no doubt Sarian was dangerous, but until now, she hadn't realize just what they were up against. Zanya leaned back with the book on her lap, her mouth suddenly so dry she could hardly swallow. If they were going to challenge him, they'd have to step up their game. That, or they might not make it out of this alive.

***

The next morning, Zanya entered the kitchen to find Peter at the stove.

He waved the spatula in his hand. "Morning."

"Good morning." Her tone was flat, but she couldn't help it. The morning was good until she ran into him—the guy trying to steal her best friend's heart. She sat at the breakfast bar, inhaling the sweet scent of freshly made pancakes.

The pan sizzled; globs of half-cooked batter clung to the spatula. Peter smiled, awkward but still charming, even though she hated to admit it to herself. "I'm glad you made it."

Yawning, she rubbed her eyes. "Made what?"

"Made it for breakfast." He tossed a hot flapjack on a plate and set it in front of her. "I'm glad you came."

"Oh." The deformed pancake was burned around the edges. "Thanks. You didn't have to make me breakfast, though. I can feed myself."

"I don't mind." He dropped another dollop into

the hot pan. "But I'm sorry to have to tell you this is about the only thing I can make. That and instant mashed potatoes." He paused, in thought. "Coffee. I can make coffee, too."

"Have you seen Tara today?"

"Yeah. She's still in her room. I just left there about fifteen minutes ago." She tensed. He was in her room. Peter shoved a huge bite in his mouth. "You want to eat? I bet you're hungry."

"No. Thanks." She padded toward the hall, and then paused. "Hey, where's Tara's room? I haven't been there yet."

He pointed with his butter knife. "She's in the main wing." His words enveloped by a full mouth of pancake. "The last door on the left. But—"

Zanya deserted Peter in the kitchen. She wasn't usually so rude, but who the hell did he think he was, anyway? Why would he have been in Tara's room? The most logical explanation made her stomach tighten. A moment later she was up the stairs and down the hall, standing in front of Tara's room. Zanya knocked, and Tara opened the door and peeked out.

"Hey!" She smiled. "Come on in." Tara swung open the door and stepped aside. "Come on, come on." She excitedly waved her in.

Zanya strode in and paused. "Wow." She scanned the space. "Nice room." The Moroccan-inspired decor was bright and festive with colors splashed over every surface. Silk pillows, an elaborate throw rug, and a plush duvet drenched in every imaginable shade of blue, red, and green.

"It's nice, right? Check this out." Tara walked to

the other side of the room and flung her curtains open, allowing sunlight to pour in through the wall of windows. The colorful decor instantly brightened and sparkled with silk accents and gold threads. "You can't beat waking up to that every morning, huh?" Tara drew in a deep breath with a satisfied smile, admiring the view.

Zanya joined her, and Tara rested her head on Zanya's shoulder. They stood together in silence, taking in the amazing scenery of acres of gardens and low-lying stone walls caring pathways among the flowers.

"It's beautiful," Zanya said.

"Definitely better the view of the cement walls and bars on the windows."

Zanya's heart ached. They'd spent so many days wishing they were somewhere else. Anywhere, just to escape that place. "How are you coping with that, by the way?"

"With what?"

"No anti-depression meds. Are you…okay?"

Tara shrugged. "Surprisingly, yeah. I feel great. I have clarity for the first time in a long time." Tara slid her arm around Zanya's waist. "I guess I owe all of that to you. If you didn't agree to stay, I'd be back there. Alone."

"I wouldn't have left you. Even if that meant me staying too."

Tara wiped a tear from her cheek and smiled. "I guess that doesn't matter anymore." She walked to her bed and sat. Her toes barely touched the floor. "So, what's up?"

The moment of peace vanished when Zanya

remembered why she came. "I wanted to have some breakfast with you, but when I went into the kitchen, you weren't there, and I didn't know where your room was." She paused, waiting for Tara to say something. "Peter was in the kitchen, so he told me." She stood quiet for another moment. Still, Tara had no reaction.

"Oh." She shrugged. "Well, that's good. I'm glad you found me. Now we can eat." Tara hopped off her bed and rummaged through a drawer of clothes.

A streak of annoyance wove through her. They'd been friends for a long time. Being blown off wasn't something Zanya took very well, even from Tara. "So, how does Peter know where your room is?"

"What do you mean, how?" Tara flung socks and folded T-shirts onto the floor. "He was here."

"And…" Zanya scratched a nervous itch on her arm. "Why exactly would Peter be in your room?"

With a shirt in her hand, Tara froze, and slowly pivoted. She pushed to her feet, dropping the garment onto the floor. "Depends." Her lips pursed. "What exactly are you insinuating?"

Zanya suddenly regretted prying. The expression on her friend's face told her she'd gone too far. "For your information, he was here to invite us to breakfast." She gestured to both of them with a sharp jab of her finger. "But he was too shy to knock on your door, so I told him I'd get you." With a moment of silence, the agitation in her features subsided. "I thought that's why you came here." She tilted her head. "You don't need to worry about me. Peter's a nice guy. He's not like that. And I wish you'd have a little faith in me." Her cheeks blazed red. "What you're thinking about...it's something I'm just not ready for yet. So, let's drop it, all right?"

Zanya mentally kicked herself. Repeatedly. "It's just that I know how guys can be. I don't want to see you get your heart broken. A boy will like you one minute, he may even say he loves you, and the next minute, he just...doesn't anymore." Tears stung Zanya's eyes.

Tara sighed, her gaze filled with a sense of empathy Zanya hated to be the recipient of. She didn't want anyone to feel bad for her. Tara snorted. "We've been friends for a long time. I know you. You can stop trying to be so tough." She hugged Zanya tightly. "Not all boys are like him. I know getting past that has been hard for you, but Peter really is different. If you get to know him, you'll see for yourself."

Zanya hugged Tara back. What had she been thinking? Tara may have been a lot of things, but a slut wasn't one of them.

"Now come on." In a sudden movement, Tara stepped back and grabbed her hand, then dragged her toward the door. "I'm so hungry, I'm about to eat my own arm."

Zanya grinned. "We wouldn't want that. Peter would be awfully disappointed during your make-out sessions...or if he decided to take up juggling and needed a partner."

Tara shot her a threatening sideways glare, then smirked and quickly left the room.

When they arrived at the kitchen, Tara's attention was immediately on Peter. Little pink hearts may as well have risen from her head and popped like little soap bubbles. It was that painfully obvious.

While Tara took a seat at the kitchen bar, Zanya leaned against the archway, observing them. Peter tugged gently on one of Tara's curls and let it go, and watched as it sprung up and bounced off her shoulder. Tara giggled and laced her fingers between his.

Zanya sighed. She'd give him credit. The boy knew how to charm. Problem was, she couldn't tell if he was trying to charm his way into Tara's heart, or into her bed.

"*Dios mío.*" Arwan walked up from behind her with his arms crossed, staring into the kitchen. "How much longer is this going to last? We need to train."

She shrugged. "I think he's gone forever."

He settled beside her and brushed his shoulder against hers. He didn't seem to notice, but she did, and the butterflies in her stomach prompted her to move away. "If he's gone, I'll have a lot of free time on my hands and nobody to spend it with." The corner of his mouth curled in a grin.

She mirrored his amused expression, and then remembered the tragic downfalls to a guy's charm. With a few mind-clearing blinks and a mental pep-talk, she renewed her oath. No guys. That was the deal she made with herself, and she would stick to it. "That's not entirely true. You have Hawa."

Arwan crinkled his nose.

"What? You don't like her? She's so warm and inviting."

"It's not that I don't like her, but she and Peter have some history. When they broke up it jaded her. She hasn't really been the same since."

Tara giggled and blushed over Peter twining his finger around her curls. Zanya decided to leave well enough alone for the moment. Maybe she'd talk to Tara about it later and give her a heads-up.

"Well," Arwan said. "I guess practice is canceled for today. I should make my rounds."

She raised an eyebrow. "Rounds?"

"I walk the perimeter at least once a day. I can show you around the grounds, unless you'd rather watch this." He gestured to Tara and Peter.

Zanya smirked. He may have been a stranger, but nothing about him seemed strange. In fact, he felt all too familiar—something in his eyes. "Okay. I guess I can handle a walk."

Her heart picked up when he caught her behind her elbow and guided her toward the back door. She swallowed her reaction and kept her pace until they stepped outside, onto the sparking sand.

The beach was windy with dark clouds clustered overhead. They strode in silence, touring the edge of the green, dense jungle encompassing the estate. Renato had said this was her home too, though it was still all so surreal. Since when did girls like her get to live in paradise?

Arwan stole a glance at her every few paces. Zanya bit the inside of her lip. What was he looking at?

"Do you like it here?"

She smiled nervously. "It's definitely a step up from the orphanage." She gathered her hair over her shoulder, taming the wild strands from whipping in the coastal wind. "What about you? How did you end up here?" His features sobered, as if she'd touched a nerve. "I didn't mean to pry."

"I guess it's only fair you know something about us now that you're here."

She'd pass on the I'll-show-you-mine-if-you-show-me-yours therapy session. "Never mind. I was just trying to be nice. Sorry I asked."

"Don't be." He smiled safely, immediately disarming her. "I've been here for some time," he said quietly. "After my mother was killed."

She exhaled as if someone had punched her in the gut. Of course it would be his mom's death she dragged to the surface. "I'm...I'm sorry." She silently cursed herself. "I didn't mean to bring that up. I know how it is to miss having a mother around."

He nodded, and his features softened. "I know you do."

Strange chirps mixed with array of foreign noises echoed from the thicket of the jungle. Vines crawled along the ground, up textured trunks, and hung from their massive branches.

"The jungle's amazing," Zanya said.

"I spend a lot of time hiking through the foothills." He approached a towering tree and rested against the smooth surface of its trunk. "There are temples you might like to see. They carry a lot of the history of the Riyata."

"Really?" The possibility of exploring had

always been completely out of reach. In fact, the possibility of anything outside the cement walls of the orphanage seemed almost unreal. "I'd like that."

From his lost, distant gaze, it was obvious his mind was wandering. His eyes seemed sad...searching.

Tara used to carry the same sadness, mostly visible in the deep lines around her eyes as she gazed out the institution windows.

Zanya had always mourned all of the years lost in that place, but she tried to keep it hidden from Tara. She had to be strong, even if she spent countless nights silently crying. They had both sacrificed so much.

Arwan rubbed the back of his neck, as if his mind had snapped back to the moment. "Come on. We should get back." He gestured to the sky. "A storm is on its way."

She tilted her face toward dark rainclouds brewing overhead. "Right. Wouldn't want to get caught in a torrential downpour."

On their way back to the house, the winds picked up, carrying her hair every which way. "So, what do you know about the stone? I want to learn more about it. I've only ever seen it in my dreams."

"I only know the common knowledge. Most Riyata know the history, but only the guardian knows everything."

"I guess I have a lot to learn."

"The sooner you learn, the sooner we can get started."

Her eyebrows knitted together. "Get started with what?"

He examined her with that same familiarity in his eyes. She shifted her weight.

"We've been waiting for a long time to find you. Meanwhile, the other side has been at work. We've lost a lot of time already, and they know it."

"They? Who are they?"

Arwan strode for a moment in silence. "It's better if you wait until the seeker arrives, like Renato said. I'm sure you'll learn all about it when the time is right." He tightened his jaw as if the words had left a bitter taste over his tongue.

"You don't really believe that, do you?"

"Whether I do or not, it's not up to me. Renato and I have different views, but I trust him. He's yet to steer us wrong."

"Yeah. He seems to think he's everyone's keeper." She huffed. "What's the deal with that, anyway?"

"Renato has led entire armies in this cause. Over the years he's watched countless men and women die to protect the stone. So if he comes across that way, it's because he is. He's our keeper, and we would all follow him into battle—even to the death."

Zanya sucked in a sharp breath. This was all much bigger than she thought. Bigger than both of them—than all of them. "It's still hard to believe this is real."

"Have some faith in yourself. We have faith in you."

She swallowed against a dry throat. "Yeah." She laughed, more from anxiety than anything. "I'm starting to get that. I don't understand how Renato is so confident in me, though. He doesn't even know me. Not really."

"He believes in you because he believed in your mother."

The black and white photo of her mother flashed through her mind. She looked so strong. So capable. Zanya had always wanted to be that person. She wanted to be so much more than a crazy orphan. "Do you really believe I can be like her?"

"Maybe this is another point Renato and I don't completely agree on."

"What do you mean?"

He dropped his gaze, sending strands of raven black hair to fall over his high cheekbones. His dark eyes searched the air as if he were searching for the right words. "I believe people are who they are. If you were born to be the guardian, that is who you are. Who you are meant to be. You can't change it."

"You'd think I'd be used to my life being totally out of my control," she said under her breath.

"You never get used to it. Abilities aren't something you can choose. You're born with what you have, and you have to live with it. That's easier for some than others."

A realization dawned on her. Peter was a healer. Hawa was nimble. Renato was strong. Marzena...well, she still hadn't gotten over the whole Children of the Corn vibe with her yet, but she seemed well-intended. But Arwan... "Are you Riyata, too?"

"My mother was a wind bender."

"Is that what you do?"

"No." He paused and scanned the beach. "Come

on. I'll show you." He led her to a cluster of purple wildflowers with a green grasshopper clung to one of them.

He flicked the flower, which caused the grasshopper to spring off and fly away in a vivid streak of lime green. "Watch carefully."

He stretched his hand over the bloom. Like the air had suddenly taken form, a haze of ripples spread around the flower. It surrounded the petals until Zanya couldn't see it clearly. The matter wavered, like the glistening surface of a creek. When he pulled his hand away, the grasshopper was perched back on the flower.

Zanya's eyes narrowed. "You made it come back?"

"By bending the space around the flower back to when the grasshopper was there. It's called bending time."

"Like time travel?"

"No. Time travel doesn't actually exist. No one can pass through folds of time without touching two points together. It's like jumping a car battery." He extended his hand toward hers, palm up. "You can't transfer energy without something to link them, which in this case..." He waited. She hesitated a moment longer, then cautiously rested her fingers over his. "Is me." The heat from his touch spread over her skin. "You understand?"

She swallowed. "Not really."

He pressed his hand firm against hers, sending a chill down the back of her arms. "Think of 'the now' as the positive, 'the past' as the negative." He arched his wrists and pressed his palms flush with hers. "I'm the cable."

She blinked, hoping he didn't notice the rush of heat in her cheeks. "I see." Zanya drew her hands back to her chest, her heart racing. His energy was intense. She cleared her throat. "Well, I don't know much about cars, but that sounds dangerous."

"If I can't complete the bend properly, it could be deadly."

"Are there a lot of time benders around?"

"No. It's a rare ability."

"It must be nice to have the power to solve so many problems in the world. Death, accidents, crime, you can go back in time and prevent them."

"Bending time is difficult with many complications, and shouldn't be done often. Abilities take practice to master. Renato taught me not to abuse what I can do. To go back in time, to change something that's already been done, would change the course of history."

She shrugged. "Who cares, as long as it changes things for the better, right?"

They continued to walk, the house now in clear sight. "Our lives, history itself, are like the ripples. If you go back and change what's already happened, it changes the ripples. They shift direction, alter course. Some end sooner. Others go on longer than originally destined. The ripples are fragile. We shouldn't manipulate them if at all possible."

It made sense of all that had happened in her life. If she hadn't been left at the orphanage, she wouldn't be who she was today. She may not have learned how to play violin. She never would have met Tara. The ripples were not only the past, but they were also the future. They held what people would become, and what they would do with their lives that made them great.

CHAPTER NINE

Zanya's legs throbbed. Sweat slicked her skin. She pushed harder to keep up with Arwan, who had hiked for the last five miles like it was a casual stroll in the park.

He veered onto a thin game path. "Do you feel like taking a detour?" She exhaled and tried not to groan. Mental note. Apparently the term "hike" actually meant "endless expedition through the jungle until your legs feel like rubber bands."

Zanya wiped away a bead of sweat tickling down her hairline. "How far, exactly?"

"Not far."

Considering his endurance, it was worth a more detailed definition. "Which is?"

He stopped and turned to face her. "Are you tired?"

"A little." She rested her hands on her knees, trying to catch her breath. "And this humidity is a killer."

"Maybe we should head back."

"No. No." She lifted her hand. "I got this.

Guardian or not, I probably need the exercise." She stood up straight, her back screaming under the effort. "Okay." She gestured ahead. "I'm right behind you."

"Just be careful." He pointed to a huge spider web stretched between two trees. "Those are poisonous."

Her eyes widened. "Is that real?"

"Why wouldn't it be?" He seemed confused by her question.

"Yeah. Right. Why wouldn't it be?" Maybe because spiders that big only belonged in *Harry Potter*. Granted, she'd only checked out the first two books from her orphanage's library. After the first spider nightmare, she was done.

She ducked around the huge silk trap and followed Arwan over the peak of a hill. Weathered stone walls and mossy steps rose from the other side—a temple buried in the overgrowth.

"I thought you would like to see this." He extended his hand as she came to a slippery slope, slicked in mud.

"I'm good. Thanks." She gripped onto a sapling and shifted down, one unstable step at a time. The sole of her shoe slid on the final step and sent her hurling back, butt first into the mud. She sighed and blew a puff of air, flying strands of hair out of her face. "Of course."

Arwan chuckled. "You sure you can't use a hand?"

She reluctantly looked up at him, his hand outstretched with an all too amused grin. "Well I'm glad someone's having a good time." She took his hand, and he hauled her back onto her feet.

Arwan searched her eyes. "I'm not laughing at you. I'm just…amazed."

"Right." She brushed of smears of dirt and pieces of dry leaves clung to her clothes. "How can someone be so absolutely clumsy, right?"

"No. It's just that you have so much power and you have no idea." He stepped back. "You'll see. And when you do…" His gaze intensified. "It'll be something amazing."

She swallowed against a dry throat. "It all still scares me."

He ventured closer to the temple, admiring the ancient features of the temple as if he'd never seen it before. "We all have something to be afraid of."

She followed him near the ruins. "So…where are we?"

"It's the temple of Ishel. She is a heaven goddess." His words were laced with a melancholy tone as he stooped beside the offering bowl. "Many people in the surrounding villages still come here and pay homage with gifts of exotic flowers, fruits, and handmade dolls."

Vines and tree branches obstructed her view of the peak. "They don't do a very good job at keeping it up."

"She was once the flower goddess. It's considered desecration to tear down the jungle growth."

Zanya carefully maneuvered toward the stone woman, who stood clear of the reaching vines. She was tall and thin with a water lily nestled in her cupped hands. Her angelic face was tipped toward the sky. Tiny wildflowers embellished the waves of hair draped over her shoulders.

Hand-woven straw dolls sat nestled at the statue's feet. "Why do people bring these dolls?"

"There is a story behind them. Do you want to hear it?" He sat on a mossy temple step and leaned back on his forearms, stretching his cotton shirt over sweat-slicked skin.

"Um...sure." Anything to distract her.

"The goddess of fertility and the god of water fell in love, bearing a beautiful daughter whom they named Ishel. She grew into the loveliest of all women.

"The god of wrath set his sights on her, and asked her father for her hand in marriage. Only Ishel loved Kinich, the sun deity. Out of adoration for Ishel, Kinich would shower her flowers in light, making them bloom and grow.

"Ignoring her wishes, Ishel's father agreed to the union between her and the god of wrath. This threw Ishel into a deep depression. She stopped tending to her flowers. They all died, and the earth became barren. Eventually her father took pity on her and revoked her union, giving his blessing for her to marry whomever she chose. Ishel rejoiced and ran into the arms of Kinich, where they conceived a child. Before their baby was born, the god of wrath took vengeance by banishing Kinich to the surface of the sun, where he would stay for all eternity."

Zanya snorted. "Well what did she expect? That they'd live happily ever after? That just doesn't happen."

"Well, soon after that, Ishel went into labor and

died in childbirth."

"Oh, this story just keeps getting better."

"It does, actually. The Maya don't believe death is the end. We…" He blinked and tightened his jaw. "They don't believe life ends when we pass from the middleworld to the afterlife."

"So, what happened to the baby?"

"Ishel entrusted her daughter to be raised by a sworn protector. Because she died in a noble way, her soul ascended to the heavens and took her place as Goddess of the sun, beside her love."

Zanya admired the weathered stone statue. "Where do the dolls come in?"

"They symbolize Ishel's love, representing their child—the product of her union with Kinich—and the remaining part of her that still roams the earth, tending to the flowers."

Zanya ran her fingers along the goddess's stone gown. It seemed somehow transparent over the delicate curves of the goddess's legs.

A tropical butterfly with brightly colored wings fluttered past her. She followed it through the air and around the stone structure. "Wow. I've never seen a butterfly like that before. It's so big!" She followed its path to a large flower where it settled, pumping its wings. "We don't have any like that back in Ohio."

He held out his hand. "Come on, there's one more place you'll want to see."

She fisted her hands and then relaxed her fingers, considering his gesture. It was a bad idea. The last time they touched, she'd felt something that scared her. Something she swore she wouldn't let in ever again.

"It's on the way. Then home, I promise."

She drew in a deep breath, stepped forward, and rested her hand in his.

***

Arwan

After another ten minutes of hiking, they had finally arrived. Arwan picked up a stick from the ground.

"What's that for?"

If he told her where they were going, it would ruin the surprise. Hopefully the creatures hadn't migrated due to the heavy rains. "You'll see."

Soon they arrived at a clearing, where hundreds of tall, thin bushes with elegant purple blooms dotted the ground. Mature trees formed a canopy overhead, while gaps in the branches allowed beams of sun to speckle the jungle floor.

"I thought you would like it here."

"It's…neat."

He chuckled. "You have no idea what it is yet."

"True…" She inspected the space. "What is it?" She shifted her weight.

Did she lie when she said he didn't make her uncomfortable? It seemed like he did. Every time he smiled at her, she evaded his gaze.

He disregarded the thought and walked forward. "Be careful. Don't touch the bushes." He blazed a path through the maze of shrubs. She followed close behind. When they reached the center, he faced her and leaned in close, hovering his lips beside her ear. "Can I hold you?" She stepped back as a clear streak of panic arched through her. He waited, patiently, for her to calm and to decide. At the slightest nod, he took her hand. "I just want to show you something. Come closer."

He slid his hand around her waist and drew against his chest. He savored the beating of her heart. He could hear it, though no ordinary human would have been able to.

Not even an ordinary timebender.

Being near Zanya allowed him to sense many things he never had before. Like the arc in her pheromones when she looked at him; the way her breath sped when he stood close; the rush of heat in her skin when he touched her.

She rested her palms against his chest. The warmth of her skin flared.

He brushed the back of his fingers over her cheek. "You're blushing."

She pressed the backs of her hands on her face, blushing more intensely. "Must be the humidity."

He caressed the silky curve of her cheek. "I hope not. You're lovely when you blush."

The aurora of light around her flared brighter. He parted his lips as the light reached out to him, soothing the chaos always blustering inside him. "Do you do that on purpose?"

Do what?"

Warm light beamed from her eyes. To tell her she was glowing wouldn't sound sane, though not much of what had happened over the last couple of weeks made much sense to her, either. "Never mind." He readied the stick in his hand. "Are you ready?"

"I think so…" She glanced down at the broken branch. "Unless you're going to beat me. Then no, not ready."

He let out a hearty laugh. "Even if I did, you could take me. But no. That's not it. Just watch." With a powerful strike, he whacked a nearby bush on its base, launching dozens of butterflies into the air.

The flight of a few caused a chain reaction, and soon the graceful creatures filled the sky. Several landed in Zanya's hair and on her arms.

Zanya tilted her head up and smiled at the array of colors gliding overhead. A butterfly rested on Arwan's shoulder, pumping its cobalt blue wings. She curled her lips and blew gently, her warm breath caressing his neck.

She didn't seem to notice, but a subtle, soft light glowed in her chest. It pulsed and churned, as if it had a life of its own. As if it was calling to him.

The rage constantly burning inside of him shed away. He lifted his eyes to hers. The world fell silent to his ears.

He pulled her closer. She braced both hands on his chest. Being near her provided the first glimpse of inner peace since he could remember.

She leaned in closer, hovering her lips over his. Her hot breath broke over his mouth.

Zanya sucked in a sharp gasp and stepped back. The panic in her eyes forced him to look away, silently cursing himself. He'd pushed her too far, too fast.

"I…" The pain streaking her voice caught him off guard. "I can't. I'm sorry."

Before he could respond, Zanya ran back toward the house, stumbling through the trees until he stood alone in the clearing. The jungle was quiet. The animals must have sensed his agitation. They always did, and became silent, as if there were a predator nearby.

He balled his fists. He should have shown more discipline. More restraint. He could put the entire mission in jeopardy over a pretty face. But deep down he knew it was more than that. She wasn't just a girl. She was the guardian. That had to come first.

Each step out of the clearing pounded against the jungle floor. When he escaped the maze of bushes, he charged his fist into the trunk of a mature tree, spitting layers of bark and redwood in every direction.

CHAPTER TEN

Zanya

Zanya darted up the stairs to her room, where she found a note tacked to her door.

The seeker has arrived. Please come see me as soon as you get in.—Renato

She didn't care about the seeker, or Renato's note. All she wanted was to see her best friend, tell her about what happened, and hopefully make some sense of it all.

He wanted to kiss her.

Why?

More importantly, why did she want him to? She'd leaned into him.

Zanya palmed her forehead. "Stupid. Stupid. Stupid."

She walked through the house, into the west wing—the most likely place Tara would be. But she was nowhere to be seen. Neither was Peter.

Something thumped overhead from the floor above. Zanya's gaze climbed the stairs that led to the bedrooms. "Tara?"

There was no reply.

She slowly scaled the steps, listening when she reached the second floor. "Tara?" She knocked on one of the doors. Zanya's gut wrenched. Just because her friend believed Peter was respectable, didn't mean it was true, or a risk Zanya was willing to take.

Another noise thumped from inside another room. Zanya crept to the next door and listened. "Tara?" More shuffling noises. If her friend was in trouble, invading their privacy was the least of her concerns. Zanya turned the knob and shoved open the door.

Her skin turned clammy and the warmth drained from her face.

A boy with dirty blond hair and crystal blue irises shot up to his feet, his strong arms and lean body tense.

Zanya's eyes widened and she stumbled back, slamming her back into the wall. "Jayden." She slid down the wall and cradled her head in her hands, swallowing down the nausea clawing up her throat. It had to be another bad dream. This couldn't be happening.

"Zanya, are you all right?" Jayden crouched beside her and rested his hand on her shoulder. Her gaze dragged from his hand and up his forearm, now covered in tattoos.

"Do. Not. Touch. Me." She narrowed her eyes as, raw, untamable heat bellowed in her gut. She slapped his hand away. "I said, don't touch me!" She pushed to her feet, hands balled into tight fists. "Don't you ever touch me! What the hell are you doing here? Who brought you here? Is this some kind of sick joke?"

"No, Zanya, calm down and I'll explain." He backed up a few steps, out of striking distance.

She jabbed her finger in the air. "Don't you dare tell me to calm down! You just disappear one day without so much as a good-bye, a note, a screw-you-I'm-leaving, and *you're* telling *me* to calm down?"

Arwan was the first to reach them, followed close behind by Tara and Peter. When Tara rounded the corner, she came to a screeching halt. Her jaw dropped open. Peter ran into the back of her in the crowded hallway.

"Okay then." Jayden turned his attention back to Arwan. "Since we've had the great pleasure of meeting already, I guess introductions aren't necessary."

"Am I the only one who doesn't know what's going on?" Peter asked.

"Apparently so. I'm Jayden, the seeker. Your boss asked for my help to find the stone."

"How did you find this place?" Arwan said.

"Well, that's a funny thing." He squared his stance. "I called to see how things were going, and your boss told me Zanya had been here for a few days already."

"You know each other?" Zanya's gaze darted between Jayden and Arwan.

Jayden scoffed. "Unfortunately."

Suddenly the heat fueling the fire in her chest fizzled out, replaced by a fierce cold that left her trembling and unable to stand. She slumped against the wall, the reality of the situation slowly sinking in. Tara shoved through the hall and hooked her arm around Zanya's waist, supporting her the best she could.

Jayden shifted toward Zanya and reached out.

"Don't, Jay." Tara held her hand out in front of her. "Just, don't."

He lowered his arm to his side. "I didn't mean to scare anyone."

Arwan shifted closer to Jayden, his glare intensified. "I don't know why she's so upset you're here, but if you bother her, you will regret it."

After a few tense moments, Arwan turned toward Zanya.

Zanya's body trembled. "I really can't do this right now."

"I don't understand," Arwan said.

"Yeah." Tara cleared her throat. "About that." She leaned in and whispered in Arwan's ear.

***

Arwan

Arwan waited in the study with the rest of the group. He glared across the room at the seeker. The same seeker he hadn't wanted there to begin with, even before Tara told him who he really was.

Zanya's ex-boyfriend.

No wonder she was hysterical. Now it all made

sense. Her apprehension. The fleeting comments of still having a broken heart. The seeker had hurt her.

Tara was the first to arrive, Zanya following close behind. Arwan stood and walked toward them. Her eyes were red and glossed over, no doubt from crying.

Zanya stared over his shoulder. He turned to see the seeker walking toward them. Arwan's jaw tightened. If the seeker were smart, he'd watch every word that came out of his mouth.

Arwan's attention snapped back to Zanya. He sensed her heartbeat now in rapid fire.

Something was wrong.

"She has a small problem with panicking," Tara said discretely. Zanya swayed on her feet. "Okay, maybe not so small." Tara steadied Zanya. "Just think of something else—one of your music pieces. What's the name of that one you like so much, from that Gadsuit song?"

Zanya clutched her chest. "*The Gadfly Suite.*"

"Whatever. Think of that."

Jayden pushed between them. Arwan stepped aside, more for Zanya's sake than anything. They may have needed the seeker's help, but if he caused any problems, Arwan wouldn't hesitate to force him to leave. A part of him wanted it to come down to that.

"Zanya." Jayden leaned and spoke in a low voice. "I know this is a lot for you, but I can explain if you just give me a chance."

Zanya jerked away from his touch. Arwan stepped closer. "Not right now." Zanya clung to Tara. "I really need to sit down."

As she walked toward the sitting area, the seeker grabbed her by the arm and spun her around. "Zanya, I—"

Arwan clenched Jayden's forearm so tight, the color flooded from his knuckles. The seeker let go of Zanya, his eyes narrowed at the vise grip.

"She said no." Arwan silently dared him to protest. His mother had told him to protect the guardian, and he would, against *anyone*.

Jayden's sharp gaze met his. "I suggest you let go of me, right now."

Arwan tightened his grip. "Or what?"

"Gentlemen." Arwan looked over his shoulder at Renato, who stood beside his desk, pipe in hand. "Shall we get started?"

Arwan released the seeker. Jayden gave one last threatening glare, then turned back to Zanya. "We'll talk later, when we have a little more privacy."

They all sat—everyone on edge and waiting for an explanation. Renato finally broke the silence. "As you are all aware, the seeker has arrived."

"Excuse me," Tara eyed Jayden like some kind of alien life form. "But what is a seeker, exactly?"

Jayden laced his fingers and leaned forward. "A seeker can see someone, even if they're far away. Not the past or the future. I can only see what's happening right now, in the present—anyone at any time, the only restriction being that I need to have a solid memory of that person. They call it *seeking*."

"Why didn't you ever tell me who you are?" Zanya said.

"I wanted to, but I couldn't."

Her eyes narrowed. "Why not?"

"First of all, you never would have believed me. How was I supposed to tell you I can see people who are thousands of miles away? You would've thought I was crazy."

"At least I wouldn't think you're a liar." Her words were laced with clear resentment. The seeker looked away. "So you ran away from the orphanage, and then what? Renato said he asked for help, so how does he know you? And how did you know who I am? I mean, who I really am?"

Arwan's shoulders grew heavy with dread. Everyone in the room understood what she meant, but only he and Renato knew the depth of their search for her. How much it took, and how many people were involved.

"I was sure you were the guardian from years of tracking," Renato explained, "but until Jayden reported back with the confirmation, and I then confirmed myself when I posed as your music teacher, I couldn't be sure. You have to understand." Renato ran his hands down his face, fatigue deepening the creases etched around his eyes. "All of the false leads. All of the years of searching, wasted. We had to be sure."

Zanya shifted in her seat, her gaze darting from Jayden to Renato. "What do you mean he had to—" Zanya lips parted.

Arwan had never been truly disappointed in his mentor, but setting her up for this wasn't right. Even if it was a small sacrifice for the greater good.

"You planted Jayden in the orphanage to spy on me?" Her voice cracked.

Jayden slid to the edge of his seat. "Zanya, it's

not like that."

"How could you?" She shot out of her chair, glaring viciously at Renato. "You told Jayden to get close to me. To make me care about him just so he could identify me? And then..." She covered her mouth with her hand. A tear rolled over the bumps of her fingers. She looked at Jayden. "That's how you left. You never really cared."

***

Zanya

Zanya ran out of the study, through the house, and all the way to the beach. She sprinted as quickly as she could, pouring her anger and confusion into fueling her feet to move faster than she thought possible.

Once she passed the cliffs, she slowed her pace. Her lungs burned, and a sharp pain stabbed into her ribs. Ahead of her were caves, casting a shadow over the sparkling sand. The gaping mouth of the entrance greeted her with an eerie chill. Nearly as tall as a two-story building, it was an enormous hole with only darkness to fill it.

She huffed and sat on a rock near the opening. Some alone time was good. Necessary, even. Her life had gone from a nightmare to a fairytale, to being the punch line of a cruel joke.

The first boy she'd ever loved was a spy. He probably never even cared about her. It was all just part of the job. A searing pain thrashed through her chest as she remembered how badly it hurt when he left. Just like that, in the middle of the night. No good-bye. No explanation. She lived in a haze of shock for weeks after, though in hindsight, the shock was better than the tidal wave of emotions that followed. She'd take shock any day.

She rested her hand over her heart and hung her head. None of it mattered now. She didn't know him anymore. Maybe she never had.

Zanya picked up a few pebbles and tossed them into the sea. The last one was light, dry, and porous. She held it up and rolled it between her fingers. Driftwood maybe. She buried her feet into the silky sand and unearthed more shards like it. Her foot bumped into a large piece, and she pulled it up, only to drop it back to the ground.

Long bones, buried in the sand—splintered, chewed, and very much human.

Bile rose in her throat. She jumped and frantically teetered over the maze of uneven rocks, but lost her balance and slammed to the ground.

Wheezing seeped from deep inside the cave's darkness. A foul stench filled the air. Her heart dropped at the sight of a brown, shriveled form crawling into the sunlight. It dragged its body over the jagged rocks. The creature's white, veiny eyes darted about in search of its target.

Zanya screamed and bolted in the opposite direction. She made it only a few steps before it caught her by the ankle and yanked her back down. Dragging her through the sand, its gurgles formed into barely discernible words. "Ssstone Guard-ian." Thousands of pointed, stained teeth lined the inside of its mouth like a monstrous shark. The beast stood to the height of two men, its bony chest sunken in, covered with thick skin that was wrinkled and split.

Zanya screamed and kicked, trying to break free as it dragged her toward its froth-smeared jaws.

A booming voice sounded like a clap of thunder. "*Muertos vivientes!*" Arwan stood with his weapon—a long, wooden stick with a curved blade on the end, glinting with the sun's reflection. The creature released her ankle and dragged its long arms back to its body.

"Who has raised you?" Arwan demanded.

The monster's voice slithered from between its teeth. "Sarian brought me forth."

"Sarian doesn't have the power to bring minions into the middleworld."

"He demands the guard-ian. We know where you hiiide."

Arwan stepped to the edge of the cliff. "I hide from no one." He leaped off the edge and landed in the sand with perfect form. The beast lashed out, and Arwan ran toward it, whipping his weapon in circles. The blade landed in its intended target and sliced open the monster's chest, leaving a gaping wound.

It hissed and recoiled. Spittle flew from its mouth as it snapped at Arwan with a twist of its bony neck.

"Zanya, run!"

He charged the beast a second time and, with a leaping strike, planted the blade deep into its hide. The creature gargled and spewed out spouts of black slime. Just as it seemed to be dying, its gargles morphed into a sinister laugh. "It is hard to kill—what is al-ready dead." It gripped the weapon with its clawed fingers and yanked it out. The minion ran its long tongue along the edge of the blade, slurping its own putrid blood.

Zanya's feet were rooted in the sand, frozen with fear.

"Zanya, I said run. Go back to the house!"

The beast took advantage of the moment of distraction and dug its talons into Arwan's back. He shouted and arched his spine, then fell to the ground.

Zanya screamed and stumbled. Her breath hitched erratically, her head spinning. The undead creature was exactly like the ones in her dreams. Her nightmares. She gripped her chest and squirmed against the urge to lie down, batting at the fog creeping along the edges of her vision from yet another panic attack.

Lying on the sand, her mind floated between darkness and light until she could no longer tell what was real. She lifted her head to see the blurry figure of Arwan still battling the monster.

He picked himself up off the ground, his shirt soaked in crimson. As the demon crawled toward her, entrails dragged behind it, its lower half completely missing.

Against the will of her failing body, Zanya clawed at the ground and fought to get to her feet. The creature hurled itself on top of her and sank its teeth into her thigh. Searing heat spiked up her leg, and a metallic taste coated her tongue. She swung drunken punches in a feeble attempt to fight back.

Arwan mounted the creature and plunged his

weapon through the back of its skull. The blade broke through its eye socket, nearly slicing into her leg. Black oozed dripped from its wound. The minion withdrew its teeth and thrashed its head side to side.

She tried to stand, but her leg was too badly mangled. A trail of blood stained the sand scarlet. Then, the rush of sick heat. It washed over her. Through her. Coiled itself around every muscle. It pulsed through every vein until her entire body was flooded with the sickness.

Zanya collapsed and heaved. Her leg tightened and seized.

Arwan speared the beast a second time, leaving it skewered and pinned to the ground.

Even with fuzzy vision, she watched Arwan continue to battle the beast.

Strong hands rested on either of her cheeks and Renato's fuzzy features came into her view. "You must fight to stay conscious." He drew his sword and ran into battle, slicing through the demon's neck with one swift downward strike, and sending its head rolling into the sea.

The monster's body went limp. It lay still before the remains sank into the earth, leaving only a black, sticky stain on the ground.

Zanya shivered and held herself tighter. It was so cold. The sickness coursed through her, and she broke out in a sweat. Sounds, smells, everything was dull.

Arwan scooped her into his arms and ran down the beach. As her vision faded, she blinked through the fog at his beautiful face.

Tired. So tired. She rested her head against his chest and listened to the lullaby of his heartbeat, then closed her eyes and drifted away.

***

Arwan

"Is she going to be all right?" Worry tore through Arwan's tone, accentuated by underlying rage that he couldn't cage. He paced beside Zanya, who lay unconscious on the healing bed.

Peter dabbed her wound with ointment. "I think so, but if you don't let me heal you, you won't be."

"I'm fine." Arwan rolled his shoulder, flinching from the dry blood that pulled at his skin. "I wasn't bitten. It's a scratch."

Tara, who had been silent since Zanya was brought in, sat in the corner, nervously bouncing her foot. Her eyes were puffy and red from crying. "When will we know for sure?"

Arwan tightened his fists as he paced. Her heartbeat was weak. He could hear that much. If she died, if Sarian took the only person he was destined to protect...A low growl vibrated in his chest. He closed his throat, cutting it off before anyone could hear.

Peter dropped more bloodstained gauze into the trash. "As soon as I see this wound close up I'll feel better. Right now it's refusing to heal."

Tara's bottom lip quaked. "What does that mean?" Tears streamed down her face.

"It just means I have to do a really good job

cleaning it before I try to heal it again. There are all kinds of broken teeth and sand embedded in the bite wound. I think the minion's saliva is like a corrosive. It's eating away at her flesh."

"Spend only as much energy as you can," Renato said. "If you can't get it to mend, we'll have to figure something else out. Healing takes energy. We cannot have two ill for the price of one."

Peter turned his back to Tara and stepped close to Renato, speaking in a low voice. Arwan's hearing was fine tuned enough to listen from across the room, no matter how low Peter whispered. "If I can't get it to mend, she'll die. I have to keep going."

Renato frowned. "Do you think it's coming to that?"

"Not if I can get it clean before infection sets in." He turned back to Zanya. "How the hell did this even happen?" Peter returned to his seat and used long-nosed tweezers to pick debris out of the gash.

"That's a good question." Arwan stood beside Peter, watching him work. "It said Sarian brought him to the middleworld. We all know that's not possible."

Not unless he had help.

Renato rubbed his hand over his five o'clock shadow. "You don't think *he* had anything to do with this?"

"That's exactly what I think. We all know Sarian doesn't have clearance for something that big. Even as a general, he needs permission, and minions aren't easy to replace. Especially one like that."

"What are you talking about?" Peter said. "You

think one of the underworld gods did him a favor?"

Arwan ignored the question. Though Renato was well aware of what this could mean, there was only so much the others should know.

Renato exhaled and dropped his gaze. "We need to find out whose bones those were. There is a local family who is missing a loved one."

"Only one?" Peter asked.

Renato nodded. "Thank God for that."

Arwan slumped against the wall. "Sarian's becoming impatient."

"Maybe that'll work in our favor. Maybe he'll expose himself more. Be more accessible—Damn it!" Peter shot up, thrashing his hand in the air. He stripped off his latex glove and threw it on the floor. The glove sizzled and disintegrated.

Tara gasped and jumped out of her chair. "What the hell is that?"

"I don't know." Peter held out his hand, burned and raw.

Arwan pressed his fingers over Zanya's wrist. "Her pulse is weakening." He couldn't hear it anymore. He rested his hand over the flickering vein. Even then, it was faint. "What's happening to her?" The warmth in her skin was fading, as were her breaths.

Peter slipped on another glove and worked to clean the wound. "This minion saliva is doing a damn good job at eating straight through my gloves." He removed his glove a second time and replaced it. "There's something still in there. I tried to pick it out, but it nicked the bone. I think it's burrowing in."

Zanya moaned, audibly grinding her teeth.

"She's waking up." Renato walked toward the open door of the healing room. "I'll get Marzena. We have to keep her unconscious." He sprinted into the hall.

Arwan took ahold of Zanya's hand and knelt beside her. "Come on, Zanya. You can fight through this. You have to."

Peter threw his tweezers on the floor, the tips twisted and mangled. Arwan squeezed her hand tighter.

Peter looked at Tara. "Get her out of here."

"What?" Tara shrieked.

"You don't want to be here. Get out." Peter's features tightened and he looked at Arwan. "Grab her leg." Arwan did what he asked. "Hold her down tight. This is going to hurt." Peter drew in a deep breath and dug his fingers into her muscle.

An ear-piercing scream tore out of Zanya's chest. Arwan pinned her flailing body the best he could without hurting her. Her back arched off the table while Peter dug deeper into the wound.

Tara screamed.

Renato returned with Marzena on his heels.

"Get Tara out of the room!" Peter shouted.

Tara sat in her chair and curled her fingers around the wood, glaring defiantly at Renato. "I'm not going anywhere. You'll have to drag me out."

Zanya let out another high-pitched scream. Arwan ground his teeth. The agony of having to restrain her tore through him. But if he didn't, she would die. That didn't make it any easier.

Peter spat out a chain of curses and then threw

something to the floor. Zanya's body collapsed onto the table. Arwan slowly backed away from her limp body. The color had drained completely from her cheeks. He pressed two fingers against her throat.

His heart dropped.

"Don't get near the tooth," Peter said. "Its nerves are still reacting."

"Back away from the guardian." Marzena rushed to her side.

"No." He slid his arms under Zanya's body and picked her up. Her arms fell limp to the sides and her head hung back. "Please, Zanya." He nestled his nose in her hair and closed his eyes. She couldn't be gone. Not when they had just found her. Not when there was more to their story than this.

CHAPTER ELEVEN

Zanya

Zanya blinked open her eyes to a dimly lit room. She recognized it from her last healing session, after Marzena rescued her from Sarian in her dreams. After she learned Sarian's true identity.

It was the healing room.

She slowly sat up; the thin sheet draped over her slid off her shoulders.

Arwan lay asleep on the floor, his hands rested behind his head and his chest rising up and down with every slow, rhythmic breath.

Her lips parted as memories flooded back through the haze. He'd risked his life to save her. He came for her.

She slid the soft cotton sheet off her lap to uncover her leg, wrapped in a white bandage. She wiggled her toes, rotated her ankle, and bent her knee—just a little. Pleased with her mobility, Zanya planted her feet on the floor. A little weight didn't cause any pain. It was only when she tried to stand that her leg failed to hold the full weight of her body.

The idea of waking Arwan to help her out of bed was ridiculous. She could do it. She'd just have to try harder. With another forward heave she made it to her feet, only for her leg to buckle again. The corner of the bed was all she had to cling onto on her way down.

Her yelp woke him, and he jumped to his feet. "What are you doing?" He grabbed her around the waist and lowered her back to the healing bed. "You shouldn't be trying to stand. Not yet."

She shivered and pulled the sheet around her shoulders. "My leg is numb. Like it's asleep."

"That'll wear off in a couple of hours."

She touched the thickly wrapped gauze. Images of the beast burst back into her mind. "I've never seen anything like that thing before." She'd been attacked by similar creatures in her dreams, but they had never crossed that gray space into the real world.

This was bad. The line was blurred, and she had a feeling that thing wasn't the last to claw its way out of her nightmares.

"You're safe now."

His silky voice pulled her out of the memory. She was safe, but only because of him. He'd fought that creature—and gotten hurt in battle. "How's your shoulder?"

"After Peter healed your leg, he took care of the scratch."

"That wasn't a scratch. Your whole shirt was soaked in blood."

"I've had worse."

That may have been true, but it didn't make her any less scared. "How did you know I needed help?"

He exhaled and rested his back against the wall. "The seeker."

Of course. Leave it up to Jayden to give her zero privacy, even after everything that had happened. "I don't like the idea of Jay being able to see me whenever he wants." Although in this case, maybe she should have been grateful. She shifted her weight on the hard, thin mattress. "Can we go somewhere else? I'm kinda uncomfortable."

He held out his hand. "Let me help you up."

She put weight on her good leg. "I think I can do it."

"Zanya—"

"No, I really think I can—" Her knee buckled and she caught herself on his shoulders. He slid his arms under her legs and around her back, scooping her off the floor.

"You're a stubborn woman, you know that?"

Zanya blew a puff of air. "Don't let Tara hear you say that. She'll gloat for the next year over someone agreeing with her." He carried her to the living room and set her down on the couch. She forced an awkward smile. "Thanks."

"Next time, I might charge a fee."

She cracked a smile—a real one this time.

His arm draped over the back of the couch behind her, the heat from his body reached through the sheet, soothing her muscles.

His gaze drifted into the air. Zanya tilted her

head, admiring the sharp angle of his jaw and the dark lashes lining his chestnut eyes. "What are you thinking about?"

He blinked and met her gaze—searching. "You hung so still in my arms. I was afraid I wouldn't get you to Peter in time." He tucked a lock of hair behind her ear.

The cold chills melted away, replaced with a rush of heat. She shrugged off the sheet in an effort to stay cool. He made her body react in ways she wasn't used to and didn't know how to handle. Maybe it would be a good idea to change the subject before she did something stupid. "Speaking of Tara…where is she?"

Arwan must have taken the hint and rested his hand in his lap, giving her some space. "She's with Peter. We weren't sure if you were going to make it. She almost fell apart. If it weren't for him, I think she might have."

"It was that bad?"

"She practically tore the room down trying to cling to the doorway while Renato dragged her out."

Zanya smirked. "Yup. That's Tara."

"Do you remember what happened after the attack?"

"Not really. It's all kind of foggy."

He nodded, his features solemn. "It may be better that way."

She sighed and rested her head in her hands. Now that Jayden had arrived, her life had gotten that much more complicated. They hadn't really spoken yet. Not really. And she had no idea if she'd have the resolve to sit with him and look him in the eye. Not without punching him in the face, first.

"Stop worrying," he said.

"Easier said than done."

"Okay. Then rest now, worry later."

He stood and pulled the sheet back over her shoulders. "You're not strong enough to walk to your room. Just sleep on the couch. It's comfortable."

"Oh, I don't think I'll be getting much sleep." She curled into a ball and hugged herself. "Not after that."

"You don't have anything to be afraid of."

"Maybe not here. But…" She dropped her gaze and swallowed. "When I fall asleep, it's a whole other story. Tara used to be there to wake me up if I had a nightmare. Now…" She curled into a tighter ball and rested her cheek on her knees.

He sat back down beside her. "If it'll help you sleep, I can stay."

Her lips parted as she struggled to seem unconcerned. But with Sarian invading her dreams, and then the creature nearly taking her leg, there was nothing she found more appealing than him staying beside her. "I…" Her stomach twisted. "That's okay. You don't have to."

"I know." He leaned against the armrest of the couch and draped his forearm over his eyes. "But I will."

She yawned and took the other side of the couch, stretching her legs out the best she could. His leg brushed against hers as he shifted to get comfortable.

Zanya melted into the cushions, completely aware of Arwan lying at the bottom of her feet. The sound of his breath was familiar—like the white noise of a fan she used to fall asleep to every night. And he was right. The couch wasn't bad. Her eyes glided closed and she exhaled a long, cleansing breath before she drifted to sleep.

***

Zanya had never experienced the brush of a man's hand trail down the crease of her back. Arwan drew her closer. Breaths passed through her lips in a sweet exhale as she combed her fingers through his silky hair. The contrast of his bronze skin against her lighter tone was striking. His muscles bulged when his arms tightened around her waist, engulfing her in a blanket of serenity. He trailed kisses down her neck, over her collarbone, and down her shoulder.

She yelped and giggled when his breath tickled against her ribs. His dark eyes, glossed with desire, searched hers. The tip of his tongue parted her lips in a deep kiss.

Zanya arched her back. She wanted to be close to him, to feel his chest against hers, to trace her fingers over the curves of his shoulders. She broke their kiss, panting, his breaths mimicking hers. Her lips found the corner of his mouth, then his jaw, and his neck.

A deep moan rumbled in his chest, tantalizing her skin. Hovering above her, he wrapped his arm around her waist and pulled her up. She hung in his arms, her head tilted back as he kissed a trail over her chest.

Her cotton panties tangled in his fingers. Her body went rigid and she grabbed his hand. "Arwan, I don't know if I'm ready."

"What do you mean, you aren't ready?" He sat up. "What did you think was going to happen?"

Her throat tightened. She thought he'd understand. "I…I don't know." Her gaze drifted through the room. Shimmering silk curtains hung over the canopy bed. A wall of windows let in light from the moon and stars above the rolling waves of the sea just outside. Where were they?

A breeze caressed her skin. In only her underclothes, she suddenly felt completely naked. Her attention shifted from their lovely beachside room to the open glass windows.

Arwan grabbed her wrist. She whimpered, searching his beautiful face. What happened to him? Why didn't he understand?

She focused on her only means of escape—the open doors leading to the beach. Before she could get to her feet, the windows slowly began to melt. Hot, dripping glass bubbled and warped into puddles on the floor. The roof rolled back like a scroll, exposing the star-speckled sky. The tiny orbs spun so quickly, they formed bright circles like twirling sparklers.

His grip tightened, bright violet now lining the irises of his eyes. It pulsed and glowed, seeping out until it covered his entire irises.

With all her strength, she kicked him away and scrambled out of the bed, falling to the wood floor with a thud and slamming her shoulder against the corner of a nightstand. She grabbed the sheet hanging over the mattress and covered herself with it. When she pushed to her feet, Sarian stood on the other side of the bed, his body no more than a silhouette in front of the light of the full moon.

She skimmed her trembling hand along the top of the table, finding the base of a heavy lamp. She gripped it as tightly as she could and waited for him to strike.

"I wish you would simply submit. It would be much easier on you."

"Get away from me." She pursed her lips, and a tear slipped over the crease of her mouth. "Please, just leave me alone."

"I'm afraid, young guardian, that simply won't happen."

***

Arwan

"Zanya, wake up." Arwan shook her by the shoulders. She moaned and whimpered. He tightened his lips and shook her again, harder this time. "Zanya."

She closed her eyes tighter and flailed her arms, slapping his chest. He didn't try to dodge her strikes. "Open your eyes." His words turned into pleading. Something was hurting her.

She froze, and with a sharp inhale, woke up. Her teary eyes searched his face. He backed away to give her space. Zanya scrambled against the arm of the couch, her gaze darting frantically around the west wing. After a moment, her back melted into the cushions.

She covered her face with her hands and let out a deep sob.

Arwan rested his hand on her arm. When she winced away from his touch, a dull pain throbbed in his heart. "He can't hurt you anymore." She didn't need to tell him what happened in her dream. Sarian would never give up.

She peeked at him from between her fingers. "How did you know?"

His scowled. "You were screaming. You were screaming at me, then him."

Zanya sat up and wiped away tears. "I was?"

"Was I hurting you?" His head hung low, bearing the shame he had known far too long. "Is that what was happening?" He couldn't have expected any less. She didn't know what he was made of. What he was capable of. Perhaps his darkness had somehow polluted her.

Zanya threw her arms around him. Her hair cascaded across his cheek, carrying the same scent of vanilla and lavender. Her hold grew tighter, and everything inside of him came alive with the need to hold her back. He wrapped his arms around her waist, embracing the warmth of her body pressed close to his.

"Zanya—"

"Thank you for waking me." Her voice quivered.

He couldn't tear Sarian out of her mind, but there was something he could do when the time was right, and he was fully prepared.

CHAPTER TWELVE

Zanya

When Zanya walked into the kitchen, Tara was already there, pouring a cup of coffee. Jayden sat at the table. It was the first time she had seen him since that night in the study. She couldn't even manage a hello.

Zanya hip-bumped Tara. "Hey, coffee is only for upperclassmen."

Tara dropped her cup to the floor, splashing caramel-colored liquid around her feet. "Zanya!" She threw her arms around Zanya's neck.

Jayden winked at her and then pushed out of his chair before leaving the kitchen. For once he left well enough alone.

"Hey," Zanya turned her attention back to her teary-eyed friend. "Pull yourself together. I really need a cup of coffee, and I think you spilled the last of it."

Tara sniffled through a smile. "I'll make some more." She filled the pot with water. "How did you sleep? Any pain in your leg?"

"It's the weirdest thing—I couldn't feel my leg when I woke up. The tingling wore off, but now I'm a little sore." Zanya touched the bandaged muscle. "But I slept fine…for the most part."

"Fine as in—you didn't have any nightmares? Or, you slept beside a hot Belizean guy, fine?" Zanya tried not to turn bright red, but judging from Tara's grin, it was an epic fail. Tara set up the rest of the coffee pot and pressed brew. "I went to check on you this morning after I woke up. When you weren't in the healing room, I found you guys on the couch."

She didn't want to worry Tara and tell her about her latest dream. There was no use.

The coffee pot gurgled, infusing the kitchen with an earthy aroma. "It's done." Zanya poured herself a mug. "Hey, where's Peter? I want to thank him for healing me."

"I'm not sure. I think he's still asleep. I haven't seen him yet this…" Her words trailed off as the ground trembled beneath her feet. Dishes in the cupboards rattled. A vase fell over and spilled water and freshly cut wildflowers onto the stone tiles.

Zanya grabbed Tara's arm. "What's going on?"

The ceiling rippled, sending dust clouds raining over them.

Arwan sprinted into the kitchen. "Get outside!" He flung open the door, letting Jayden and Renato run outside onto the beach. Zanya and Tara followed, then stood with Arwan, watching the home they had grown to love fall under attack.

It rocked back and forth like a massive

146

earthquake had struck its foundation. Thick trails of churned soil ran along the coast, leaving the rest of the ground undisturbed.

Terracotta shingles slid off the roof and smashed into dozens of pieces around them. Hawa was beside them in a split second. She pointed down the beach. "Sarian's here."

Arwan's fists tightened. "In person?"

Hawa nodded.

Arwan rested his hand on Zanya's shoulder. "Stay out here. I'll be right back." He ran inside as Zanya followed the rest of the group toward the jungle. There was no telling how long the house could stand under the attacks, and they couldn't be anywhere nearby if it collapsed.

Arwan burst out of the door, glaive in his clenched hand. Sarian was closer. Zanya could now smell his bitter scent overtake the crisp, salty air. As tense moments ticked by, his thin figure grew closer until she could see the violet in his eyes.

Tara held onto Zanya's arm, her face paled to stark white. "Peter! Peter's in the house!" She bolted onto the open beach.

Zanya gasped and reached out for her. "Tara. No! Get back here!"

Sarian's attention shifted to Tara. He struck the ground and sent a small vibration that threw her to the sand.

Renato ran at Sarian from behind and swung his sword, aiming to kill. The blade cut through the air and came within a wisp of Sarian's throat before a dark layer of light flashed. The weapon bounced back and Renato stumbled in the sand, the sword ringing from the defensive shield. Jayden rushed to his side.

Sarian sighed, both hands rested on the brass grip of his cane. "You see. That is exactly why I have never felt welcome around your kind. Thankfully, this time I came prepared for such poor hospitality." He honed in on Zanya. "Young guardian, I knew you wouldn't be far."

Arwan stepped beside her, joined by Hawa.

"Leave her," Renato ordered.

Sarian cupped his fingers around his chin. "You haven't properly introduced me to your friends, young guardian, although it seems one of them needs no introduction at all." He bowed to Arwan with his cold eyes trained on him. "It's been quite some time."

Arwan's features were as hard as stone.

Sarian shifted his attention to Tara, lying in the sand. "And she must be—ahhh, yes, your friend. I've met her in your dreams. I'm sure you remember. I was the one slicing her throat while you screamed her name, always arriving just moments too late to save her."

Arwan stepped forward, placing himself in front of Zanya.

A deep groan rumbled through the air, making the hairs on her arms stand on edge.

Zanya heard it, felt it, deep in her bones. It must have come from Sarian, but she couldn't be sure.

One thing was for certain, he had something up his sleeve or he wouldn't be there. All she could do was swallow the fear bubbling in her chest and try to appear brave.

Sarian laughed, though it sounded more like a hiss. "Poor boy. He thinks he can defend you. He has always played the martyr. Ahh, to be young and in love again." His eyes darkened with magic. He swung his cane, projecting a dark cloud at Zanya. She threw her hands out to shield herself, and when nothing happened, opened her eyes to see the mass floating in front of her.

Power flickered on her fingertips. It built and spread into her hands, down her arms and to her chest.

Zanya slowly reached out and pressed her fingers against the wavering mass. It was cold and sick—a product of black magic. She peered through its transparent walls to the distorted image of Sarian on the other side.

The light in her chest flickered on. Instinct took over and she threw her hands out, striking the cloud as hard as she could. It projected through the air and struck Sarian to the ground with enough force to send his body skidding along the sand. When he scrambled to his feet, his face was red and his mouth tight.

"You will regret that." His gaze flickered to Tara with a calculating grin. With a wave of his hand, Tara's body was dragged across the sand by some invisible force. He grabbed her by her arm and yanked her up.

"No!" Zanya lunged toward Tara, followed by Jayden, who attacked from behind, but Sarian's shield expanded and encompassed both him and Tara. It flashed deep violet with every pound of Zanya's fists and Jayden's blows.

She fell to her knees. "Let her go!"

"The time for dreams is over now, guardian." His eyes narrowed. "Here is where the real fun begins." He hit the ground with his cane, and with a burst of violet light, they vanished.

Zanya pounded her fists on the sand. "Tara! Where did he take her?" She raked her fingers over the ground where they stood. "Where are they?" She stared desperately up at Jayden, then at Arwan. "We have to get her back! Why are you just standing there?" She stood, sand sticking to her hands and knees. "What the hell's wrong with you? Why aren't you doing anything? We have to get her back!" Arwan and Renato didn't even try to rescue her.

With a solemn expression, Renato rested his hand on her shoulder. "There was nothing we could do, Zanya. His shield is impenetrable."

Her chest ached with agonizing images of what Tara would soon endure. And she would know, after so many nights spent with that sadistic monster. It was the one thing she kept hidden—how terrible it really was.

Arwan walked to her side. "We will get her back."

If anyone could help, it was him. Even if he didn't really care about her at all, he wouldn't let her best friend die. She was innocent, and the little she knew about Arwan assured her he was better than that. "You. You can go back. You can take us back before he took her. We can save her."

Arwan and Renato held each other's gaze, as if they knew something she didn't. As if neither of them were willing to go after Tara. "No!" Zanya jabbed her finger in the air. "You have to take us back. She's my best friend. If Sarian kills her..." She couldn't finish the sentence aloud, but if he killed Tara, he may as well kill her, too. Zanya curled her fingers around Arwan's cotton T-shirt. "Please." The single word came out in a trembling whisper.

Arwan wrapped his arms around her and pulled her to his chest. He hovered his lips beside her ear. "Hold your breath."

Renato leaped forward. "No!"

She did as Arwan said before Renato could stop them. The air churned and ripples formed around them until the beach became distorted and the clear matter pressed on their bodies. It was as if she had jumped into a sinkhole. The immense pressure made the smallest movement difficult, and breathing impossible.

As quickly as the ripples formed, they vanished. Zanya stood beside Arwan on the beach while the house swayed, under attack. Zanya's eyes grew wide. Had they just jumped through time? There was a tiny part of her that still didn't believe it was possible.

Hawa arrived and pointed down the coast, just as she had done before. "Sarian's here."

Zanya searched around them, but Tara was nowhere to be seen. "Where is she?" The bronze tone of Arwan's skin had paled, sweat trickling down his forehead. "Arwan, what's happening?"

"I can't explain it." He peered down the coast at Sarian's approach. "We've gone back. She should be here."

Something was terribly wrong.

Sarian walked with a purpose, showing no interest in Renato or the continued attack on the house. "Did you really think that little trick would work?" Sarian said. "Or perhaps you forgot who you're dealing with."

Zanya walked toward him, but Arwan reached out, stopping her after just a few paces. "Where is she?"

Sarian studied her with a slight grin. "I didn't expect such boldness from you. I assumed you took after your mother, a cowardly *whore*." His gaze flashed to Arwan. "Well, perhaps you do take after her in some ways."

A deep cooling sensation spread through Zanya's veins and the light in her chest burst to life. A typhoon of inner power crashed through her senses. It was even stronger than before, and she'd take what she could get—especially now. Zanya balled her fists. "My mother was no such thing."

"You should learn how to speak with respect."

Zanya's skin burned as if it was on fire.

"Zanya." Jayden touched her shoulder and quickly recoiled, sucking in a sharp breath through his teeth.

She raised her hands to see a storm of electrical currents flickering over her body. She looked over Sarian's shoulder at Renato, who lowered his sword and stepped back.

Zanya examined her hands as the bright current sparked between her fingers. She looked Sarian in the eyes. "You will return my friend. Unharmed."

Sarian held up a limp piece of flesh with locks of blood-soaked curls hanging from his fingers. "Consider that the price for destroying my minion." He tossed the piece of scalp to the sand. "Next, it will be her head." He struck the earth with his cane and disappeared in a blast of light.

CHAPTER THIRTEEN

Zanya stared down at the tangled mess of flesh covered in blood and sand. Stomach acid rose in her throat. That couldn't belong to Tara. Red curls shimmered under the sun. She cupped her hand over her mouth and turned away. Good God, it was hers.

Renato draped his arm over her shoulder. "Let's go inside." He lead her away. "Our home is still standing. That much we can be thankful for. We will get Tara back. I give you my word."

Slowly, they reentered the house, stepping over splintered wood and shattered glass. As they walked through the kitchen, broken dishes lay scattered on the floor. The grandfather clock in the foyer had fallen, its weights and chains spilled out onto the hardwood.

"Where's Marzena?" Hawa asked.

"She left last night. It's of no consequence. She wouldn't have been able to help."

Hawa scoffed. "Maybe she could have kept her little friend from running—" She froze and her eyes widened with a gasped. "Peter!" She disappeared from sight in a streak of color. Zanya dashed to keep up with the rest of the group as they flooded into the west wing.

When she burst through the door, Hawa shouted from the upper floor. "He's up here. I need help!" She followed Renato up the stairs into Peter's bedroom to find Hawa yanking on the solid wooden beam with all her might. The color of her face morphed into brighter shades of red as she strained under the immense effort.

The beam was as long as the room, thick, and unbelievably heavy. Renato wrapped a single hand around the wooden slab, and in one mighty heave, lifted it off Peter, allowing Arwan and Jayden to drag him out. Hawa screamed frantically, running her hands over his contorted frame.

"No, Peter, wake up." Her trembling hands hovering over his chest. "You have to wake up."

Renato carried their wounded friend to the healing room. Zanya clung to Arwan's arm, waiting to see if any life still lingered in Peter's limp body. Peter may not have been her favorite person, but she didn't want him to die. And with Tara gone, Zanya would give almost anything to take back all the times she'd been so cold and crass. She'd never forgive herself if he didn't get through this.

Renato laid Peter on the healing bed and tore open his shirt to expose his chest—black, blue, and sunken in from the impact and weight. Bruises formed in front of Zanya's eyes as more blood pooled under his skin.

Jayden winced.

Zanya turned away. Arwan placed his steady

hand on her back. The room was deathly quiet.

Hawa sobbed in the corner, falling to pieces. It wasn't right. She may have been a lot of things, but nobody should watch someone they care about take their final breaths.

Zanya walked to Hawa's side and took her by the shoulders, turning her away from Peter. "You don't want to see him like this."

Hawa's lips quivered. "He can't die." Her voice was broken and cracked. "I love him. He can't die."

Zanya's heart ached. Arwan did say Hawa and Peter once dated, but with the girl's fierce façade, Zanya didn't peg her as the girlfriend type. Maybe that was why they broke up. Maybe it was something more. Either way, the girl was always so tough, so unreadable. Now, she was broken and sobbing for just one more day. "He's not going to die. Renato will help him. He'll be fine." Zanya spoke with the best sure and steady tone she could, hoping it would mask her uncertainty.

It all made sense—the nasty remarks, the sharp tones, and the I-don't-give-a-shit attitude. The girl may have not been warm, but she could love, and she loved Peter. More than anyone understood. Jayden took Hawa's hand and led her toward the exit. He glanced over his shoulder, and in that moment, Zanya couldn't refuse to acknowledge him. She smiled softly and nodded.

Once they were out of the room, she returned to Arwan's side, and watched in horror while Renato began to administer CPR.

Renato's mouth contorted with desperation as he pumped Peter's chest, pausing only to take his pulse. "Come on, Peter, breathe. Breathe, damn it!" He continued to pound his chest, then pushed several breaths into his lungs. Renato stopped to listen for a heartbeat.

The room fell silent.

So silent.

Zanya cringed when Hawa's frantic scream echoed through the halls, followed by Jayden's hushed voice, offering what little comfort he could.

***

There was no laughter, no joking, and no storytelling. They simply sat in the kitchen, each lost in their own thoughts. The rooms seemed colder, less joyful, and less inviting. It was as if the house itself was heartbroken that Tara was gone.

Renato called Marzena home. He insisted she was the most qualified to find Tara after Jayden's efforts had failed. It took her three days to get back. They were the longest three days of Zanya's life.

When Marzena entered the kitchen, everyone paused. She stood, motionless and brilliant as always, but with a sadness lingering behind her emerald eyes. "I cannot locate Tara. I see only darkness and static."

"Same for me when I seek her," Jayden said. "Sarian too. It's like they're...nowhere." He slumped down in a bar chair. It wasn't often he was so gloomy. Jayden usually took things with a grain of salt. That, or he was strong enough to hide emotion—good, bad or indifferent.

Renato patted Jayden on the shoulder. "You see,

you could have done nothing more than you already have."

"Wherever he is keeping her," Marzena said, "he has made sure we cannot locate her with our abilities."

"We have to find her." Zanya slammed her fist on the table. "We were so close to losing Peter, and I won't just give up and leave her to die." She would do whatever it took. *Whatever* it took.

Renato now paced her. "We will find another way."

None of them could possibly know how important Tara was to her. She wasn't just Zanya's friend. Tara was her sister, her other half. The idea of losing her forever was more than she could bear.

Jayden rested his hand over hers. "We'll find her. I'll keep working at it. She's my friend too."

He was right. Spy or not, he'd spent years in that orphanage, just like they had.

Jayden looked at Arwan, who narrowed his eyes at Jay's hand over hers. Jayden grinned. "What's the matter, Arnie? Do I intimidate you?"

Arwan scoffed. "Nobody intimidates me."

Were they seriously fighting at a time like this? "First of all." Zanya pulled her hand from under Jayden's. "I'm still pissed at you. Second, I just lost my best friend. I haven't been able to eat, sleep, or even think coherently. I don't know where she is, or if she's even alive." She pushed out of her chair. "There are bigger things to worry about right now than you two measuring your egos."

Zanya walked out of the kitchen, and somehow ended up in the music room. She slid down the wall and wrapped her arms around her knees.

There were times she had to be strong. Then there were the times she was by herself and allowed her emotions to break through. So, surrounded by instruments, with a melody swaying in her mind, she broke down, counting all of the *what ifs*.

What if she grew up knowing of her role in this world?

What if she had never met Tara and put her in so much danger?

What if she were better…stronger…a leader, like Renato was so sure she was.

Zanya searched for the beautiful, mahogany violin, finding it rested on a silk pillow in its case. She lifted it out, running her fingers over its sleek, curvy lines.

She reached for the bow and rested it against the strings. With a single pass, a note stretched into the air. She smiled softly. The bow glided over the strings like ball bearings over marble. Flawlessly.

She tucked the chin rest under her chin and drew in a deep breath. With her fingers pressed over the strings, she pulled the bow across the violin, playing the Romance movement of *The Gadfly Suite*—her favorite movement.

The familiarity of the notes filled the void in her chest, allowing her to breathe. The bow and violin danced in a ballet of suffering and beauty, caressing each other like lovers. They conjured a magic she couldn't explain. A healing power, maybe. Healing for her heart.

The wooden floor creaked. Zanya opened her eyes and stopped playing.

Jayden leaned against the doorframe.

He crossed the room, his shoulders moving with every stride. The same shoulders she'd cried on, leaned on, depended on. It was the first moment they'd been alone together since he came back. The pain of betrayal stabbed at her.

"You've always played so beautifully." The familiar tone of his voice carried such tenderness. He lifted the violin out of her hands and set it aside. "I was never very good."

She returned the bow to its case, brushing her fingers over the horsetail and cherry wood one last time. "You were actually pretty terrible."

Jayden took her hands and turned her palms to the sky. He brushed his thumbs over the creases. Some were scars, others were natural folds of her skin. "You have the hands of a violinist; long fingers and strong wrists. You've gotten even better since…"

She wanted to forgive him and put this all behind her, but it wasn't that easy. Did he think he could put her through hell, then pop back up out of nowhere and not face the consequences? "Go ahead. Say it." She yanked her hands out of his. "Since you left. Since you vanished, more like it."

He locked eyes with her. It was so much like him, to not be afraid of anything—even her reaction to his pathetic excuses. Because whatever he had to say wouldn't be enough.

"I argued with Renato for days to let me stay, but he said it would be safer and easier for you once I was gone. I've watched over you. I never forgot…I never forgot about us." He leaned in to kiss her.

She pushed him back with a scoff. "Are you kidding me? You think you can just come back and make it all right with a kiss? Do I look like some Disney princess in need of being rescued?"

"I know you're angry, but we're right for each other. We always have been."

As heavy as Zanya's heart was, in that moment it somehow became even heavier. "In all the years that we've been friends, did I ever hurt you?"

He dropped his gaze and exhaled. "No."

"You meant more to me than anything. You and Tara were all I had." Her voice hitched in her throat.

He glided his fingers up her arm. Zanya jerked back. They stood together in silence for a stretched, tense moment before he spoke. "The last time we saw each other...do you remember?"

Zanya didn't respond, the memory too harsh to recall.

"That night, standing in the cafeteria..." He smirked. "It was all we had. Just our dorm rooms, the hallways, and the gardens, but only during the day. So we went to the cafeteria—"

"You broke in, is more like it."

He chuckled. "Yeah. You were scared we'd get caught."

"And we did. I got like twenty hours of psych time for that."

His smile widened. "But it was worth it." His crystal blue eyes met hers. "That was the night I was sure you were the guardian. You gave yourself away. The energy built inside you. The light wasn't there, but the cold that rushed over your skin was enough. When I kissed you..." He leaned in closer.

"That's when it happened. That's when I knew you loved me. That we belonged together."

How dare he drag her through this again? She glared. "You knew how much I cared about you and you left anyway. When you said you loved me that night..." Her gaze softened. "Did you even mean it?"

"I meant it, Zanya. I loved you. I still do."

She winced at his words and stepped back. "I don't know what you want from me. You've been gone for over six months. All I know is that I have to find a way to get Tara back. Nothing else matters right now."

He nodded, his mouth turned down in a tight-lipped frown. He shoved his hands in his pockets, which immediately reminded her of Peter. Another streak of pain shot through her.

She walked toward the exit. "I'm going to see how Peter's doing." She paused at the door. "I'm sure he's bored all alone in his room."

CHAPTER FOURTEEN

Zanya sat with her legs crossed on the floor of the study, piles of books stacked around her. After Jayden's seeking efforts fell flat and Marzena's attempts yielded no result, it was time to take matters into her own hands. Arwan and Hawa joined in, assisting in the research.

There were countless books in the library, many of them handwritten journals. Zanya picked one up and admired the antique finish. "Where did these all come from, anyway?"

"All of what?" Hawa never tore her focus away from her book.

"All of these." She slid the hand-crafted journal across the floor to Hawa, who picked it up.

"It's a scribe's journal."

"Which is?"

"A-scribe's-journal," Hawa repeated slowly.

Zanya grabbed another book from beside her. "Saying it slower doesn't help clarify anything."

"She doesn't know these things yet," Arwan said.

Hawa rolled her eyes. "A scribe's journal is exactly what it sounds like. The journal of a scribe. The writings of the original Mayan civilization were almost lost during the Spanish conquests. Though a lot of the cities were already abandoned, the Spaniards invaded what was left and burned most of the literature. Anything written on papyrus and bark was destroyed, and the language became forbidden to speak. These are what survived."

"Whoa. You guys must have everything they ever wrote."

"Not even close. The books in our library are just the ones that were smuggled out of the villages. The elders hid them until Renato built this house. Now they're kept here for safekeeping."

"So, they're history books." It was half question, half statement.

Hawa shrugged. "Pretty much. History, religious rituals, all that. Anything the scribes could record about our history. It's all here."

Renato entered the study and paused, raising an eyebrow at the mess of books. "What are you doing?"

"Hoping to find something useful," Zanya said. "I'm thinking if Jay or Marzena couldn't find Sarian, maybe there's something here that can help."

He continued to his desk. "Anything interesting?"

"No, not yet." Zanya sighed. "Plenty of uninteresting stuff, though." She displayed the journal in her hand. "This is part two." Her gaze scaled up the shelves. "I must have left part one up there."

With a bit of bravery, she climbed the ladder to the top. Stretching on her tiptoes, Zanya stretched for the title and caught it with her fingertips. "Got it." She slid it out.

"I don't think you're going to find what you need in that one either," Hawa said.

Zanya climbed down the ladder, relieved when she planted her feet firmly on the floor. "How would you know what we're going to find?"

"Because we've been reading for hours."

Zanya exhaled and set the book on Renato's desk. Hawa was right. They had been at it all day. Her throbbing eyes were testament to how many pages she'd searched through.

Tara could be anywhere in the world, and they were just a few people in a library. No high-tech tracking equipment. Not even a clue where to start. Zanya hung her head and rubbed her eyes. For the first time, the idea of not getting Tara back became a real possibility.

Hawa rested her hand on Zanya's arm. "Hey...I didn't mean—" Hawa pulled away and glanced at Arwan. "I think this is your, you know, area of expertise."

Arwan drew Zanya close and rested his chin on the top of her head. "I think we should take a break."

Zanya sniffled. "Do you think we'll get her back?"

"Yes, I do. But you've been at this for hours. Come on, let me make you some tea. We'll drink it on the veranda."

Zanya followed him toward the door. She nearly stepped over a book lying on the floor, but decided to pick it up. Renato would go nuts if she left his precious library a mess.

She paused and flipped through the pages, stopping on one with an image of an ominous shadow rising from the ground. Zanya furrowed her brow as she read the caption beneath it.

We have assumed that Sarian was the worst threat to our existence. Today is a woeful day for man, for we have discovered there will be a being that, with the desire in his heart, could be far worse. The Star has fallen.

"Zanya." Arwan waited for her near the door. "Tea?"

It could hold a clue. Instead of shelving the journal, she tucked it under her arm. "Yeah, I'm coming."

***

Arwan

The following evening, Arwan sat at the table for dinner. Zanya made stir-fry from the fresh shrimp Hawa brought from the market. He leaned over the plate and inhaled the flavorful aroma of lemon, thyme, and rosemary. His mouth watered.

Peter limped into the kitchen holding his ribs. "I

have an idea."

"Peter. You shouldn't be out of bed." Zanya pulled out a chair for him to sit. Peter moaned, lowering himself into the seat. "What's so important that you walked all the way here from the west wing?"

Peter leaned forward on the table, anticipation building in the room with a long pause. "We can go back."

Hawa exhaled, picking at her food. "We already tried that."

"No. We can go way back. Back further than Sarian thinks we can go. Just hear me out. This all started when Zanya's mother was captured by Sarian, right?" Peter looked at Renato. "How long ago was that?"

"Ellie left seventeen years ago. If we could go back—and allow me to bring emphasis to if—we would need to return to where I last saw her, our last shared link."

Bending time was hard, and seventeen years was farther than Arwan had ever thought of going back. An hour, a few days, maybe.

"So what if we went back seventeen years," Peter continued, "before she was captured. We can get the stone before Sarian does. I know it's a long shot, but if Arwan can do it, if he can take us back that far—"

Zanya bolted out of her chair. "Peter, you're a genius!"

Arwan's gut wrenched. He tightened his jaw. It was a suicide mission.

She studied the faces of everyone in the room.

"What? You guys are acting like you don't think this is an amazing idea."

Arwan ran his fingers through his hair. "Going back that far is dangerous. Not just for you, but for me as well. We would be stuck in the bend for too long. We wouldn't survive it."

"Are you trying to tell me you want to sit and do nothing when we have a chance to really make a difference?"

He narrowed his eyes. "If anyone wants to find him, I do. Trust that."

Marzena placed her tiny hand over Renato's.

"But...we can't...If they—" Renato fumbled over his words.

What he wouldn't give to know what Marzena was saying. Hopefully she was backing him up. There was too much on the line. They had to find another way.

After a few tense moments, Renato squared his jaw. "No. Absolutely not. We are not even going to attempt it."

Arwan nodded. "We'll figure something else out."

"What?" Zanya gripped onto the chair. "It's the best idea we've had since...ever!"

"Arwan is right," Renato said. "It would be much too dangerous. I'm sorry."

"Well, I'm not just going to sit here and do nothing while you guys shoot down every decent idea we come up with. You may not care about Tara, but I'm not going to just stand around while Sarian—"

"Stop," Peter said sternly. "Don't say it. I

can't...I can't even think about it."

Her features softened. "I'm sorry, Pete. I didn't mean..." Zanya locked her eyes with Renato. "You brought me here to help find the stone. I agreed to stay. Now Tara needs us, and I'll put her before anything."

After a tense, quiet moment, Renato's eyes softened. "Very well."

Arwan sat up straight. "This is not an option." He did his best to ignore Zanya's quickening pulse. She was afraid, and she had every right to be. Her best friend's life was on the line, but he would do what he had to in order to keep Zanya safe. "I won't do it." Arwan stood, his shoulders tense.

"What do you mean you won't do it?"

"It's too dangerous. Don't you remember how it was to stand in the bend?" The heavy weight on their chests. The strain on his muscles, tearing them from the inside out. It was agony.

Zanya shifted her weight, her eyes pleading. "If we don't try, the stone could be lost and Tara will die. We will all die. Sarian will eventually break the obedience spell. Once he does, this'll all be over. We'll be outnumbered and overpowered."

"I can't..." Arwan shook his head. "I won't do it." He left the room.

"You should go talk to him," Peter said from the kitchen, just loud enough for him to hear.

No amount of talking would change his mind. He walked through the halls to the west wing, and up the stairs.

"Hey, wait a second!" Zanya's voice called from the bottom floor.

"Leave me alone, Zanya." He clenched his jaw to the sound of her footsteps pounding on the stairs.

"To hell with that. You have to talk to me."

He walked into his room and shut the door. Talking wouldn't change anything.

She flung the door open, crashing the handle against the wall. "What is wrong with you!"

Arwan turned to face her and ranted in Spanish. *"Ever since you showed up, life as I know it has changed. Drina thinks I can save you somehow, but I can't even save myself. My mother tells me to protect and embrace you, but all you do is pull away. I scare you. And you should be frightened. You don't know me, and you never can. So if you really want to know what's wrong with me, it's that I'm completely wrong for you, and I know it, but I can't stop wanting you."*

Zanya stood with her arms crossed, fingers tapping on her biceps.

Arwan snapped his jaw shut and composed himself. Thankfully she didn't understand a word, though a part of him wished she had.

"Are you finished?" she asked, glaring.

He ran his hands through his hair, pulling it out of his face. "What do you want from me?"

"I want you to listen." She stepped toward him. "You're not going to help because it's too dangerous. I'm bound to run into danger. It's my job to protect the stone."

"If you run into danger, it won't be by my doing."

She threw her hands in the air. "Well, you can't protect me from everything. I'll go after Sarian with

170

or without you. My chances are better with you. So…please."

The darkness inside of him clawed through his gut and wound around his spine. He tensed and clenched his fists, fighting it down. "Do you have any idea what would happen to us if I failed to keep the ripples intact? We would all die, and not pleasantly. Do you think it's how you see it in the movies? You pull a lever on a time machine and suddenly you're standing in the past? It's much more complicated than that."

Zanya's eyes narrowed further, this time accompanied by flickers of energy darting over her skin. "We don't have any other choice."

He inspected the pulses of electricity dancing over her skin. It was as if she was covered in diamond dust, glittering and changing with every movement.

She was the most beautiful creature he'd ever seen.

He slowly closed the distance between them and ran his fingers through her strands of dark, wavy hair. Sparks of energy jumped over his hand, cooling his skin. "Don't you get it, you stubborn girl?"

Her gaze was defiant and strong. "That you're refusing to help? That you're running away when I need you the most?"

He dropped his hand to his side, her energy slipping through his fingers. "I won't do it. You're asking me to assist you in a suicide mission."

Zanya turned away from him and paced the room. His gaze drifted to the back wall, to the sketches of his mother. It was so strange to think he had just seen her, and yet she was so far away. Her dark hair was pulled back, showcasing her heart-shaped face.

He'd spent so many years believing she was ashamed of him.

Zanya must have noticed him admiring the drawings. She turned and looked at them. "Are those the drawings of your mother you mentioned on the beach?" He didn't reply. Zanya examined them more closely. "You have her eyes, you know. She was lovely." She turned to face him, and the desperation behind her gaze nearly broke him. "I know how it is to grow up without a mom around. It leaves you feeling kind of...empty, huh?" She sighed and rested her hand on his arm. The warmth of her skin spread through him. "I know you think it's your job to protect me." She huffed. "It's kind of obvious I'm not exactly excelling at my job description. But just for a minute, consider what you'd do if you had the chance to see your mother one last time. Even if it were just for a second. Just to know what it's like to be hugged—" Her throat closed around the word, tears welled in her eyes.

Because of his mother, for the first time since he could remember, he was given a choice. A choice to either continue to run, or do what his mother said he was set on this world to do.

Protect the guardian.

Embrace her.

Keep her close, and stop fighting his destiny.

"For the longest time I believed she was ashamed." He caressed her cheek. "You and

I...we're not so different. We both had to make a choice. You chose to be brave while I chose to hide." A smile curled his lips. "I suppose the old man was right, after all. We choose who we want to be. That takes bravery and faith, something I admire very much in you."

The light in Zanya's chest flickered on and electricity sparked between their bodies. Arwan examined her with fascination. She lifted her hands to see her skin illuminated with a soft white light. "This keeps happening when I'm around you. I'm starting to think it's not a coincidence." She took his hands and laced their fingers together.

"Your skin is like ice."

"It's the light." The electricity jumped to his fingers and crept around his hand, up his wrist. "Tickles, doesn't it?" The sparks traveled up his arm and around his shoulder, causing his hair to stand up. Zanya laughed. "It's a good look on you."

He smoothed down his hair. The energy popped and then vanished like a surge of static electricity. "What do you think triggers it?"

"I'm not sure." Her pulse quickened.

He touched her again, causing the light in her chest to glow brighter.

She arched an eyebrow. "Oh, you think you're really funny, don't you?"

He grinned "Occasionally." In that moment, he'd give anything for his life to be normal. No Sarian. No underworld. No darkness clashing inside of him. Just the touch of a beautiful woman, and the knowledge she cared about him. Wanted him. Needed him.

His breath hitched when she rested her hand on his chest. She shifted closer, her eyes searching his. "This isn't a good idea." She traced the curves of his muscles.

His heart raced under her touch. "I know."

"Someone's going to get hurt." Her gaze landed on his mouth.

"Maybe." He wound his arm around her waist and pulled her closer. Time wasn't like the butterfly field. Rather than pushing him away, she curled her fingers around his shirt, her body temperature rising. He could smell the adrenaline coursing through her. The hairs on his arms stood on edge. "It won't be you."

She smiled softly, as if teasing him to kiss her. "It's always me."

He tucked strands of hair behind her ear, his hand lingering over her jaw. "*It won't be you.*"

She leaned in and kissed him, her lips like warm velvet. She wrapped her arms around his neck and leaned into him.

He parted his lips, deepening their kiss. She sucked in a sharp breath through her nose when he crushed her against his chest. Her tongue rolled over his, commanding every ounce of restraint.

She let out a small sigh, her fingers gently resting on his jaw. When he pulled away, her eyes fluttered open. "I'm going to take that as a yes, you'll help."

He searched her eyes, then looked at his mother's drawings. Zanya would go after Sarian with or without him. At least if he were there, he could keep her safe. "On one condition."

"Let's hear it."

"Promise to put your safety before anything or anyone. No exceptions."

"It's a deal."

CHAPTER FIFTEEN

Arwan waited in the study.

The seeker sat across from him, staring at the doorway.

Peter walked in, making the seeker scowl. It was obvious he was waiting for Zanya to arrive. This time, he would be doing himself a favor to watch how he treated her.

Arwan's attention returned to Peter, who was walking better now. His arm wasn't in a sling anymore, and he only had a slight limp. His healing abilities did him well.

Renato stood from behind his desk, puffing his pipe. "I hope your accommodations are comfortable."

The seeker pivoted in his seat. "Yeah. They're good, thanks."

Zanya's quiet footsteps caught Arwan's attention. He stood and walked through the room, meeting her halfway.

"Ken-doll-Prince Charming-Casanova hybrid," Jayden scoffed under his breath. "What a douche."

If Arwan were anyone other than who he was, he wouldn't have heard the seeker. The guy had a real chip on his shoulder, but Arwan wouldn't play into it. More tension was the last thing Zanya needed.

Zanya gave a brilliant smile. "Hey."

"Are you ready for this?" The road ahead was going to be rough. He doubted she understood just how difficult it would be.

Zanya's smile vanished and she shifted her weight. "I don't have much of a choice."

They walked to the sofa, where he sat beside her. The seeker trained his gaze on Zanya. Arwan didn't need to be a mind reader to know what was reeling through his head. He wanted her.

"So, are we doing this, or what?" The seeker sat back in his seat. "Or should I say, *can* you do this?"

"I'm going to try." Arwan rested his arm over the back of the couch behind Zanya's shoulders. The seeker's glare intensified. "I've never been back that far," Arwan continued. "I always thought it was impossible. Time bending has restrictions, limitations. But I've been thinking. If we measure the time it takes to go back every minute, we can safely figure out how long it would take to go back seventeen years."

Renato's eyes brightened. "That's brilliant."

Jayden huffed. "Of course it's brilliant. Everything that comes out of his mouth is laced in magic and pixie dust." The seeker pushed out of his seat. "Let's stop wasting time."

"*Bueno.*" Arwan stood and held his hand out to Zanya.

"I think she can get off the couch without you

carrying her." Jayden stalked toward the exit.

"Maybe you're angry because you weren't man enough to treat her like a lady."

Jayden froze. "What the hell did you just say?" He turned, his shoulders rising and falling with each breath.

"Ohhh nooo," Hawa said in a low tone.

The seeker stepped toward him. "Not man enough? I treated her like gold!" His shouts made Zanya wince. Jayden seemed to notice her reaction. He reeled himself back and lowered his voice. "He's not the only one who knows a good thing when he sees it, you know."

Zanya's head cocked slightly. "What do you mean?" Her cheeks flushed pink when she realized what had happened. She shot out of her seat and marched toward him. Jay quickly stepped back. "It serves you right! What, you think my life is some kind of channel you can tune in to and watch anytime you want? How dare you seek me without my permission? Who said I want you peeking in on what I'm doing anytime you feel like it?"

Jayden's nostrils flared. "More like *who* you're doing."

Zanya balled her fists, and without a word in response, crossed her arms over her chest, curling her sleeves tight around her fingers.

Arwan fought the instinctual desire to tear the seeker apart. That wasn't him. But that wasn't who he'd chosen to be.

"Zanya." Jayden shifted closer to her and spoke in a whisper. "Why do you make it so damn hard to talk to you? I just want to explain, but every time I do, you turn it into a kick-Jayden-in-the-balls party. What do I have to do for you to listen to me?" Zanya shook her head, still not saying a word. "There's no getting through to you, is there?" Jayden dropped his shoulders. "Fuck it." He cupped her face in his hands and kissed her.

She shoved him away, tearing their lips apart. Zanya gripped her chest, sucking in labored, shallow breaths. "What the hell, Jayden!" She staggered back.

Something inside Arwan snapped, and his world was washed in red. He struck out and wrapped his hand around the seeker's throat, lifting him off the ground. The seeker's feet dangled off the floor, cutting off his breath. Muffled grunts barreled in his chest.

The beast inside of him squeezed his hand tighter. The seeker's eyes widened and he kicked harder, struggling to break free.

Renato grabbed Arwan from behind and pulled back on his shoulders, but he wouldn't budge. "Let him go, Arwan! Let go. You're going to kill him!"

Jayden's eyes glossed with pressure. He used what little leverage he had to punch Arwan in the jaw, but it didn't break his focus.

Renato heaved Arwan back. "Let him go!" Renato's voice was distorted in his ears.

Jayden's eyes rolled in the back of his head.

Zanya grabbed his arms and pulled on him. The warmth of her skin broke the hold of his inner darkness. He looked at Zanya. Her cheeks were pale and her eyes wide. This wasn't who he wanted to be. Arwan blinked and let go of the seeker, letting him fall to the floor.

Zanya's breath skipped and her knees buckled. He caught her before her body hit the floor.

Jayden writhed and gasped, rubbing the tender half circle around his throat. "What the fuck is wrong with you?" His voice was horse as he choked out the words.

Peter rushed to Zanya's side and pressed his hand over her forehead. "She passed out." His hand rested on her chest. "Her heart's beating a million miles an hour. Her pulse is..." He pressed two fingers over her wrist and waited in silence. "Good God. One ninety-two."

***

Zanya

Zanya sat up in bed, still a little hazy from her fainting spell. Whatever had come over Arwan, she'd never seen anything like it. Even Renato couldn't move him, and she had watched him pull a solid wood beam off of Peter with one hand.

There was a knock on her door. She startled. "Who is it?"

"It's Jay."

She rolled her eyes. "Go away."

"Zanya, we have to talk about this."

"I don't want to talk to you."

There was a short pause. "Well, you can't just sit on your bed all day...and stop glaring at me."

Her eyes widened. How dare he seek her, especially after what happened in the study. She sprang out of bed and flung open the door. "What!"

He rested his arm on the doorframe. "Can I come in?"

"No."

"Then can you come out?"

"No!"

He pursed his lips into a tight line. "Stop being so stubborn."

"You're calling me stubborn?" She jabbed her finger at his chest. "You have some nerve."

"I need to have nerves of steel to be around you."

She propped her hands on her hips. "Well if I'm so unnerving, why are you here?"

"Because I fell in love with an unnerving, stubborn girl who drives me nuts." His jaw snapped shut.

"Yeah. I believed that once."

He hung his head. "I'm sorry, Zanya. I didn't mean…" He sighed. "I don't want to fight. How can I fix this?"

She shrugged and crossed her arms. "You had no right to kiss me. None."

His frown deepened. "Yeah, I'm starting to realize that. I just wish there was something I could do to fix this. Fix us."

"Not everything broken can be fixed."

He met her gaze. "Don't tell me that."

"Well, what do you want me to say? That it's so fan-freaking-tastically awesome that you pretended to care about me for a job?" She snorted. "You have some nerve."

"Yeah, well it didn't exactly go as planned for me, either."

"Yeah. Okay."

"You don't believe me?"

Exhaustion washed over her, and she slumped against the doorframe. "I don't know what to believe anymore. My entire life has been one, big, cruel joke. Whatever higher powers are out there, they've been using me as their personal jester, pointing and laughing while I run into every booby trap they've set." She dragged herself through her room and sat on her bed. Jayden lingered in the doorway as she played dolefully with the seam of her shirt. "Are you just going to stand there?"

"You said I couldn't come in."

"Well, if you don't, you'll just stand in the hall and watch me with your sixth sense anyway."

He stepped in and shut the door. "So what do we do now?" He crossed the room and sat beside her.

"I need to find Arwan. He's probably really upset with himself."

"I don't know about being upset with himself, but I'd say he's upset."

"What do you mean? Have you talked to him?"

"No, but I saw him for about five seconds this morning before he took off."

"Where?"

Jayden shrugged. "Do I look like a babysitter?"

His attention wandered, and he peered through the open door to her bathroom. "Well, that's hardly fair. I have to share one with dumb and dumber."

She shot him a your-next-words-could-be-your-last glare.

He raised his hands in defeat. "Fine. Peter and Arnie."

"That's not his name."

"I think it fits him." He lay down and stared at the ceiling. "He reminds me of that guy from Sesame Street. What's his name, with the best friend?"

"Bert and Ernie?"

"Ernie! That's what I'll call him."

"If you want me to kill you." Electricity sparked over her skin, but then fizzled out. Too bad, it would have been so satisfying to zap him. Just once.

Jayden's grin vanished. "Apparently your taste has changed."

"No it hasn't. It just…expanded."

He pushed up on his forearms. "So you still think I'm hot?"

"I did not say that."

"But you didn't *not* say it, either."

She jabbed a finger at him. "Don't push it." There was a knock at the door. Zanya immediately tensed. "Who is it?"

"Arwan. May I come in?"

Zanya jumped off the bed. "Uh…" She stared at Jayden with wide eyes, biting her lip. After a moment of considering her options, she let out a long exhale. It wasn't like she could shove Jayden in her closet. That would look even worse, like she was trying to hide him. "Yeah. Come in."

Arwan opened the door and poked his head in the room. Jayden threw up a peace sign. Arwan parted his lips as if he was going to say something to Jay, but didn't. Instead, looked at Zanya. "Renato wants you to keep studying the abilities of the stone. I'm working with him on the time bending issue, but you should be ready if we figure out a solution. He thought I should tell you rather than ask Marzena. She was worried you were too exhausted for her telepathy." He looked at Jay. "I'll let her know you're feeling better." He slipped back out and shut the door.

Zanya stared at the door. "Great! Now he thinks I was in here with you. That we were…together."

Jayden rocked up to a sitting position. "You were sitting right beside me. I would classify that as together, wouldn't you?"

She balled her fists. "You are—"

"Handsome? Charming? Irresistible?"

"A royal pain in my ass. Get out!"

***

Arwan

The tiny grass hut with a triangle roof was finally in sight. Though Arwan had seen that same hut a thousand times, today it seemed different. Perhaps it was the heartache he carried with him. Either way, he was sure Drina wouldn't be surprised to see him.

Standing outside the mud-spackled walls, he pushed aside the fabric covering the entrance of her home. "*Tía* Drina?"

There was a pause before a familiar rickety voice replied from behind him. "I t'ought you would be here today." Drina struggled with a stack of wood in her arms. He scooped the weight off of the aging woman's bones. She wiped sweat from her forehead, then waved him forward. "Inside."

Arwan ducked through the door and set the firewood onto the grass mat. "You knew I was coming?"

Drina shooed away her graying black hair and scooped a handful of water over her face from the terracotta basin. "You forget who you are talking to, hmm?" Drina puckered her lips while inspecting him from top to bottom. She waved her finger in the air. "Somet'ing is different about you. T'ere is somet'ing weighing you down. Your heart bleeds." She threw wood onto the fire. Flames caressed the curves of the bark, engulfing them with red and orange. "So, you tell me what bot'ers you, and Drina will do her best to help." She plopped on the floor and signaled for him to join her.

Arwan sat across from her, his legs tucked under him and his chest pushed out.

He recalled the stories Drina had told him of tribe leaders gathering around a fire so many years ago. Warriors with painted chests and faces, and armor made of animal bone, all of them participating in the grave discussion of the future of man.

He drew in a deep breath, cuing the wrinkles around Drina's eyes to deepen with observation. "Love can destroy you if you expect it to feed your soul." Arwan nodded in understanding. He wanted nothing more than to allow himself to be happy. But the darkness inside him was not worthy. Worse, it was dangerous. "Your love must be selfless. The guardian will love you in return, only if she knows who she gives her heart to."

"She won't want me if she knows who I am." He ground his teeth. "No one could. I almost allowed it through. I couldn't control it, and nearly killed someone…because of how I feel about her."

After a silent moment, Drina reached for something near the firewood, and then whopped him on top of his head with a stick. Arwan jumped and rubbed the sore spot on his scalp. "Enough of feeling bad for yourself." Drina waved the broken branch in his face, her wrinkles puckered into a scowl. Grunts pushed out of her throat as she got to her feet and stared down at him.

Arwan stood so he wouldn't be at perfect beating level. "What was that for?" The woman had lost her mind.

Drina grabbed him by his earlobe. "Pitiful boy sits. Does not'ing but rolls in mud like an elephant in the heat." Arwan stumbled under her lead, half-crouched while Drina dragged him out of the hut and to the bank of a stream.

When she finally let go, Arwan stood up straight, nearly two heads taller than her. He rubbed his ear without the slightest clue how to respond. Drina was a lot of things, but truly insane wasn't on the top of the list. Something had set her off, and he was better off to shut his mouth and listen.

She poked him in the stomach with the stick. "The power inside you did not flare because of a weakness, but from finding someone who you care for more than yourself. Your balance." She pointed to the water. "You are who you are, and you know what the ripples of fate can do. And you fear them." She threw the stick in the water, causing a school of guppies to scatter in every direction. "But you forget. When the surface stands too still, not'ing changes." Her rickety fingers wavered in front of him. "The ripples are progress." She perched her fists on her hips. "But you…" She shook her head, her bushy eyebrows pushed downward. "You will never find happiness."

Arwan's chest constricted. In all the years he'd known Drina, she was never wrong. Not in her predictions, not in her advice. She knew him inside and out, and the truth that had come from her lips nearly sent him crumbling to the ground. "You are too selfish. Too scared." She waved her hand in the air as if shooing away a mosquito. "Too weak." The old woman slowly waddled back to her grass hut. "Your mot'er was wrong." Her voice faded with every step. "You are still not ready."

He crouched and stared into the mirror surface of the slow-moving creek. It had been a long time since he was brave enough to look at himself in the mirror.

Zanya was right. He did have his mother's eyes.

He squared his jaw as a well of determination roared to life. It was deep, savage, and fierce. He pushed his chest out and leaned closer to the water's surface.

He wouldn't be like the guppies, clustered together because they were too afraid to venture out alone. They may be up against the general of the underworld, but he'd be damned if he'd let Zanya face Sarian alone.

Not when he was the only one who could.

He slapped the surface of the water, scattering

the tiny fish and distorting his reflection. There were so many days he didn't feel human. As the water pacified and regained its smooth surface, the reflection that stared back at him was much different than before.

The person he saw now was filled with purpose.

CHAPTER SIXTEEN

Zanya

The next morning, Zanya walked into the kitchen while humming a classical tune. What happened with Arwan seeing Jayden in her bedroom was an issue she would just have to deal with later. Now, she needed to find a way to go back.

She grabbed a bagel and some coffee, and then headed to the study. Renato smoked his pipe, as he usually did, sending clouds of smoke billowing into the air.

She bit a chunk from the bagel. "That'll kill you, ya know."

He smirked. "I have been smoking a pipe for a thousand years. I believe I'm past the point of concern."

She chuckled as she leaned over his desk and peered at dozens of math problems scribbled on a sheet of paper. "What are you doing?"

"Arwan and I did several practice sessions this morning. It only took a few before I was able to calculate an estimated travel time." He offered her the mathematical Rubix Cube.

"Uh-uh. You'll have to explain this to me. I was never very good at math."

"From what I understand, Arwan is extremely vigilant. I estimate it would take a total of seventeen minutes to bend time back by seventeen years. One minute per year, which is extraordinary."

"But, when we were in the bend, we couldn't breathe. We can't last seventeen minutes with no air."

"No, we cannot." Leaning back in his chair, he rubbed his chin. "Perhaps we should be asking *how* we can breathe while in the bend."

"It was like a truck was parked on my chest. Even if we found some kind of oxygen mask, how would we get one with a tank that could withstand the pressure?"

"It is possible we could use deep-sea diving tanks. They are designed to withstand tremendous amounts of pressure."

"And what if they don't work right? What if the tubes burst or something comes loose? Besides, oxygen is really flammable. What if one of the tanks was cracked or leaked? It could explode and kill us all."

Renato sat in silence, his chair creaking as he rocked back and forth. "Very good points." He rubbed his chin. "What if we can find a way that is not normal? A truly abnormal means, indeed."

He picked up the phone and dialed a number. It took only a moment before he began conversing in a strange language. Minutes later, he hung up the phone and stood.

Zanya gestured to the phone. "What language were you just speaking?"

"Yucatec is a Mayan dialect."

"I didn't know you spoke Mayan."

"It's actually my first language. It was only later I learned Spanish, and then English."

"Wow, you're trilingual?" She was lucky to slide by with a passing grade in French class in the orphanage.

"I'm what they would call a polyglot. I speak Yucatec, Spanish, English, and then German, Arabic, and a bit of Mandarin."

Zanya sighed. "Of course you do."

"When you've been alive as long as I have, you either spend quite a bit of time being bored, or you learn something. I chose the latter."

"How many Mayan languages are there?"

"It's not a question of how many languages. It's a question of dialects. Over the years, there have been numerous variations formed throughout Central America. I believe now there are over forty different accents, although Yucatec is most commonly spoken, and the dialect I suggest you learn. It should only take you a few years, with some practice."

Just the thought of studying another language made her head spin. "Yeah, maybe," she lied. Time to change the subject before he handed her another stack of books. "What was that phone call about?"

"That was a friend of mine. He's a collector of rare and endangered artifacts."

"What, like an archeologist?"

"No. More like a mad scientist of sorts."

Zanya's eyebrows shot up. "So you're asking Victor Frankenstein for help now?"

Renato laughed. "A *Frankenstein* fan, are we?"

"Not me. Tara." Zanya grinned, recalling Halloween movie night at the orphanage. *Frankenstein* was always Tara's favorite, even though she'd seen it a dozen times.

Zanya's attention was pulled back to Renato while he gathered papers from his desk. He turned to her and rested his hand on her shoulder. "I suggest you go ready yourself. Thursday will be a big day for you."

"Thursday?" She shifted her weight. "What's Thursday?"

"Thursday, we travel to see your mother."

His hand slipped from her shoulder, and Zanya stared after him as he left the study. She'd always pictured reuniting with her mom. The magical moment in which her mother would hug her and confess how she'd tirelessly searched for her all these years. Zanya always imagined she would be happy. Overjoyed, even. But instead, she found herself with a knot in her gut.

"Okay then." She smoothed down her shirt. "In three days, I'll meet my mother."

***

Zanya spent the next few days reviewing the books and spending more time than she cared to admit swallowing down the metallic taste from rattled nerves.

As promised, she sat in her room, studying the books Renato had given her. She yawned and picked one up titled: '*Abilities*'.

That was it.

Just a single word to mark a book that must have been a thousand pages long.

The thick, leather cover was tied closed with twine. She carefully undid the knot and opened the cover.

Pg. 1: Healing

Pg. 266: Transformation

Pg. 592: Sprinting

Pg. 783: Strength

Pg. 991: Currents

Peter was a healer, and Hawa a sprinter. Renato had strength, which apparently she'd have too. But she'd never heard of transformation or currents.

She flipped to page two hundred twenty-six, where the bold lettering marked the chapter.

There was a sketch of a woman on the right, and to the left stood a sketch of an elderly man. Her eyes narrowed as she read the text scribbled beneath it.

Transformation is an ability of moderate talent. One must have focus to master this ability.

"Focus," Zanya said to herself. "I could do that."

Step one. Clear your mind. Find your center and breathe deep. Be aware of your entire body. The tips of your fingers, your limbs, your heartbeat. Do not allow any distractions to divide your focus. The Riyata must be completely neutral in both emotion and mind to accomplish this ability.

Zanya stood from her bed and propped the book on a pillow to face her. "Okay." She drew in a deep breath, shaking out her hands. "Deep breaths. Tranquility."

Step two. Picture your body changing. Do not just believe it can happen, but actively play the process through your mind, as if it is happening at that very moment. If the target has long hair, the Riyata must imagine their hair growing. If the target has colored skin, the Riyata must picture the color of their skin changing. It is vital to allow the process to take place in order to transform successfully.

Step three. Transform. Voice, appearance and even clothing can be changed in this process. Once the transformation is complete, the form may be held until the Riyata wills themselves to change back. To transform back, the Riyata must repeat the above steps in order to return to their natural form.

"Um…okay." She stretched her neck side to side. The book said this ability was of moderate difficulty. If she could throw up a force field, maybe she could do this, too. But who did she want to change into? Someone she was familiar with. Someone she could hold a mental image of without any doubt of their appearance.

"Tara it is." She drew in another deep breath and relaxed her muscles. Using yoga breaths she learned in group therapy at the orphanage, she centered herself in the quiet room. Her eyes were closed. Her breaths rhythmic. Her heart drummed in her ears and her limbs fell limp. She cleared her mind and focused only on Tara.

Tara had freckles. Lots of them.

The skin on Zanya's cheeks burned as if she had stood in the sun for too long.

And red, curly hair that ended just past her shoulders.

Her scalp tingled and pinched.

How was she supposed to stay focused when everything she changed, hurt?

She swallowed; her concentration was slipping. She pulled in another breath and exhaled slowly through her mouth, centering herself.

Her voice was—

There was a knock at her door.

Zanya gasped and her eyes flew open. "What!" she shouted in her own voice. Apparently that part hadn't taken.

There was a long pause. "It's me, Peter."

What the hell was Peter doing at her bedroom door at—she checked the clock hung on her wall— eleven at night. "Um…" Zanya turned and looked in the mirror. Her eyes widened and she stumbled back, tumbling over her bed and onto the floor. She knocked her elbow on the nightstand and groaned. "Damn it."

"Are you okay?" He asked through the door.

Zanya buried her fingers in red, curly hair. "No. Definitely not okay."

The knob rattled. "You sound like you need help."

"No. No you can't come in!" She jumped to her feet and threw herself at the vanity. Freckles dotted her own olive completion. She crinkled her nose. The red hair looked like a bad wig.

"I just came to check up on you. Renato's been worried about you."

Zanya spun to face the door. She couldn't let Peter see her like this. She smoothed down the coarse curls. "I can't talk right now. Maybe later. Tell Renato I'm fine."

There was a streak of silence. "Are you?" His tone had taken a softer edge.

Zanya shifted her weight. Shooting him down might make Peter think she was hiding something. He didn't need any more stress than he already had.

"Just, hang on." She closed her eyes and drew in a deep breath. "Clear your mind," she whispered. Her limbs grew heavy. Her breaths softened. With a mental image of herself to focus on, her scalp and cheeks pinched and tingled.

She opened her eyes and looked in the mirror, and released a long exhale. She ran her fingers through strands of brown, wavy hair and over her cheeks, now freckle-free.

Note to self. Moderate meant hard.

She could only imagine how difficult the advanced abilities would be.

Zanya walked to her door and pulled it open. She stuck her head out into the empty hall. "Peter?" When there was no response, she leaned against the doorframe. Too bad. He sounded like he needed to talk.

She shut the door and walked back to her bed. She scooped up the book and snapped it shut, tying it closed with the twine. Maybe she needed to be bonded with the stone to do these things. Maybe Sarian was right. Without her stone, she was worthless.

Zanya collapsed into bed, staring up at the ceiling, where she drifted off to sleep.

The next morning was welcomed with rays of crisp sun shining through her window and a knock on her door. She sat up in bed. "Come in."

Hawa swung it open. "It's time. Get up and get ready." She was dressed like an assassin, with knee-high leather boots and several weapons strapped to her belt.

Zanya crawled out of bed. "Why are you dressed

like that?"

"We're going to get the stone, remember?" She planted her hand on her hip. "Or has all of this escaped you?"

Zanya stood, covering her mouth through a yawn. "No, of course not. But..." The row of daggers gleamed in the light. She raised her brow. "I don't have any weapons. Do I need any?"

Hawa grabbed the door handle. "Zanya, you are a weapon. Now get out of bed before the boys come up to find you like this. It'll be my ass Renato chews on if you're not ready in time."

After cleaning up and getting dressed, Zanya made her way outside onto the beach. She didn't have a huge wardrobe of clothes to choose from, but what she did have fitted her fine. Because there was no way of telling what exactly they'd encounter, she chose a pair of yoga pants and a tank top with cardigan to layer over.

Once she got outside, everyone in the group looked just as dangerous as Hawa.

Jayden came out the back door and jogged across the beach. A bow in his hand and a quiver of arrows bunched in a holster on his back.

Since when did he become an archer?

Marzena glided out and settled beside Renato.

Peter and Arwan were both dressed in cotton clothes with leather patches on their elbows and knees, weapons strapped to their own holsters.

"Marzena will link my mind with Arwan's," Renato said. "In order to take us to Ellie, he has to see our last link in time."

Jayden handed Renato something that resembled

a high-tech toolbox.

"What is that?"

"These are our oxygen masks." Renato set the box on a weathered table and opened it to reveal a pile of slimy, twisting creatures flailing their slippery bodies toward the sun.

Zanya jumped back, clutching her stomach. "Those are our masks? What are they?"

He removed one from the box. Its wide, flat body covered his entire hand. Renato held it at arm's length as the worm reached for his face. "These are the first ancestors of the modern-day fluke worm. They have been kept alive in a lab that belongs to a very close friend of mine, who enjoys collecting...unique antiquities. They are very resilient, surviving for thousands of years in the harshest conditions and most inhospitable climates."

"And what exactly are we going to do with them?"

Renato braced his hand on Hawa's shoulder. It was clear from her curled lip she wasn't happy to have the creature near her, but that didn't stop her from backing away. She nodded.

Zanya watched what seemed like a horror movie as Renato lifted the parasite to her face. The worm elevated the top half of its body, and then launched toward her. It expanded to a thick, flat mask, sticking to Hawa's nose and mouth. Hawa gasped and choked as the worm latched on.

Zanya screamed and stumbled back. Hawa righted herself just as the parasite attached a set of suction cups to her face. Its flat body rose up and down, and after a moment of concentration, Hawa's chest pumped in unison, both her and the creature breathing in a rhythmic pattern.

The parasite formed an armored, glossy mask, muscles rippling and contracting over her mouth and nose.

"The parasite does not drink blood." Renato reached for another worm. "Nor does it eat from flesh. Instead, it needs what we produce; carbon dioxide. Much like a plant, it absorbs gasses and produces oxygen, but at a much faster rate. As it recycles the carbon dioxide we exhale, it filters it and passes oxygen back into our lungs via an organ it extends into the nasal cavity. The parasite was usually found on cattle and livestock, but was soon discovered to have other useful qualities, such as allowing humans to breathe in unstable conditions."

He really expected her to put that thing on her face. She shook her head. "No. No way am I letting that thing near me."

Jayden stepped forward. "If you don't do this, you won't be able to go with us, and we'll have to try to get the stone without you."

"Ellie may not believe us, and she won't let the stone go without a fight," Renato said. "We could all die trying."

Zanya swayed, pushing down the urge to gag.

"I don't like it either," Jayden said. "But it's the only way we can survive the trip."

Bile rose in her throat. The bitter, acidic liquid coated the back of her tongue.

"Zanya." Arwan's smooth voice was like a breath of fresh air. "It's the only way."

She swallowed and looked at Arwan. "Will you

hold my hand? It's just that…these things really freak me out."

Arwan followed her to Renato, who held the parasite away from his own face. Arwan took her hand. "Try not to panic I know it'll be hard, but try."

Without warning, it hit Zanya's face. She gasped. Bad idea. Cold and wet, a thick muscle of slithering slime flooded her mouth. The worm spread over Zanya's nose, cutting off her air. She tried to inhale, but found nothing but mucus to fill her lungs. The creature extended a lubricated tube into her nose, to the back of her throat.

Arwan held her hands tight as she struggled to break free. The parasite created an airtight seal. Its body flattened as small suction cups gripped onto her skin.

Her lungs burned and ached for air.

She started to panic.

Trying to shake Arwan's hands loose from hers, she shouted, her voice muffled under the parasite's body. Her head spinning, she made one last effort, and pushed every ounce of breath from her lungs. Just before Zanya thought she was going to pass out, the parasite's body expanded, filling her lungs with a gust of fresh, crisp air.

Her eyes wide with terror, Zanya drew in a deep breath.

"Breathe slowly." Arwan let go of her hands.

She sucked in several deep breaths before she realized it was actually working.

Renato continued on to the others. Zanya cringed and decided not to watch while the other "masks" were applied.

"When we emerge from the time bend, you can remove the parasites." Renato said loudly to the group. "I'll take their transporting tank with us. When you want to remove them, simply hold your breath. They will assume you are dead and will quickly fall away in search for another host."

Peter helped Renato apply his parasite, and they huddled together in a tight circle. Renato rested his hand firmly on Arwan's shoulder, and then nodded to Marzena, who stood several yards away on the sand. She closed her eyes. Renato flinched, as did Arwan—a reaction to their minds being invaded.

Arwan's muscles flexed as he stretched the bend around them until it completely encompassed the group. Heavy matter filled the space, pressing on Zanya's skin and clothes, making it difficult to move. The parasites squirmed, probably equally uncomfortable under the pressure.

Arwan's face paled. The tendons in his hands were visibly strained to keep the ripples intact.

It seemed like forever in the bend. A long, stretched moment of purgatory, not in the past, present or future. They were nowhere and everywhere at the same time.

Finally, the ripples began to fade. Zanya sighed with relief as the pressure lifted from her chest, and the bend vanished.

Arwan swayed, then stumbled in the sand, sweat trickling down his forehead.

Zanya caught him around the torso.

He nodded and lifted his hand, still unable to speak with the parasite attached to him.

It was like his life energy had been drained.

Zanya examined the beach where they stood when the bend began. There were differences in the scenery. The large palm near the house was now a tiny sapling that stood only four or five feet tall, and the house seemed slightly newer.

Renato swiped his hand across his throat in a cutting motion. In a spell of silence void of movement, Peter's parasite was the first to fall away. He gasped and gagged when the worm extracted its tube from his nose. The process wasn't pretty, but it was necessary. Everyone else followed suit.

Renato retrieved the parasites and placed them safely in the transport case. They advanced toward the house on high alert. Jayden drew an arrow and readied it in his bow.

Peter crouched beside Renato. "Should we knock?"

Renato shook his head and signaled to the veranda.

Arwan crept toward the patio and silently hopped over the guardrail. Peering into the French doors, he signaled it was all clear.

The rest of the group followed over the rail, some more gracefully than others.

Renato set down the transport tank and grabbed the door handles. "All of you stay here. I have to talk to Ellie alone. I don't want to frighten her in her condition."

Her condition? Zanya's breath stalled and she backed away from the doors, one slow, stunned footstep at a time.

Peter hurried beside her. "Zanya." He tugged on her arm.

She stared into the kitchen with wide eyes. "Peter, this is too weird. I'm going to finally meet my mother, but she won't have any idea who I am. She's never seen me before, and she's still…" The word caught in her throat. It bounced around her mind, wreaking havoc on her sanity before it finally drifted through her lips. "…pregnant."

"It's going to be fine. Just stay calm. We'll get the stone, go home, and this'll all be over with."

Footsteps came from the side of the house. Arwan reached over his shoulder and unclasped his glaive from its holster. Jayden took aim and drew back his arrow.

"What are you doing here?" a woman's voice said from behind them.

Everyone turned.

Jayden loosened the tension on his bow.

Zanya gazed upon her mother, who hadn't changed a bit from the photo that sat beside her bed.

"Answer my question. Who are you, and what do you want?"

Hawa nudged Zanya, urging her to step forward. But she couldn't. Her feet were rooted to the ground and coherent words were trapped in a mental haze. She could do little more than stare, star-struck at the most stunning woman she'd ever seen.

Wind churned and circled around Eleuia. Like a vicious thunderstorm had been conjured from thin air, electricity sparked over her mother's skin. "Then you have come to die."

CHAPTER SEVENTEEN

Eleuia stood tall, her delicate hand raised with a bright light churning in her palm.

"She thinks we're here to steal the stone." Peter shielded his eyes against the roar of the wind. "You have to do something!"

Zanya's hair whipped at her cheeks, blown in the sandstorm whirling around them. She squinted and also shielded her eyes with her hands, rising to her feet against the force of the cyclone. "Mom…"

Eleuia's gaze fixed on her. Her lips parted and the wind slowed until the electricity pulsing in her fingers vanished. She rested her hand gently over her swollen belly.

Zanya stared her mother's face. It may as well have been a mirror. She had the same gray eyes, same long, dark hair.

"It can't be," Eleuia whispered.

Peter stood up and stepped forward. "Renato's with us. He went searching for you in the house."

Eleuia scanned the other faces in the group, settling on Hawa. She waved them forward.

"Quickly, come inside." They filed in and spread through the familiar kitchen. The granite countertops glistened the same way they did almost twenty years in the future. "How is this possible? Is it true?" She remained focused on Zanya.

Her hands shaking, Zanya laced her fingers together to calm them long enough to draw in a deep breath. She recalled a lifetime of wishes, tears, and all the things she wanted to say. She hoped to be graceful and eloquent, but all she could manage was a simple, forced reply. "Yes, it's true."

Her mother stood as still as her photo. Zanya seized the opportunity to memorize the curves of her lips and the warmth of her eyes. She was even more stunning than in her picture, with a soft illumination surrounding her skin.

They gazed at each other for another fleeting moment. Eleuia's bottom lip trembled. "You're so beautiful." She threw her arms around Zanya.

A hard bump pressed against Zanya's stomach. She jumped back from her mother's belly. Inside that bump was…her.

Renato skidded into the kitchen. When Eleuia spun around, he wasted no time in scooping her into his arms and spinning her in a circle.

"Renato." She giggled. "Please, put me down, brother."

"Oh, I'm sorry, Ellie." He carefully lowered her back to the hardwood floor. "I've missed you." He kissed her cheek. "So, you've seen her then?" He looked at Zanya.

She nodded. "I did."

Suddenly it occurred to Zanya that Hawa was

there too. Zanya grabbed her cousin's arm and guided her forward. "This is your niece, Hawa."

Hawa stood like a deer in headlights.

Eleuia's posture was tall, her chin tilted up as if she were royalty. "I recognized you the moment I saw you on the veranda. I also remember the day you were born. Your mother was never happier than on that day. She was a fine woman, and would have been extremely proud of you." She touched Hawa's chin lightly. "You're lovely, like her."

Hawa simply nodded, and then stepped back.

"And who are the rest of these children?"

Renato began the introductions. "This is Peter, our healer." Peter nodded and smiled.

"Jayden, our seeker." Jayden gave a nod.

"And this is Arwan. He is our timebender."

Zanya shifted beside him and smiled softly.

Eleuia's gaze darted from her to Arwan a few times. "I see."

"Then, of course, Hawa," Renato continued, "and Marzena would have loved to come—"

Eleuia's eyes lit up. "Marzena still lives in the house?"

"Yes. She linked my memory with Arwan's, allowing us to come here."

"I would have loved to see her again. I miss her terribly."

"I will be sure to send your good wishes." He rested his hand on the small of her back. "But now, we need to talk."

They relocated to the familiar study. Zanya sat across from her mother beside the fireplace. Their happy reunion moment was short-lived, with more important matters to discuss. Primarily, the stone.

"If you are here, then this must mean I failed." Eleuia propped a pillow behind her lower back when she sat in a leather armchair, the light from the fire flickering over her face.

Renato gave a reluctant nod.

She sighed, stroking her belly. "Tell me. What has he done with the stone?"

"Nothing yet." Renato reached for his pipe, but found nothing in the inner pocket of his jacket. Zanya had never seen him so nervous. He smoothed down the lapel of his coat, more times than necessary. "We came from seventeen years in the future."

"Even with a timebender, how is that possible?"

"It seems he's more efficient than we anticipated. It took him only seventeen minutes to travel here."

She paused, the creases around her eyes deepening.

If they told her how they were in the bend for so long without dying, it would probably make her throw up, being pregnant and all. "Don't ask," Zanya said. "Really, you don't want to know."

Renato leaned forward. "Sarian has not been able to break the obedience spell, but he may be getting close. His magic is stronger than it was in your time."

"But if my daughter is alive, you have a guardian. Has she not been protecting the stone?" Her gaze darted between her and Renato. "What aren't you telling me, brother?"

"Wait." Zanya leaned forward in her chair. All

those years. All this time. Was it possible? "You don't know?"

Eleuia's eyes narrowed. "Know what?"

Renato looked at Zanya. "Perhaps you should be the one to tell her."

"I, uh…I was raised in an orphanage."

Eleuia's lips parted as she shielded her belly. "Where was your father?"

Zanya shrugged. "I don't know. I've never met him."

Her horrified expression suddenly turned fierce. She peered at her brother. "He put her in an orphanage? An orphanage!"

Her entire life she thought her mom had abandoned her. Some days Zanya was so angry with her mom for leaving, she'd hoped to see her just once; just once, to tell her how being such a coward ruined her life. Now it all just seemed to vanish into thin air.

"He must have known what he was doing," Renato said. "He was not Riyata. He knew he could not protect Zanya if Sarian found him. As hard as it is to understand, he did the right thing."

"But…if she has not been with the stone, she has never bonded with it."

"That is why we are here."

Eleuia pushed out of her chair and held out her hand to Zanya. "Come. If this is what the future holds for our people, you must bond with the stone immediately."

Zanya stood and took her mother's hand, following her through the familiar halls, up the spiral staircase, and into her bedroom.

Eleuia approached her bed, reached behind her pillow, and pulled out a velvet bag. A light glowed from inside. She slipped out a brilliant, oval-shaped stone and caressed it, smiling tenderly.

The light in Zanya's chest flickered on. Zanya leaned forward, the orb in her chest churning with life. The stone's beauty nearly stole her breath away.

"This is the stone of Muuk'Ich. It is enchanted, powerful, and very much alive." She held it out. "This is what I gave my life to protect."

Zanya extended her fingers to the stone, but hesitated. "Can I touch it?"

Eleuia's slowly shook her head and pulled it back to her chest, stroking its smooth surface.

Zanya dropped her hand to her side. "What's wrong?"

"It doesn't recognize you, but that's probably because you're not technically born yet." She smiled softly and gazed down at her belly.

Zanya cringed. Imagining herself, like that, in her mother's womb. It made every muscle in her body rigid. She tried to brush it off, even if it went against her better nature. They had bigger problems at the moment. "So…what do we do?"

Eleuia lifted the stone to her lips and whispered in another language—the same language Renato spoke on the phone. The stone reacted with colors of blue and white, churning with bright light.

Zanya's light in her chest matched the stone's vibrancy.

Eleuia extended it. "Here."

Slowly, she reached out with cupped hands.

Eleuia entrusted her with the stone. It was heavier than it was in her dreams, and it was cold as ice.

The light inside of it vanished.

Zanya lifted it to eye level and peered through its translucent walls. "What happened—" Searing pain shot through her palm and up her wrist. She screamed and dropped the stone to the bed, then held out her shaking hands, now covered in burns. "What the hell—"

"Shh." Her mother cradled Zanya's hands in hers, looking her in the eyes. "Listen to me." Zanya froze. "I know I haven't been there to teach you about your skills, but you have a natural ability."

Zanya swallowed against the pain. "How do you know?"

"Without the stone you've managed to conjure your own light. That's only possible if you have a tremendous amount of inner power. But you have to believe in yourself."

Zanya nodded, the raw skin now rising with blisters. She wanted to fist her hands but the pain was too intense. She blinked and flinched at her mother's touch.

"Heal." Eleuia let go of Zanya's hands. "Come now. You can do it."

Zanya stared down at the fluid-filled bubbles. "I've never done it before."

"Concentrate. Clear your mind."

Zanya snorted. "I tried the three-step program before. It didn't work very well."

"Transformation?" Zanya nodded, prompting a soft laugh from her mother. "The first time I tried to transform, I attempted to change into your uncle. I thought it would be hilarious."

"It wasn't, I'm gathering?"

"For him it was. I panicked and couldn't calm down enough to change back."

Zanya smiled through the pain. "So how did you?"

"Practice. Now clear your mind and imagine the burns healing. Believe they are, and they will."

Zanya closed her eyes and did as her mother instructed. With several deep breaths, she focused on the raw skin, and imagined the burns slowly fading away. The pain subsided. When Zanya blinked open her eyes, the skin on her palms was flawless. She smiled. "I did it."

"That you did." Eleuia's chin was raised and chest pushed out.

Zanya glanced at the stone. "What about the stone? I'm not trying that twice."

Her mother rested her hands over her swollen belly. "This has never been done before."

"So…" Her gut wrenched over the possibility of failure.

"I don't know." Eleuia met her gaze. "I really don't know."

Eleuia slipped the stone back in to its pouch. "Here." She extended it.

Zanya shifted back. "Do you think it's safe?"

"In the pouch it can't hurt you. Maybe holding onto it will make the stone feel more comfortable."

Zanya arched an eyebrow. "Make the stone…feel?"

"The stone is not simply a rock. It is a miracle. A one of a kind gesture bestowed upon all Riyata by the heavens. Once you bond with the stone and become its guardian, it will be your soul mate. It will feel your pain, and you will feel its pain. When you are sorrowful, it will show compassion. When you are joyful, it will celebrate your happiness. It becomes a part of you, since you are, in fact, a part of it."

Zanya crossed her arms and stretched her sleeves over her hands. "That sounds…invasive."

"It is at times. The stone's whispers become a part of you."

"It talks?"

"It communicates through emotion. When it's scared, you'll feel it. When it's unsure, you will be, too." Zanya examined the velvet pouch in her mother's grasp. "In order to bond with the stone, you must first accept your responsibility toward it. Once you do that, there is only one way out." Eleuia shifted toward her with an intense gaze. "This is very important. Possibly the most important thing I can teach you.

"The only way for you to surrender your position as the guardian is to pass it to an heir. A blood heir. Do you understand what I'm saying?" Zanya nodded. "It is that, or death. Those are the only two options. Is this what you want?"

Among all this chaos, Zanya had never asked herself what she wanted. What would this mean for her? Immortality. An unimaginable responsibility. How would the rest of her long life play out? Would she be lonely? Always looking over her shoulder? Was that really the kind of life she wanted to live?

Her mother sat in front of her, radiant and strong.

She had been the guardian for centuries, protecting the stone at all costs.

Eleuia sighed and shifted off of the bed. "I'll be right back." She glanced to the bathroom door. "I guess I should thank you ahead of time for using my bladder as a trampoline."

Zanya's eyes widened. "Sorry?"

Eleuia giggled. "I'll just be a minute." When she vanished into the bathroom, Zanya relaxed against the headboard. Seeing her mother pregnant would never be normal. Granted, seeing her mother at all wasn't normal, either.

Hell, nothing about her life had been normal.

Ever.

She groaned and rubbed her hands over her face, then stared down at the stone. "I get it. I do. I wouldn't want to give her up, either." She puffed out a breath of air. "Not for me, at least." Zanya's muscles eased as fatigue set in. Traveling through the time bend had stripped her energy. Arwan must have been completely drained.

Alone in the room, she hummed a tune. The notes rose out of her throat with such ease, she hardly realized she was doing it. The velvet pouch beside her glowed from a light inside. She paused and sat up straighter, watching it. The light dimmed until it vanished completely. She hummed a few more notes, causing the stone to illuminate.

"Really. You like my tune?" She carefully picked up the pouch and rolled it in her hands. The cold of the stone pushed through the pouch, pressing onto her skin. She continued to hum until the stone's whispers returned—like a thread was attached to her heart, and the stone was tugging on it.

"Um…" She glanced at the bathroom door. "Mom?" It was so weird saying that.

"Be right out," she called through the closed bathroom door.

She returned her attention to the stone. Something stirred inside of her. Something familiar and encouraging. It had to be what her mother spoke about. The emotions of the stone channeling through her.

Zanya tugged the string to the pouch until it fell open. "I'm going to make you a deal. I'll hold you if you don't burn my face off." She paused before taking it out. "Deal?" There was no booming voice or clear affirmation, but there wasn't scolding heat, either. "I'll take that as a yes." With a leap of faith, she tugged off the velvet pouch and slipped the stone into her hand.

She immediately cringed with anticipation—and not the good kind. When pain didn't shoot up her arm, she relaxed and smiled. "There. That wasn't so bad."

Indiscernible whispers echoed in her ears. They floated all around her, from every direction. She searched the room, alarmed at first. But soon it became clear it was the stone speaking to her. It was…happy. Joy coursed through her, making her blood rush. Zanya smiled. Suddenly a jolt of fierce protectiveness crawled through her, like a maternal instinct that overpowered all other emotion. In that moment there was nothing more important than keeping the stone safe.

This stone was the reason she never had a mother. The reason she had grown up with no family. It was her legacy, the only part of her mother that was truly still alive.

Zanya nodded. "Yes. This is what I want."

A burst of light exploded through the room, like a star projecting its final moments of life. Zanya's body quaked as the stone's memories crashed through her like a tidal wave. Every place it had been, every set of hands it had touched, every pain or joy it experienced.

The stone encouraged her, prompted her to subdue the light with pure will. Zanya grasped at the rays with her mind until it bowed and bent into awkward shapes while she reeled it in with an invisible tether. Finally it submitted, and settled into an oval shape in the center of her chest.

When Zanya opened her eyes, the light in the room was gone, and was now a pulsing orb between her breasts.

Panting, she cradled the stone to her chest. "Whoa."

The toilet flushed from the bathroom and the door swung open. Her mother walked out, her belly leading the way. When her gaze landed on Zanya, she stopped and smiled.

***

Arwan

Arwan sat with Renato, Peter, and Hawa in silence, waiting for Zanya and her mother to come back downstairs. The room was quiet and the air so tense, he could barely breathe.

Everything was riding on the success of this trip.

Absolutely everything.

"How long is this going to take?" Hawa asked in her typical sharp tone.

He'd learned not to take it personally. Some people were friendly. Others weren't. He had suspicions Hawa had experienced her share of life struggles. And just like with anything, some came out unfazed, while others were eternally jaded.

Creaking of floorboards stole Arwan's attention. He stood and turned to the staircase. His pulse quickened. If Zanya could not bond with the stone, there would be nowhere to turn.

Eleuia was the first to appear, followed by Zanya, who cradled something in her hands. He peered at the object, no larger than a mango. Arwan froze when he caught a glint of movement from inside the object.

It was the stone.

Everyone watched and waited for them to reach the sitting area. Eleuia smiled gracefully, her shoulders pulled back and her chin raised when she stopped in front of them. "My reign as the guardian has come to an end." She looked at Zanya. "Zanya is your leader now. Follow her. Believe in her. She'll need your support and guidance in the difficult times ahead."

Zanya paused and held her mother's hand. "Mom...just so you know, if you've been wondering, my life hasn't been terrible." Eleuia's eyes filled with tears. "I've always been taken care of, and I have the most amazing friends. I wish my best friend Tara was here to meet you. You would have loved her." Zanya hung her head. "Sarian has her."

"I never would have given you up if it was not my only option. Sarian would have killed us both. I'm thankful at least you survived." A tear streaked down her cheek. "I would not wish capture by him on my worst of enemies. I know you will exceed my expectations as the guardian. After all…" She wiped away the tear and smiled. "You are your mother's daughter."

Zanya threw her arms around her mother and pushed down a sob.

"I love you more than you'll ever know, Zanya."

They held on to each other for a moment longer before reluctantly letting go. Eleuia looked at Renato and nodded.

"It's time to go, Zanya."

She turned to her uncle. "But…but we just got here."

"Soon I'll be leaving," Eleuia said.

"Leaving? But…come with us. You can come with us."

Eleuia hung her head, admiring her belly. "I have no idea of the consequences—"

"Who cares about the damn consequences? Who cares how it changes things? You can stay with me."

Eleuia smiled, though it seemed a little sad. She stroked Zanya's hair. "Let me have a moment with your timebender first. We'll have to work out some details." She glanced at Arwan, who shifted his weight. He couldn't bring her back. Not while she was pregnant. Not without a way for her to breathe. "Come, time bender. Let the others get ready while we speak."

Arwan glanced at the others, and then followed her into the greeting room. Eleuia closed the wooden double doors. When they clicked shut, she paused, her hands still resting on the handles and her back facing him. "Timebender." She turned, her gaze soft and warm. "What are you doing with Renato, dear boy?"

He lifted his head and steadied his breathing. "I've been with him almost all my life."

"Your ability is rare."

He didn't respond.

"We both know exactly how rare it is. You must have some light in your soul." His muscles tensed. His darkness had been left undetected, and he would not give her reason for alarm. Not now. "I'm grateful to see you with her." Eleuia rested her hand on his cheek. "She cares for you."

His breath stalled. "How do you know?"

She smiled softly. "It's in her eyes. It's always in a woman's eyes." She walked to a large recliner in the center of the room. "Please tell Zanya and my brother I love them." She grabbed a duffle bag from the chair. He hadn't noticed it when he came in. "I know Zanya won't understand that I have to leave. You'll help her through it, won't you?" She rested her hand on her belly. "I can't risk her safety for anything. Now that I've given up my reign as the guardian, if Zanya does not live to her current age…"

"There would be no hope."

"Hope." Eleuia lifted her gaze and met his. "That's what she'll give to the world, as long as she's alive."

Arwan held his breath through a stretch of silence. Eleuia wiped away a tear from her cheek and crossed the room to another door at the back. She grabbed the handle and paused. "Thank you, timebender."

He nodded. "Find peace."

She glanced over her shoulder. "Find peace." Eleuia opened the door, letting light spill in from outside. She walked out and closed the door, leaving him alone in the room.

He stood still and silent. There was a knock on the double doors. "Mom?" Zanya's voice called from the other side. She pushed it open. "We have a small setback, but nothing..." She scanned the room. "Where's my mom?"

Arwan dropped his gaze. "I'm sorry." He glanced at the door at the back of the room, still ajar.

"She left?" She rushed through the room and flung open the door to a walkway outside. "Mom?" Zanya whimpered. "Mom!" Zanya slowly turned toward him in a stunned haze. "How could you let her leave?"

He would hold her, but he was probably the last person she wanted at the moment. "She had no choice."

CHAPTER EIGHTEEN

Zanya

Zanya stood at the back of the room, staring at the closed door.

"What do you mean, she left?" Renato said. "That's impossible."

Tears stung Zanya's eyes. "It's not impossible." Her throat was sore from holding back tears. "She left once." She shrugged. "She left again."

Renato rested his hand on her shoulder. "I'm sure she didn't want to."

Zanya nodded. "I know." It was all so complicated. There were years of history she knew nothing about. So many reasons why. But it still hurt to think of the future they could have had. "I was stupid for thinking she could come back with us."

Jayden gently nudged her with his elbow. "It wasn't stupid."

"At the very least, you got the stone," Hawa said. "And that means your mom trusted you with it, which should mean something."

"She is absolutely right." Renato pushed out his chest. "It means everything."

Arwan gestured to the French doors off the kitchen. "We should go. It's getting late."

They returned to the beach, where they applied the parasites one last time and stood in the bend. The ripples vibrated and bubbled around them for what seemed like a lifetime.

Zanya peered through the translucent walls of the time bend at a dark figure looming in the sand.

The bend was struck with a violent blow. Arwan's groan was muffled in Zanya's ears. Another blow sent a crack down the center. A shockwave thrashed through her. She clenched her fists.

Another blow tore open the fault line, searing Zanya's skin. She pushed away when the heat intensified, but she was trapped. They were all trapped.

Hawa shrieked, her face contorting in agony as red blisters formed over her cheeks.

Another blow opened an inferno of fire and light writhing inside.

Zanya turned her head away from the flames. The weight of the time bend pinned her hands down from shielding her face. The blaze whipped her skin, singeing the hairs on her arms to follicles of ash.

It was exactly like Arwan had said. They could all die a terrible death if he failed to complete the bend. And they would. They would burn.

The fire crept out of the crack like a trail of lava.

Zanya ground her teeth and screamed as another flame slashed across her leg. The stench of burned flesh filled her nose.

The dark figure lingered beyond in sight as if it were taunting her, savoring the moment before it sent them all to their graves. Before it could finish the job, the beast doubled over in the sand. A mighty roar gnarled through the air.

The blurry figure of Marzena stood in the distance, her hands raised over her head, seawater churning around her. It took only a moment to realize she wasn't standing on the beach, but on the water's surface, her eyes as black as obsidian.

Her mental assault on the beast gave Arwan just enough time to complete the journey through time. When the wall of ripples vanished, they stood scorched, scalded, and barely alive. Arwan tore the parasite off his face and collapsed, burns covering his hands and arms, almost beyond recognition.

Zanya tore hers off, though it didn't take much effort. It seemed the parasite was already half-dead. She spit and threw the creature to the burning sand. A flame whipped Zanya to the ground. She cracked her head against a rock. Her vision blurred as she writhed in the sand, struggling to scramble to her feet. Once she had, Zanya swayed like a drunkard as fuzzy figures darted around her.

She brushed her fingers over a bump on her head that throbbed with every heartbeat. Zanya caught sight of a figure sprawled in the ground. She stumbled toward Arwan's motionless body, making it only a few steps before her legs buckled and she collapsed.

Bleeding, burned, and incapacitated, Zanya lay there fighting to remain conscious. Until she failed.

***

There was no way of telling how long she'd been out, but when she came to, Zanya still laid on the beach, Arwan nowhere to be seen. For a fleeting moment she was relieved. It was over. The fight was won and whatever attacked them was gone.

But when she lifted her head, a completely different picture was in front of her.

Arwan sliced at a dark figure that darted out of striking distance. The creature lashed out with a vicious swing of its claws.

She rolled onto her stomach and forced herself to her hands and knees, her ribs aching under the effort.

The black beast growled and lunged at Arwan, who aimed his glaive at its sternum and drove the blade through its chest. The monster gurgled and collapsed.

Zanya crawled to a palm tree, pain shooting through her body as open wounds burned with heightened intensity, the sand grinding into her raw skin. With her fingers dug into the jagged bark, she clung to the tree for support and pulled herself to her feet. In the distance, the silhouette of a creature stalked down the shore.

Her stone called out to her for rescue while it was carried away. She gasped and searched the ground, only to realize she'd lost the stone when she was knocked unconscious.

She pushed away from the tree and ran toward the beast. Sunlight reflected off the sand and made it impossible to keep a clear view of it as it stalked in the opposite direction, away from the fight.

Before she could catch up, the monster-like figure knelt and then launched into the air. With a flash of its wings, it rose above the trees and vanished into the distance.

She hadn't been the guardian for more than a few hours and had already broken the one, cardinal rule. Protect the stone.

The stone cried out to her, its pain tearing at their tethered souls.

"Zanya!" Peter grabbed her arm. It hurt, but she didn't care anymore. Nothing mattered now that the stone was back in Sarian's grasp. She turned to Peter. "They took it." She swallowed down a sob. "I had one job. One..."

Peter sifted his fingers through her hair, making her wince when he brushed over her swollen bump. "You have a concussion. Hold still." Soothing heat eased the wave of pain in her temples.

Her energy returned, stabilizing her body and clearing her mind. Energy flickered over her skin. "Thanks, Pete." She turned toward the battle raging on the beach. "Go get the others. I need to find my stone." She closed her eyes and summoned her new seeking ability to locate the creature. Or at least tried. It was like peering through a wall of smoke at first. As she concentrated harder, an image formed through the haze.

Peter grabbed her arm again, tearing away her focus. "We need you here. We can't fight the demons alone." He pointed down the beach. With her vision sharp, she could see them clearly now— tall creatures with black, leathery wings protruding from their shoulder blades. "We need you to stay and fight or we might not live through this."

Hawa screamed when one of the monsters dug into her forearm with its claws. She leaped away and flung a row of throwing stars. Razor-sharp edges planted into the monster's shoulder, but the creature only brushed them away. Its wounds quickly healed.

Were those...gargoyles? No, they were a hundred times larger than the flat-faced statues perched on old churches. There was no way she could fight one of those. They were rippled with muscle, with long whipping tails and talon-like hands.

"They regenerate!" Hawa flung more throwing stars through the air.

Renato swung at his target with his sword. "Cut off their heads or pierce their hearts." One of the beasts jumped clear over his head and landed behind him with a thud.

Peter ran to his defense.

Jayden shot several arrows into the chest of one of the creatures, then spun around and projected more into another. "We don't have anything to cut their heads off with. You're the only one with a sword."

Zanya searched the skies. The beast that took her stone was probably miles away by now, over rocky mountainsides and thick jungle, completely out of reach.

Half running, half flying, a beast charged and was on top of her in a fraction of a second. She screamed and threw up her hands, inadvertently creating a force field that sent the demon hurling back.

It glared at Zanya with fiery red eyes. From under its wing it removed a whip made of flames and fury, a tool from hell at its command. A deep growl built in its chest, and through its gaping jaws it bellowed a massive roar.

Zanya stumbled back and fell to the ground. With the whip in one hand, it grabbed Zanya by her hair with the other and yanked her up. Inches from the beast's face, each foul breath stunk like rotting flesh. It let out another roar, flinging strings of saliva from its jaws.

This was the beast that broke open the time bend. The leader. And it was after her.

It lifted the flaming whip to her cheek, burning a welt into her skin.

The creature roared and arched, dropping Zanya to the ground. It spun around with three arrows protruding from its back. The creature's tail whipped through the air and sliced open Zanya's torso. She gripped her stomach as her skin separated, and warm liquid stained her shirt scarlet.

The searing pain spread through her gut and chest, making every breath more labored than the last. This was no panic attack. She'd had enough to tell the difference. This was something else entirely—as though a ball python had slithered into her chest and wrapped itself around her lungs. With each exhale, its grip tightened.

The creature raised its nose in the air, the scent of her blood catching its attention. She frantically pressed on her wound to stop the bleeding, but the scarlet liquid coated her shirt and fingers. There was no masking it. The animal lunged at her. Its claws barely grazed her skin when something jerked it back.

Arwan wrestled the creature from behind, his glaive wedged against the beast's throat. The demon tried to attack with its tail, barely missing Arwan's head. The second time its tail swished by, Arwan caught it and thrust the bone tip through the beast's back, into its heart.

"Watch out for the tails. They're poisoned." He let go of the creature and its lifeless body crashed to the ground.

Arwan stooped beside Zanya and examined her wound. "I'll be right back." He left for only a moment before he returned and dropped to his knees. His glaive's holster was filled with seawater. "Zanya, listen to me. This is going to hurt. Their tails excrete venom. You aren't going to heal unless I flush the wound." He positioned his holster. "Are you ready?"

She ground her teeth, held her breath, and nodded.

When he tipped the holster, saltwater flooded the wound. She screamed, and Arwan held her hand, the only comfort she found in the wall of relentless pain. After what seemed like forever trapped in agony, the pain subsided.

"I'm going to run out of ammo soon," Jayden shouted from down the beach. "We've got to do something."

Arwan glanced at the others still in battle. "Can you stand?"

"I think so. I'll try." He grabbed her hand and helped her to her feet. "I'm okay. Just go." Shouts came from behind them, mixed with growls and hisses. Her eyes grew wide. "Go help them!" She grabbed his shirt and pulled him close. "Just be careful."

He cradled her cheek and, after a moment of hesitation, ran into battle.

With quivering hands, Zanya lifted her shirt to reveal an open gash, drizzling blood.

I know I can heal. Come on, heal. She closed her eyes and drew in a deep breath. *Concentrate. Find your center.*

She channeled energy to the torn flesh. There was a tingling sensation, followed by tugging. Her skin knitted together, closing the wound until it was no more than a discolored blemish.

"Duck!" Hawa launched a series of daggers through the air. They flew over Renato's head and sank into the beast's chest. Renato spun and lopped off the creature's head.

Jayden slipped his bow over a beast's neck and twisted the string into a tourniquet, cutting off its air. "I'm out of arrows!"

Under armed, her group exhausted and beaten, and with powerful demons on the attack, her hope dwindled.

"I have to be able to do something. Think, Zanya." Her mind raced frantically while she concocted a plan. Her stomach dropped when she settled on their best option.

She'd tried it once and ended up looking like a circus clown with bad makeup. Now that she was bonded with the stone, maybe her powers would be stronger.

Maybe…

But maybe wasn't a chance she could afford to take. A successful attempt at transformation was the only way they could call off the beasts without anyone getting hurt.

If she screwed up, all of their lives would be on the line.

"We can't hold them back!" Hawa threw more bladed stars. "We have to run."

Renato sliced at another creature with his sword. "You go. You're the only one who can outrun them."

"I'm not leaving you!" Hawa shouted.

It was now or never.

She focused, honed on her new inner power from bonding with the stone. The light in her chest churned.

Breathe deep.

Clear your mind.

Find your center.

She formed a clear picture of Sarian, recalling his appearance from head to toe. She had to remember every detail, which wouldn't be very hard considering he'd haunted her for so many years.

Black hair. Even blacker eyes. A pointed nose. Sharp, cold eyes.

Her muscles twitched and her vision went black.

She panicked, sure she had done something terribly wrong.

But when her vision returned, she stood in the sand, the cold brass of a cane leaning into her palm. With no time to adjust to her new appearance, she smoothed out her coat and stepped forward.

"Enough!" She nearly screeched, startled by the sound of Sarian's baritone voice. "The stone is safe. They can do me no harm now that it is back in my possession. Leave now and return..." She had no clue where they should go other than... "Home."

The raging battle came to a sudden halt. The beasts backed away from the attack, giving Arwan and Renato the space to shift their focus to her—him.

The largest creature approached. Its shadow covered her entirely when they stood toe to toe. Zanya puffed out her chest and straightened her back to seem as tall as she could. She swallowed, doing her best to muffle her trembling breaths. With salvaged courage, she looked the beast in its eyes.

"I said, return home." Zanya dug the brass foot of her cane into the sand. "Dare you defy me?"

The creature pushed its nose closer to her, inhaled, and leaked a low growl.

She had forgotten one of Sarian's defining characteristics—his bitter stench. She concentrated on her memory of the foul rank, and repressed a gag when the smell seeped from her skin.

The incubus jerked its head back. It turned and bellowed from deep in its chest. The rest of the creatures hissed in response.

With Zanya's friends still on the defensive, the

smaller demons took flight.

The beast in front of Zanya crouched, gave a gurgled snarl, and leaped into the air.

Zanya exhaled in relief. It was the first time she'd exercised her changing ability. Now if she could figure out how to change back...

Renato charged toward her with a warrior's cry, prepared to kill. She gasped and threw up her hands. The blade sliced through the air just as Zanya pushed out a burst of light, throwing Renato back. He skidded along the ground, his sword half buried in the sand beside him. "Renato, it's me, Zanya." She clenched her fist, bore down, and willed her body back to its normal state.

It was only then the full force of the transformation tore through her. She hadn't noticed it when her adrenaline was pumping, but now that imminent death was no longer present, morphing hurt like hell.

Renato stared at her with a gaping mouth and scrambled to his feet. "Fantastic." A fascinated light twinkled in his eye. "I've never seen anything like it."

She slumped her shoulders and let out a deep breath. "Yeah, neither have I. It was something I read in one of those books you gave me. I can't believe that actually worked."

Renato laughed. "Brilliant. Just brilliant."

Zanya turned and peered at the sky, still tuned in to the stone's pleas for rescue. "Don't get too happy. Something terrible has happened."

CHAPTER NINETEEN

Renato picked his sword up off the sand. "As long as we are all here, we live to fight another day." He slid the gleaming blade back into its hilt. "We will get the stone back, that is for certain."

"Yeah?" Hawa grudgingly accepted help from Peter for her wounds. "You think we'll get it back, or was that our last chance gone down the drain?"

"Calm down," Peter said.

She yanked her arm away from him, leaving the cut only partially healed. "Don't tell me to calm down." She glared at Renato. "As long as we're all alive and well, my ass. We aren't all well, in case you haven't noticed."

"Be thankful we are alive," Renato said.

"Yeah, barely. And now the stone is gone and we're back at square one." She gestured to Zanya. "And you, our fearless leader." The sarcasm in her tone made Zanya cringe. "All you care about is getting your little friend back, and the stone is a distant second. Get your priorities straight, *Stone Guardian*." Hawa stormed back toward the house.

"Wait…" Zanya stepped forward, her gaze trained on the windows to Tara's bedroom. "If we went back and changed the past…" She sprinted into the house, accidently shoulder-checkering Hawa before scaling the stairs. Ignoring Hawa's chain of curse words, Zanya slowed her pace as she approached Tara's bedroom door. "Please be there, please be there." She held her breath and turned the handle, entering the room.

A mess of blankets and lumpy pillows were piled on the mattress. Tara had to be there, just under the covers. It was the only thing that made sense. They'd gone back, changed the sequence of events, and altered the future.

Please let her see bright red hair and her freckled cheeks.

She wrapped her fingers around the blankets, and with a deep breath, tore away the covers.

There was nothing more than cold, tangled sheets.

Zanya cupped her hands over her face and fell to her knees. She wanted to scream, cry, and destroy everything in her path. But most of all, she wanted her best friend back.

The sound of a flushing toilet sent Zanya springing to her feet. The bathroom door swung open and Tara stepped out, groggy, her hair a tousled mess. Tara rubbed her eyes, blinking through the bright sun filtering into her room. "What time is it?"

Zanya threw her arms around Tara and buried her face into the messy layers of curly red hair.

"What happened? What's wrong?" She looked

down at Zanya's bloodstained shirt. "Oh my God, you're hurt!"

Zanya sniffled. "No, I'm fine. Everything is just right. Exactly how it should be."

"Why are you crying? And what's all over your clothes?" Tara's eyes narrowed. "Did Jay do something? I swear—"

"No, no. It's nothing like that." Zanya tilted her head, admiring the familiar warmth of Tara's pinkish skin. "I'm just glad you're back."

Tara perched her hands on her hips. "What the hell are you talking about? Back from where?"

"You don't remember being taken?"

"I wasn't taken anywhere." She pressed the back of her hand against Zanya's forehead. "Are you all right? Have you been getting enough sleep? You look, well…like crap."

If she only knew what they had been through to find her, but none of that mattered now. Every effort was worth it, because her best friend—no, her sister—was home, and she could breathe again. "I'm…" Zanya smiled. "Fantastic."

"That's good to hear." She examined Zanya's shirt. "You should go change out of those filthy clothes. You're a mess. Plus, whatever that is—" She crinkled her nose. "It smells funny." Her eyes brightened. "Anyway, I'm starving. Maybe Peter's making pancakes."

How could she forget about Peter? He'd been just as worried. Zanya shouldn't keep him waiting longer than necessary. She grabbed Tara by her wrist and dragged her out into the hall.

When their eyes met, Peter dashed up the stairs,

two at a time, and scooped Tara into his arms.

***

After going to sleep that night, Zanya opened her eyes in the dark space. There was no doubt in her mind where she was. No beautiful beachside bedroom with silk draperies. No wall of windows or crashing waves against dark shores.

Sarian stood in front of her, his frail frame recognizable even in the dark. His shadow limped toward her. "Hello, young guardian."

She backed up. "Get away from me."

"I'm not here to harm you, dear. I merely wish to give my sincere congratulations on your bonding." He extended his hand with a tiny box sitting in his palm.

Her chest jumped, and the light in her chest burst to life. "I don't need your help, and I don't want anything from you but my stone."

Zanya forced herself to her feet. Something was really, really wrong. There was no way he would just turn the other cheek and be Mr. Nice Guy all of a sudden.

"You once asked me what I wanted." He stepped closer. "With your rather intrusive dreamwalker interrupting us, I never had the opportunity to respond." His posture was relaxed and his face seemed more pleasant than she'd ever seen before. He almost looked…handsome.

"An alliance. You and I, we could rule the middleworld together."

The gleam in his eye. It had been there all along,

and she hadn't recognized it until now. But as Sarian's tongue caressed the fold of his lips and his gaze hungrily devoured her figure, it was clear.

He wanted *her*.

Suspicion confirmed. This was really, really bad.

"You are power and beauty wrapped in one. An ideal combination." Zanya cringed and stepped away. Just the thought of him wanting her in that way made her stomach churn. "I will be perfectly forthright. I wish for you to be my queen. We would be untouchable. The Stone Guardian on the throne beside the mightiest of kings."

"I would never form an alliance with you."

He stood still and silent. A quiver of fear rolled over her skin. She had learned when he was quiet was when he was most dangerous.

He lunged forward and clamped his hand around Zanya's throat. She grasped onto his wrist, choking beneath his solid hold. "Do not forget who you are speaking to." The harshness of his voice sent terror screaming through her. He loosened his grip, just enough to allow her to breathe. She coughed and sucked in shallow breaths. "Or perhaps I should remind you of what I am capable of in your dreams." He raised the handle of his cane to her face and trailed it down her cheek, then leaned in close to her lips. "So beautiful." She clenched her eyes shut, just in time for the brass handle to deliver a bone-shattering blow. Zanya shrieked and held her face. He let her go, spilling her onto the ground.

"You don't know him as well as you think, my dear. Your timebender—as he calls himself—has more to him than he leads you to believe. In fact, he and I, we aren't as different as you think."

Sarian turned and walked into the darkness. He paused, tilting his cane side to side, as if in contemplation. "By the way," He faced her. "How is your friend? She and I got to know each other quite well." He grinned. "She is very loyal to you. With all the suffering she endured, she didn't breathe a word. Not even a hint." He watched Zanya, rage parading behind his eyes. He was out to hurt her in ways much deeper than cuts and bruises. "Do you really think you got her back against my will? I never planned to kill her. Not when I knew how it would tear you apart." He gave her his back and limped into the darkness. "Next time, I might not be so kind."

CHAPTER TWENTY

Alone on the beach, Zanya's mind drifted past the distant waves. The skies this time of the year were gray, and the water plunged more violently against the cliffside. Sea birds stopped flying for enjoyment. Instead, they huddled in large colonies on the cliffs.

Yes, change was underway, not only in the season, but in her life as well.

"The weather's getting colder." Jayden strolled toward her from behind.

Zanya turned. "How long have you been there?"

"A few minutes. You looked so peaceful; I didn't want to bother you."

Peaceful was the opposite of what she was feeling, but there was nothing he could do to make it better.

The coastal winds infused her hair and tickled her nose with a hint of salt. It was a scent she'd grown to love. "I don't think I'll ever forget the smell of the sea."

"What are you doing out here alone, anyway?"

He sat beside her on the cool sand.

"I just needed to get away."

"Away from what?"

She brushed hair away from her face. "Just…away."

Jayden leaned back on his forearms, squinting up at the overcast. "So, in this getaway, is anyone allowed to come with you?"

"I thought the idea of getting away was to be alone."

"It's always more fun when someone goes with you." Jayden sat up and inspected her face, then frowned. "Unless the person you really want isn't anywhere around." When she didn't reply, he stood and brushed off grains of sand stuck to his clothes. "Sorry to bother you." He turned and meandered down the beach.

Zanya stared after him. "I wouldn't go down there if I were you."

"Why not?"

"Because Peter finally convinced Tara to go swimming with him, and they're spending some alone time together." She needed a serious brain bleach to forget the image of them making out against the rocks.

"If you knew that, why would you go down there?" He shifted his weight, his eyes narrowing. "You sought them, didn't you?"

"I was just trying to find Tara. I wasn't spying."

"So, it's okay for you to seek your best friend, but I can't seek mine?"

She stilled. "I'm your best friend?"

"Yes, and friends watch out for each other. Talk

240

about the pot calling the kettle black." He turned and walked back toward the house.

Zanya stood up, brushing the sand off her clothes. She was already in a shitty mood, and agitating her wasn't going to end well—for him. "The difference is that you weren't just checking up on me. You *were* spying."

He spun around. "First of all, I have no idea what you're talking about. That guy you were batting your eyelashes at could have taken advantage of you or hurt you. I was just making sure you were safe. And a good thing I did. There's something wrong with him. Like, something really fucking wrong."

"Who the hell do you think you are? You completely invaded my privacy! Now you're calling him some kind of monster, and all because he didn't appreciate you throwing yourself at me." Her voice had risen to a near shout.

"Your privacy doesn't matter compared to your safety. And…fine! I'm sorry, okay?"

She threw her hands up in the air. "This is ridiculous. I'm a big girl. I can draw my own conclusions, and you conclusion is you can't just go kissing people."

"You're not *people*. You were my girlfriend."

"Exactly. I *was*. You need to get a grip on that."

"Yeah. I'm realizing that." Jayden kicked at the sand. "What are you going to do now?"

She shrugged. "My friends are all I have. If you can be my friend, we'll be okay. If not…" She couldn't tell him to leave. Not after everything. "Well, even if you can't, you're still important to me."

He tilted his head, trying to get a better look at her face, hidden behind drapes of long, wavy hair. "I'm important to you?"

"Yeah. I mean…you're a jerk. Don't get me wrong. But…you're my friend."

He stepped toward her. "I want more than that."

She held his gaze, steady and sure. "You threw that chance away when you left."

"You've got to stop holding that against me. I told you, I had no choice."

That was such a load of crap. He kept saying he was forced to leave, but Jayden couldn't be forced into doing anything he didn't want to do. That much she knew about him from years of his stubborn pride. "If you really loved me, you would have stayed. Hell or high water, you wouldn't have left me there. You chose to go, and then you chose to barge back into my life, unannounced and uninvited."

His eyes narrowed. "What you mean to say is unwanted. I barged back into your life, unannounced and unwanted." He backed away. "Well, you won't have to worry about me barging into your life anymore. I'll leave you alone." He walked up the beach and disappeared into the house.

So that was it. He was just going to throw a temper tantrum and run away—again. She should be used to people leaving when things got rough, though it never hurt less.

As she meandered back toward the home, the tides whispered to her; waves rolling onto the beach, bubbling with white water, and then retreating again. But when the whispers formed words, Zanya stopped and listened.

Her heart flooded with misery, as if someone had reached inside her chest and torn it out with a hot iron.

It was her stone. From wherever Sarian held it captive, it managed to break through the barrier to deliver a message.

The obedience spell was failing.

Her light bolted to life so violently, her back arched and her chest jerked toward the sky. Behind her lids played a succession of images.

Raging water.

Flashes of light.

A tree, hanging onto the edge of a cliff with vines consuming the trunk.

Flashes of light.

She gasped and held her breath when ice cold shocked her skin.

White water and bubbles.

Flashes of light.

Her lungs burned.

Flashes of light.

The water roared in her ears.

Flashes of light.

Her throat tightened.

Flashes of light.

Panic streaked through her. She couldn't breathe.

Flashes of light.

She ground her teeth and swallowed down the need to pull in a breath.

The soft glow of something, pinched between

two rocks. A string, from what she could tell, swayed in the water's current.

When her light flickered off, her eyes flew open and she collapsed to the sand. She gasped and coughed, choking on the memory. Her body shook as she struggled to stand. The vision had torn through her. She'd never experienced anything like it.

One thing she knew for sure.

That wasn't her stone.

When her stone spoke to her, she *felt* it.

This was more like an infliction—a vision she had no way to control.

She had to go there. She had to find the place with the waterfall.

It took longer than usual to make it to the house. The more she walked, the lighter her muscles became. After she had walked through a few wings, she was as good as new. Maybe it was that whole healing thing that helped her recover so fast, though it was hard to tell.

When she reached the north wing, Zanya knocked on the door. It creaked open and Hawa peeked out. Her hair in a tight ponytail, she resembled a black leopard. "Yes?"

"I need your help."

Hawa rolled her eyes. "What now?"

"Listen. I'm coming to you because I think you can help me. I need to go out. You—I think—can take me there."

She arched a perfectly shaped eyebrow. "Why me?"

"Because you don't care about keeping me safe."

Hawa opened the door a bit wider. "Sounds like an adventure."

"Yeah." Zanya shrugged. "I guess you could call it that."

***

It took almost an hour to get to the place from her vision. When they arrived, Zanya followed Hawa out of the car. Soft soil sank under her feet in the humid night air.

"Where to now?" Hawa stepped out of the car and shut the door behind her.

Even with the Jeep's headlights, the waterfall was shrouded in darkness. Its presence would have been cloaked completely if the water weren't for the roaring rush of the water. A light mist coated her skin.

"I'm not completely sure." Zanya listened carefully, half expecting a booming voice to echo down from the skies and direct her where to go.

"Well I seriously hope you didn't drag us out here for nothing. I'm missing my beauty rest to take you on this little excursion."

Zanya held up her hand. "Just...shut up for a second."

Hawa huffed and swatted at the bugs swarming around the light from the headlights. "Make this quick, would you? I don't particularly want to be eaten alive."

The jungle's sounds were deafening. Zanya carefully walked forward, every step more unsure than the last. Staggering around in the jungle at night wasn't exactly smart, but her vision was so strong, she wasn't left with a choice. It was either follow the clues or not sleep again—ever.

She scanned the jungle foliage.

"Anything?" Hawa called from behind her.

Zanya's scanned the jagged cliffside to the top, where silky moonlight cast over a single tree. Vines wrapped around the trunk as if they were eating it alive. "I think I got something." She glanced over her shoulder at Hawa. "This way."

She scouted the easiest way up the side of the cliff, spotting what may have been a game trail. Without a second thought she pushed forward, stumbling over rocks and thick branches on her way.

"Hey!"

Zanya ignored Hawa's calls. Her pulse quickened with every step toward the tree. She had to get to it. She needed to see what was there.

"Hey, crazy woman. Does being the guardian give you night vision, too?"

"I have to get to that tree." She clawed at the ground and scrambled her way there until she reached the top of the cliff. When she looked down at the car, Hawa's silhouette was carved into bright beams from headlights.

Hawa cupped her hands around her mouth. "You're going to get yourself killed!"

Zanya reached the tree, the toes of her shoes close to the edge of the cliff. The tree grew in an awkward spot, tilted over the edge. She rested her hand on the trunk and peered over at the raging water below.

Vertigo made her head spin. She pushed back, her stomach lurching into her throat.

Her vision had brought her to the tree, and then…

"Oh, hell no." She stole another glance over the cliff. "This is so not a good idea." Her muscles rigid, she ground her teeth and then stripped off the outer layer of clothes. "I've finally lost it."

"What the hell are you doing?" Hawa yelled.

"I don't know!" Her shouts echoed through the jungle. She tossed her sweater on the ground and gathered all of the courage she had, which under the circumstances had to be a lot. She curled her lip. "This better be worth it."

She ran forward, and with the third step, she hit air. Zanya flailed her arms as she fell to the churning pool below. When she hit the white water, her first instinct was to gasp from the shock of cold. Instead she swallowed down the urge and kicked as hard as she could.

Panic streaked through her as she fought to find the surface. The water tossed her in every direction. Bubbles swirled in circles and her hair floated all around her.

A warm glow caught her eye. She searched below, but the waterfall's power swept her away.

The glow streaked past her again. Her lungs were on fire, and the idea of retrieving whatever was there became a distant second to taking a breath. She kicked and scrambled until she found rock and skimmed her hands along its slick surface to the top. She pulled in the most wonderful air she'd ever breathed, and then another. Water fell over her head, pushing hair into her face.

"Are you fucking crazy or do you have a death wish?" Hawa stood at the edge of the lake, flailing her arms in the air.

"There's something down there."

Hawa paused, and then threw her arms out to the sides. "Great. There's something down there." She paced. "I need your help, she said. It'll be an adventure, she said." Hawa laughed. "Just great."

"I have to get it."

Hawa turned toward her. "Don't you dare. Renato will kill me if something happens to you."

Zanya shivered. She had to retrieve the glowing object. She tightened her jaw. "This better be worth it." She drew in a deep breath and dunked under.

Peering through the churning water, the glow broke through. She pushed off the rock and kicked toward it, reaching out to catch the string with the tips of her fingers. With one firm tug, the pendant came loose.

The current grabbed her and dragged her underneath the waterfall. The water punched her in the gut and in the ribs, battering her against sharp rocks.

Her limbs went limp.

Her head pounded with every heartbeat.

The need to find oxygen had all but vanished as her vision blurred.

The current carried her out from under the waterfall and pushed her motionless body into the center of the lake.

She wanted to swim to the surface.

She wanted to, but couldn't.

Her limbs were heavy and the will to fight slipped away.

Someone grabbed hold of her arm and tugged her to the surface. She gasped when a cool breeze caressed her cheek, and she tilted her head back to see Hawa's blurry features.

Zanya blinked through beads of water. "You look like a drowned rat." The words croaked from her throat.

"Yeah. Thanks." Hawa dragged her to the edge and onto land, then collapsed beside her, her chest heaving. "You are one stupid, crazy girl."

"I know." Zanya lifted her hand with the wicker pendant folded in her fingers. "But it was worth it."

***

Arwan

Arwan paced in the foyer. He had heard Hawa and Zanya leave, but it had been hours since then and they still hadn't returned. He glanced out the window at the sky, now streaked with colors of a dawning day. Something was wrong. He had to find them, which would mean telling Renato he was aware they left and didn't stop them. There was no doubt his mentor would be furious, but it was out of his hands now.

The doorknob jiggled. Arwan paused and watched, listening to whispers from the other side of the door. His eyes narrowed. When the door pushed open, Hawa met his gaze and her shoulders slumped forward. "Fantastic."

Zanya followed her, both of them sopping wet.

Strands of wet hair were stuck to Zanya's neck and cheeks. She cleared her throat and glanced at Hawa. "Hey. What are you doing up?"

Arwan stepped toward Hawa, who immediately stepped back.

"Where have you been?" The words pushed through his clenched jaw.

"Hey, calm down, cowboy. It's fine. We're fine." Hawa smoothed out her wet shirt. "Can't say the same for my clothes, though." She shot a glare at Zanya.

She shrugged. "Sorry."

Arwan shifted his attention to the guardian. "What's going on?"

She gathered hair over her shoulder. "I had this thing I had to do. It's kind of hard to explain."

He glared. "Amuse me."

Zanya froze, then dropped her hands to her sides. "Why do you seem so pissed off?"

Arwan clenched and unclenched his fists. "Do you have any clue what would have happened if you got hurt?"

"Well…" She rubbed the back of her head. "It seems like the whole healing thing is working in my favor."

He widened his eyes. "You did get hurt?"

"It was just a scratch," Hawa said. "Calm down."

He shouted a few lines in Spanish, telling Hawa just how irresponsible she was for allowing Zanya to put herself in harm's way. Their entire plan would have fallen apart if Zanya didn't return.

Hawa scoffed and perched her hand on her hip.

"You have some damn nerve. You should be thanking me, and instead you're acting like a lunatic." He opened his mouth to say something else, but she pushed out her palm. "Whatever. I'm going to change." Hawa stomped off, leaving him alone in the foyer with Zanya.

She shifted her weight. "I have a feeling I missed something."

"What was so important?" He scanned her for any injuries. There was a streak of blood on the shoulder of her shirt, but she didn't seem to be in any pain.

Zanya dug in her pocket and pulled out a wicker pendant dangling from a thin rope. "I had to get it."

He inspected it a moment before speaking. "You went to get a piece of jewelry?"

"Well…" She glanced at it. "Yeah. Kind of. I had this vision and—"

Arwan grabbed her shoulders. "What were you thinking?"

Her features hardened and she craned her neck, looking at his hand rested on her shoulder. "Get your hands off of me."

"You could have gotten yourself killed."

"I said…" She drew in a deep breath, as if trying to calm herself. "Get your hands off of me. Now."

He searched her face, and then stepped back. "Why didn't you ask me to help?"

"Now I can't do anything without your permission? Maybe you have the wrong idea of what we are. You're not my boss or my protector. I can handle myself."

His heart clenched. "I didn't mean it like that."

251

"Well you sure as hell are acting like you know what's best for me." She shoved the pendant back in her pocket. "I didn't ask for a babysitter, okay? So…" She eyed him. "Back off."

"Back off?" He ground his teeth. "Do you have any idea how long we've searched for you? Do you have any idea how many people have died, for you!"

"I don't know what you're talking about. I didn't ask for anyone to—"

"You didn't have to!" His shouts echoed through the foyer. He reeled himself back, his gazed locked with hers. "You should be training. You should be putting your time and energy into learning how to use your powers and getting the stone back. Into finding Sarian. We have to find him!"

"Why is it so important to you, anyway?"

Arwan turned his face away from her.

"Oh. So there's more to this than I thought."

He scowled. "He may not have killed my mother, but he helped the person who did. For that, he deserves to die."

"So that's it. That's why this whole thing has been so important to you. Why *I'm* so important to you."

He furrowed his brows. "That's what you think?"

"I don't know. You tell me. I thought you were different. That I could…" Her cheeks flushed.

"Zanya." He reached out to her, but she pulled back.

"It's okay. I get it." She shivered and curled her arms around herself.

He ached to hold her. Comfort her.

"You don't have to pretend anymore, Arwan." Her features hardened. "I'll try harder to find Sarian. That's my job, after all. That's why I'm here."

CHAPTER TWENTY-ONE

Zanya

Settled on the sofa in Renato's study, Zanya shut her eyes and used telepathy to call everyone to a meeting. She tried to be as gentle as possible, recalling how much it hurt when Marzena first climbed into her head. Even though she was hesitant, Renato insisted she use her powers as much as possible. Practice makes perfect.

One by one, they sluggishly strode in at the early morning hour.

Arwan was the last to arrive, wearing a pair of striped shorts and a tight white T-shirt. She hated how he always looked like he'd just stepped out of the pages of an Abercrombie and Fitch ad without even the slightest effort.

He pulled back strands of hair fallen around his face. Completely avoiding eye contact, he found a seat on one of the two leather armchairs.

Jayden strode in and plopped on the couch beside her. He threw his arm over her shoulder.

"Good morning, beautiful."

Zanya rolled the pendant between her fingers. She didn't know why, but it calm her. "I thought you were mad at me," she said to Jayden in a low voice.

He shrugged. "I could never stay mad at you for long."

That may have been true, but Arwan was proving to be the polar opposite. She sensed his avoidance. They hadn't spoken since last night, making the air thick with tension.

Renato held a book when he took front and center. "Marzena and I have spent a tremendous amount of time in research. We've found a connection, one that may prove helpful in locating Sarian. When Tara was taken, he most likely brought her to where he is hiding. It's where he would have been most comfortable interrogating her."

Zanya winced. There was only one thing he could have meant by 'interrogating.' He was trying to handle the topic delicately, but it still made her skin crawl. She gripped the pendant tighter.

"So..." Peter took Tara's hand, waiting for Renato to elaborate.

"So if Marzena can search Tara's mind for some kind of link buried deep in her subconscious, we may be able to locate him."

"That seems like a good idea," Zanya said. "We should try it."

Renato struck a long wooden match and glided the flame over the chamber of his pipe. "There's a catch."

Jayden huffed. "There's always a catch."

"If I can help, I'll do it," Tara said. "Even if it's not easy."

Marzena used her mind to speak to the group. Thankfully, Zanya had gotten used to the mental invasion now that she had access to her own strengths. "Tara, my dear. Entering the mind can be difficult, and sometimes painful. Usually, if the subject is open to me looking into their memories, the discomfort can be avoided. In this case, however, I will need to reach very deep inside your subconscious."

Tara frowned. "So, it'll be painful?"

"The memory of your experience with Sarian has been locked away, separated from the rest of your mind because in reality, when we went back and changed the path of history, it was undone. But no memory is ever completely lost. Reaching them is possible, but not without risk."

"What risk?" Zanya asked.

"It may bring Tara's recollection of her time with Sarian to the surface."

Zanya's features hardened. "No. There's no way we're going to do it."

"Zanya, if I can help find the stone, I want to do it. I'm the only one without abilities here, and all I've been is dead weight—"

"That's not true," Peter said.

"Yes it is. I know it sounds bad to say, but it's the truth. If I can do this one thing—"

"You don't want to remember. Trust me." She had spent years with that monster climbing in her head. She wouldn't let Tara go through the same

256

thing.

"I agree with Zanya," Renato said. "It's settled then. We will find another way."

Tara leaned forward, her red curls now matching the shade spread over her cheeks. "Excuse me, but I'm the one in question here. What about how *I* feel? Doesn't that matter?"

"Of course it does," Renato replied. "But certain things should be left in the past."

"There isn't any other way to find this guy, and if Marzena doesn't find anything in my head, then we're no worse for wear."

"And if she does find something?" Peter asked. "Then what? You'll have all those memories to cope with. God knows what they'll be."

***

Two days later, Renato called everyone back to the study. Pacing in front of his desk, he cradled a book to his chest. "We have been asking all the wrong questions. We have been trying to figure out where Sarian is hiding, while we should have been asking *when* he is hiding." His pacing stopped. "He has been sheltering his whereabouts not at a secret location, but in the past, which is why neither Marzena nor Jayden have been able to track him."

"How did you figure that out?" Zanya asked.

Tara cleared her throat. "I, uh, I let Marzena..." She tapped her temple. "You know..."

"You let her dig around in your head?" Zanya's disbelief changed to uncertainty, which grew into anger. She stood up, glaring at Marzena. "I thought we agreed? How could you do this?"

Renato stepped forward. "Zanya, it was Tara's choice to make. She wanted to help. She insisted. They did nothing wrong. It was a brave, unselfish act. You should be very proud of her."

"Proud?" Zanya's turned to Renato. "But you agreed with us that it was too big of a risk."

"That was until Tara spoke to me in private. Nothing I could have said would have changed her mind."

Zanya rested back on the sofa. "Fantastic. Now you guys are plotting behind my back."

"I think you're being a little unreasonable," Arwan mumbled.

Zanya's eyes narrowed. "You would think that." If he was trying to get on her nerves, it was working. She looked at Tara. "Are you okay? Do you remember anything?"

She shook her head. "I did have a gnarly migraine after she finished. Peter fixed it, and everything's fine. There's seriously no reason to be upset."

Zanya examined her friend. She seemed okay, and she was acting normal enough. Besides, Tara would tell her if something went wrong. The tension in Zanya's muscles gave way. Of course Tara would tell her. They were best friends.

"Very well," Renato said. "The information Tara provided led me to examine the 1800s. The strongest indication being a symbol on a flag." He opened the book in his hands and displayed a large flag on its pages. "It's a royal family crest. I should have known better. I'm a fool for not realizing the possibility sooner."

"So what are we going to do?" Peter asked.

"We must find a way to travel back to Victorian London."

"Can't we just use the parasites again?" Jayden said.

Renato shook his head. "I'm afraid not. Even if the parasites could withstand that length of time in the bend, it would surely kill Arwan."

"What if Peter heals him while we're traveling?" Tara suggested.

"That was a possibility I considered, but I'm afraid our abilities are disabled while in the bend."

"And what do you mean, we?" Zanya said. "You're not coming. It's too dangerous."

Tara crossed her arms. "Oh, I'm coming. You can't leave me behind while you go gallivanting around the Victorian era."

"You're not coming," Zanya said again.

"Yes—I am."

Peter took Tara's hand. "I'll stay behind with her."

Tara's jaw dropped open. "Peter, I want to go."

"I'm sorry, but I have to agree with Zanya on this one. It's too dangerous. You could get hurt."

"Actually," Renato interrupted, "we need Peter with us in case someone gets injured."

Peter gestured to Zanya. "She has the healing ability now, too."

"Which she hasn't learned to use accurately enough yet. And what if Zanya gets injured? What if several of us are hurt simultaneously? We cannot risk you staying behind."

Tara displayed a smug grin. "So it's settled. I'm going."

Zanya pushed her hands down on the cushion of the couch and leaned forward. "No, you're not."

"Well I'm not leaving Tara alone," Peter said.

He must have been crazy. Here she was trying to keep Tara safe, and Peter was ruining it. "What if she gets taken by Sarian again? It was a pure stroke of luck we got her back last time. She's the only one of us without abilities. She's too vulnerable."

Tara scoffed. "So since you have abilities and I don't, you don't want me around?"

"You know that's not what I mean. I'm trying to protect you." Hell, she was starting to sound like Arwan.

"I know. You're always watching out for me…but I'm still coming."

Zanya dug her fingers into the cushion. "You're so stubborn."

Bobbing her foot, Tara shrugged. "And you wonder why we're best friends."

Zanya leaned back and folded her arms over her chest.

"If Peter will not come with us unless Tara accompanies him, then we have no choice but to bring them both. We will all keep a close eye on her."

Zanya weighed their options. She hated to admit it, but Renato was right about Peter. They needed him to come. "Fine, but you have to promise to stay safe. I couldn't stand losing you again."

Tara clapped her hands in delight. Zanya rolled her eyes. Of course Tara would celebrate that she was about to walk straight into a hot zone. She was fearless. Unfortunately, that quality wasn't always smart.

Zanya couldn't help but noticed Arwan's grin.

"I'm glad you're getting such a kick out of this," she snapped.

His grin widened. "I can't help it." He met her gaze. "You're incredibly cute when you're angry."

Zanya parted her lips. She wanted to shout at him, hit him—or better yet, zap him. How dare he go from cold to hot so quickly? Give the impression he only cared about her for one reason, and then drop the, you're incredibly cute, line.

"Now that we have that settled, we can move on to the means by which we will get there," Renato said.

They all waited for him to reveal his plan. Several horrifying possibilities traipsed through Zanya's imagination.

Renato searched the faces in the room. "Anyone?"

Zanya sat up straight. "What do you mean? You don't know?"

"I haven't the slightest idea."

That was a first. Renato always knew the answer. She perked up when she remembered something she'd read in a scribe's journal. "Wait." She stood and walked to a bookshelf, searching for the right title.

Renato joined her and waited while she sifted through the titles. She stole a glance at him every so often as he examined the pendant in her hand. "What do you have there?"

She held it up. "To be honest, I'm not sure."

Renato gently took the necklace.

She searched the shelves while he gave the pendant a closer look.

"Zanya…"

The scribe's journal had to be there somewhere. If she could just find the right one…

"This is the symbol of Cualli, flower goddess of the middleworld. The daughter of Ishel."

Zanya froze and tore her attention away from her search.

"Where did you get this?"

"I was led to it, by a vision. It was at the bottom of a waterfall."

"Amazing." He examined the piece closer. "The Maya believe water is a portal to the underworld. Someone must have tossed this into the lake while pleading for help. It's very old."

Zanya peered at it. "How old?"

"Hundreds of years. And it hasn't been affected by the water." He turned it over, running his fingers along the lines. "It's in perfect condition. This means something."

"Like what?"

"It means, Zanya, that we are no longer working alone. The middleworld deities are aware of our struggles and have joined our fight."

She stared at the pendant that suddenly took on a whole new meaning. "That—is from a goddess?"

Renato nodded and handed it back to her. It was so beautiful, like artwork. And the way it made her feel was even more remarkable. It steadied her hand, gave her reassurance. Almost like her stone, but in a different way. Why, she'd had no idea—until now.

After a few more moments of searching, she plucked the book from the shelf. "Here it is. She might be able to take us back." Zanya flipped through the pages, then handed it to Renato.

"She, who?" Tara asked.

Renato rubbed his chin, studying the pages. "This would be incredibly dangerous."

"If you can't come up with a solution, I'm pretty sure this is the only way."

Renato drew in a deep breath. "Very well." He tossed the book on his desk and turned to the rest of the group. "Contessa."

Marzena gripped Renato's arm, a grave expression hardening her tiny features.

"I know." Renato patted her hand, as if trying to reassure her. "But Zanya is right. It is quite likely our only option."

"Do you know Contessa?" Zanya asked. Marzena's eyes darted to her, narrow and dark. It was disturbing to see the face of a small child so cold and fierce.

"Contessa was once Sarian's lover," Renato explained. "He manipulated her, and eventually convinced her to kill his mother. When she did, his mother's darkness was woven into Contessa's soul. He soon grew tired of her and attempted to kill her by stabbing her through the heart. She survived, but only by black magic, and now lives on borrowed time."

"How do you borrow time?" Hawa said.

"By stealing the souls of others, and using them

to fuel her own existence."

Zanya slowly sat back down on the couch. "I, uh…I didn't know that."

"And she does not work for free. If we are going to ask for her patronage, we must offer her payment. It is usually a heavy price."

"I mean, we aren't poor," Hawa said. "We could sell some shares in the stocks we're invested in and just pay her off."

Renato frowned. "Unlikely."

Zanya swallowed, her hands iced over. This lady was a lot worse than she'd originally thought. Maybe it was a bad idea. Jayden took her hand. "Don't worry; it'll be fine."

"How do we find her?" Peter asked.

"She currently resides in Moscow. It is where she has lived for centuries. We will travel there and begin our search. I have an feeling that once we land in her town, she will come for us."

CHAPTER TWENTY-TWO

Zanya found her window seat on the commercial jet and settled in. The chair was plush and comfortable with a touch screen television in the seat back in front of her. She had never flown before.

So far, so good.

Jayden walked down the narrow aisle and paused beside her while inspecting his ticket. He frowned and then continued toward the back of the plane.

Marzena took her seat beside Renato. The stewardess crouched and handed Marzena a captain's wing pin, fussing over how cute Marzena's freckles were, and what a big girl she was for flying in first class with her daddy.

Zanya stifled a laugh. If that stewardess didn't back off soon, she may end up with an unexplained migraine for the rest of the flight.

Tara stopped beside Zanya's seat. "This is so awesome." Her elated squeak made the child passing behind her giggle. "Can you believe we're going to Russia? I've never flown first class before."

"Tara, you've never flown before."

She paused, her lips parted while she took a moment to think. "Well, maybe that's true, but this is still awesome."

Zanya laughed. "Yeah, it's pretty great." And it was—for the most part. She scanned the plane for Arwan, but he wasn't anywhere in sight.

A man of reasonable girth standing behind Tara cleared his throat. Tara rolled her eyes. "Don't have a heart attack. I'm going." She smiled at Zanya. "I'll see you in Moscow!" She trotted to her seat.

Zanya's chest tightened when she spotted Arwan walking down the aisle. A group of girls giggled and whispered as he passed. She couldn't blame them for seeing exactly what she did—muscles packed under a fitted shirt and smoky eyes. Still, that didn't stop her from wanting to slap them upside the head.

He double checked his seat number, slid his bag under the seat beside Zanya and plopped down. He smiled softly, then leaned back in his chair and closed his eyes.

The pilot made an announcement, the Fasten Seat Belt sign pinged on, and Zanya gripped the armrest as if she were riding a roller coaster. The engines roared and she watched the ground move out the window. The acceleration pinned her against her seat, and as the plane's tires lifted off the ground. Her stomach dropped. Suddenly she didn't appreciate the idea of riding thirty thousand feet in the air with no control over going up or down. The plane bobbed and shook.

She drew in a deep breath, groping inside her pocket for the pendant Cualli had given her. She'd gotten accustomed to carrying it around everywhere, especially since it helped her stay calm. She pulled in another deep breath and closed her eyes, humming a few notes to herself, and finding comfort in the melody. The pendant seemed to grow warm in her palm. She curled her fingers around it and continued humming.

"You really like that thing, don't you?"

She opened her eyes to find Arwan examining the necklace in her hand. "So you're talking to me now?" She didn't make any effort to mask the sarcasm in her tone. The plane pitched again. She sucked in a breath and held it, rubbing her fingers over the wicker pendant. When the plane stabilized, she continued to hum. The melody was muffled in her ears from the altitude change. "Is it going to be like this the whole flight?"

"Do you want me to get Peter?"

"No, it's fine." She glanced at him. "Thanks."

He pulled a bottle of water out of his carryon and dampened a napkin. "Here." He pressed it over her forehead and along her temples. The cool water soothed the heat flushing her face. She slid her fingers up his forearm. She missed his touch so much, it was almost unbearable.

He pulled away, causing a streak of pain to spike in her chest. "I have something for you."

Please don't let it be Dramamine and an airsick bag.

He reached in his back pocket and took out a small, teal box with a silver heart charm dangling off the top.

Her breath hitched. "What's this?"

"It's a birthday gift. I got it at the airport." He extended it to her. "There's not much in the way of gifts in the jungle."

She touched the tiny silver charm. There was no way she would be able to set things straight if she opened this box first, so folded down the tray table and placed it in front of her. "I think need to talk."

"I know. Just, let me say something first."

Of course. He was going to give her the whole "it's not you, it's me" speech, and whatever was waiting for her in that box was his way of softening the blow.

Arwan turned toward her in his seat, his shoulders rigid. He seemed nervous, which made sense. Her hands began to shake. She couldn't stand it anymore. "Just do it. Just get it over with."

"If that's what you want." It was. Like a bandage—the faster, the better. He cleared his throat. "I admire you, Zanya." He touched her cheek. "I am fascinated by you. I'm entranced by you." Every word came out softer than the next. He dropped his hand from her cheek. "You're so many things I'm not, and I know I shouldn't care about you. Not the way I do."

She blinked. "What?"

"I refuse to lose you. I know I deserve to, but please don't give up on me. We can take it slow."

The genuine warmth behind his gaze was affirmation enough. She swallowed. "Slow is good."

His chest jumped. She saw it, felt it in the flinch

of his fingers entwined in hers. "Is that a yes?"

She wanted nothing more than to just say yes and kiss him. God, she had wanted to taste his lips for so long—more than just a soft, sweet kiss. But if they were going to work, he had to understand. "Under two conditions. No more questions about my friendship with Jayden. We're just friends. That's it. No more. Not ever."

"And the second one?"

She stared down at the pendant. "I'm not your responsibility. I don't ever want you to treat me like that again."

Arwan responded by picking up the tiny box and holding it out to her. "Deal. Now open your gift."

And just like that, everything was in place. Tara was home, her and Arwan were back to normal—whatever that was—and Jayden…well, he was still Jayden, sitting a few rows back, strumming an air guitar. However crazy and insane her life was, it wouldn't be the same without him, or the other people she'd gotten to know. Her family.

She snatched the box and tilted open the lid. Her breath caught in her throat, and she hooked the short chain around her fingers, pulling out the butterfly bracelet. Colored gemstones glittered inside the wings that ended in a scroll tip.

"It's beautiful." Nobody had ever given her a birthday gift before. Sure, her friends did what they could; fresh-picked wildflowers, an extra portion of dessert in the cafeteria, but nothing like this. "It's so thoughtful." Arwan took the bracelet and clasped it around her wrist.

"Why butterflies?"

The edges of his mouth pulled into a grin. "I remembered the butterfly field."

Her cheeks flushed with heat. It wasn't exactly the best memory they had together. She'd pushed him away and run off, leaving him in the middle of the jungle. "So…you're a glutton for punishment?"

He smiled. It was the first wide, brilliant smile she'd ever seen. "I guess you could say that."

***

The next day, the group stood in the lobby of their hotel, waiting for Renato to finish checking in.

Zanya flipped up her jacket collar and yawned.

Tara hadn't slept well last night. The sound of her entangled in her sheets, getting up and down out of bed, and deep nightmare-induced moans kept Zanya up most of the night. It wasn't like Tara to have nightmares. She usually slept like a rock. What was even stranger was how she left the room, and didn't come back until morning.

Tara finally stepped off the elevator and dragged herself beside Zanya, rubbing her puffy eyes.

"Hey. How are you feeling?"

Tara yawned. "I'm fine."

"Yeah, right. Where have you been all night?"

"Sorry about that. I didn't mean to wake you up."

Zanya shrugged. "You know me. I'm used to sleeping like crap. But you…"

"I'm fine, Zanya." Her tone was sharp—probably grumpy from the lack of sleep. "It's just the jet lag."

Renato finally arrived, and the group huddled around him. "Since we don't know exactly where Contessa lives, I suggest we break up into groups." He reached into a plastic bag and removed several cell phones. "These are international phones I purchased in town this morning. I took the liberty of programming each other's numbers into the devices. They will work anywhere in the world, so from now on, please keep them with you."

"Nice." Jayden snatched his and played with the settings.

"If you want to break into groups, you may, but please stay with at least one other person at all times. Keep your eyes and ears open. If you get in trouble, auto dial me immediately. And if you spot Contessa, text the group your location."

"How will we know who she is?" Hawa said.

"When you see her, you will know. There is no mistaking a powerful witch for a commoner."

"Witch? She's a witch?" Tara's harsh whisper made Marzena scowl.

"She uses her extraordinary beauty to lure men into bed before consuming their souls. You may call her a siren, a witch, a succubus, or a bandit of life. Whatever you call her, be sure not to underestimate her abilities." Renato gestured to the guys. "And do not allow her to seduce you."

"Isn't she like, a thousand years old?" Jayden smirked. "Talk about cougar syndrome."

"This is no matter to take lightly!" Marzena's voice amplified in Zanya's ears, threatening to buckle her knees. Several people in the lobby stopped their conversations and stared. Marzena lowered her head and returned to silence.

Renato waited for the people to go back to their business as Zanya steadied herself, squinting through a sharp pain in her temples. Marzena gave her an apologetic glance.

"Marzena is right," Renato said in a hushed tone. "Contessa may be old in years, but her appearance is untouched by time, and she is deadly."

Peter took Tara's hand. "Got it."

"Let's do this." Hawa slapped Jayden on the arm. "Come on."

"Um…okay." He turned to Zanya. "Be careful."

"We will." She shifted closer to Arwan. Jayden pursed his lips into a tight line, and then followed Hawa out the door.

"We're on the other end of the phone if you need us," Renato said, standing close to Marzena. "Just call."

Zanya followed Arwan out of the hotel and onto the sidewalk. The air was crisp and cold. The inside of her nose burned with every breath. "Where do we start?"

"Anywhere, I guess."

They started to walk, and kept walking, weaving between residential roads, tiny stone paths, under bridges, and in every other direction they could think of. Hours later, Zanya's feet ached, and worse, they hadn't found even a hint of Contessa's whereabouts. "So we're just going to wander around all day until we bump into her on the streets?"

"Renato said she would locate us if we made ourselves available."

She stopped and slumped against a brick wall. "I'm exhausted."

"Maybe we should get something to eat." He squinted up at the sky. "It's nearly two o'clock. We've been walking for almost five hours."

Her stomach growled at the mere thought of food. "That sounds like a really good idea." Her phone buzzed in her pocket, and she pulled it out and read the text from Tara.

Contessa is here in the food district. Hurry. Peter's in trouble.

Zanya snapped her phone shut. "Tara found her, but something's wrong. They're in the food district."

They ran at an annoyingly-slow pace—human speed. Arwan was fast, but now Zanya was faster, and she couldn't wait for him. "I can get there quicker than you. I'll go ahead and meet you there."

"Be careful."

Zanya sprinted ahead, darting behind buildings so as not to be seen or have her photo accidentally taken by an unsuspecting tourist. When she was forced to weave through crowds, she ran at human pace as quickly as she could without appearing unnatural. As soon as she was shielded from the public eye, she pressed on the gas.

Tiny stores and modest Russian homes passed by in a blur, as did the textured stone pathway and rows of bicycles chained to racks. It all seemed to just melt into a streak of color—just like Hawa looked when she sprinted. Still, Zanya remained hypersensitive to obstacles in her way. She dodged through alleys, under clotheslines, and around the

273

occasional stray dog with ease.

Emerged from behind a massive building was an entire block filled with wooden carts loaded with fresh fruit. She screeched to a halt and closed her eyes in search for Tara, finding her beside a brick wall yards away. After careful maneuvering through hustling crowds, she grabbed her friend's arm.

Tara spun around and jerked away, her eyes wide with fear. "Oh, it's you!"

"Where's Peter?" Zanya pressed her back against the stone wall, keeping her eye out for Arwan.

"He followed Contessa into that alley. He told me I had to stay here."

"What?" Zanya peeked around the sharp brick corner into the narrow, abandoned street. "You let him follow her alone?"

"I couldn't stop him." Tara was getting hysterical, and they couldn't risk her making a scene.

"Okay." She braced her hands on Tara's shoulders. "Listen to me. Everyone else will be here in just a minute." She pointed her finger at the ground. "Stay. Right. Here. Do you understand me? Do not move from this spot, or I'll assume you're in trouble." She let go of Tara and stepped back. "I'm going to get Peter."

Careful, quiet steps. That's what she made, creeping along the damp, narrow alley. The tall buildings towered on both sides, snuffing out the sun and reducing the temperature enough to cause the tips of Zanya's fingers to tingle with frostbite. She spied into doorways that sat ajar, in bare windows, and down smaller walkways leading to dead ends. Calling out for Peter would only give away her position.

The element of surprise was the only thing she had in her favor.

"Poor girl," a lustrous voice purred from behind her. Zanya jumped and spun to see a striking, red-haired woman standing in the center of the alley. "You honestly believe you have the element of surprise?" Her hazel eyes, accented by a corseted emerald-green dress, were more calculating than Zanya was comfortable with. It was Contessa. She knew it, without a shadow of a doubt, just like Renato said.

Zanya gathered her confidence, or at least the appearance of. "It's a pleasure to meet you."

"I must say. I am surprised to see you wandering the streets with no chaperone. A young lady with your exceptional abilities should use more discretion while traveling. You flaunt your powers as if no one would dare to rob you of them." The chill in her tone was subtle, but unmistakable. Contessa's eyes flickered with darkness, and her placid expression only deepened the fear gripping Zanya's throat. "Where are the rest of your comrades?"

Zanya swallowed in an attempt to restore moisture to her dry mouth. She had to play it cool or she'd ruin any chance they had of finding Peter, or convincing Contessa that helping them was in her best interest. "They'll be here soon. In fact, you might know where one of them is right now. My friend Peter came up missing, and we're worried about him."

"Ah, the brown-haired boy with dark blue eyes?"

Zanya nodded.

"Yes, he followed me into the alley, spouting poetry of my beauty. Many men have presented me with ballads, although his were quite flattering." Contessa's pink tongue caressed her lips. "He shows promise to be an ambitious lover."

After what Renato said about Contessa's romantic life, there was no way that could be a good thing. But there was one offer Zanya could present that might be more appealing. "I have something more interesting, if you're willing to make a trade."

Contessa arched an eyebrow. "What would you have to offer that could bring me more pleasure than him?"

The only thing a woman with a chip on her shoulder would want. "Revenge on Sarian."

The dark, rolling magic in her irises was visible even from where Zanya stood. Contessa's features morphed and flashed with glimpses of something inhuman lurking just under her milky skin. "Heed my warning. If you plan to take the boy without fulfilling your proposition, you will be remorseful."

Zanya shook her head. "I promise. I won't go back on my word."

Contessa's eyes returned to normal, as did her porcelain skin. She studied Zanya. "Hmm. The word of a Stone Guardian. Very well." Contessa removed a flawless hand from her fur warmer and pulled a key from the bust of her dress. "Any adversary of Sarian is an ally of mine."

CHAPTER TWENTY-THREE

Arwan

In Contessa's kitchen, Arwan inhaled the aroma of spices as the witched poured each of them tea. The copper kettle in hand, she filled Renato's cup.

His mentor seemed so calm. So reserved.

A slick of sweat collected on Arwan's brow. He wiped it away and swallowed down the urge to heave.

Renato's gaze flickered to him, and he gave a single nod as if asking if he was all right.

Arwan couldn't respond. His muscles pulled so tight he could barely breathe. He blinked hard, trying to swat away the fog edging his vision.

Being around Contessa was agonizing. Her darkness sparked against his, instigating his natural instinct.

Arwan curled his fingers around the arms of the wooden chair he sat in, squeezing them as tight as he could. If Zanya was only aware of what dark urges were pouring through him, she would never look at him the same again.

Contessa's sparkling eyes landed on him. Her gaze dragged over his body.

It was as if she wanted to taunt him.

His darkness flared and he looked at Zanya, his blood rushing with savage heat. He clenched his jaw and closed his eyes, remembering his mother's face and the warmth of her smile. He reached for Zanya's hand and squeezed it. The gesture seemed to catch her off guard, but she squeezed his hand in return.

She leaned close to him. "Are you okay?"

He forced a nod and then opened his eyes, regaining his focus.

Jayden stared down at the drink, his lips pressed together. Hawa, who mimicked Renato's demeanor, sat across from him with her legs crossed and a casual tilt of her head.

Contessa leaned over the table and poured a dollop of cream in Arwan's tea. He avoided her gaze and instead stared into the steaming liquid, the colors twisting like a cyclone.

"What kind of tea is this?" Tara asked.

"It is a homemade blend of black tea, spices, bat's blood, and eye of newt."

Tara stared at her cup in horror.

Contessa snarled. "It is a mixture of cinnamon, cardamom, mint leaves, and clove, you puerile girl. Worry not, it carries no incantation."

Renato was the first to sip the brew and set the delicate china cup back on its matching saucer. "It's delicious. Thank you, Contessa. Your hospitality is greatly appreciated. But I believe we still have a small matter to clear up before proceeding."

"Ah, yes. The boy. I will wake him momentarily."

"Wake him up from what? What'd you do to him?" Tara's probing clearly annoyed Contessa.

"Certain things are better not divulged, young lady." She leaned back in her chair. "Although you are fortunate to have arrived when you did. I've been feeling rather…" She sighed and glided her fingers along her chest, "unsatisfied."

Arwan coughed. He pressed his fist over his mouth, his chest heaving as Contessa's carnal desire poured over him.

Zanya rested her hand on his shoulder. "Maybe you should go outside."

"Yes, perhaps the boy dislikes my tea," she said, grinning.

Tara crossed her arms. "Are you going to wake up Peter or what?"

Contessa stared at Tara for a moment, then turned her attention to Renato. "Does the girl always speak so obtusely?"

"I apologize. My pupils have no knowledge in the practices of black magic."

"One cannot practice what they are. The state of someone's being is far beyond the repetitive, mundane rituals of the pagan people. I do not practice dark magic, my dear gentleman." She leaned forward with a devious grin. "I am dark magic."

Zanya's hand trembled.

"Yes, of course. My apologies. Nonetheless, I would like to know of Peter's whereabouts and condition, if you would be so kind. I'm rather fond of him, and I take personal responsibility for his safety."

Contessa sipped her tea. "Is that so? Yet you were nowhere to be found when he fell to his knees, pleading for my adoration." She laughed to herself. "A man's propensity to bring a lady to bed will never cease to amaze me."

Tara shot out of her chair. "Are you saying Peter wanted to sleep with you?"

Contessa slowly placed her cup on the table. "Ah. You are the boy's lover."

Tara's cheeks blazed a brilliant red. "He's my boyfriend."

"Of course he is. Well, feel no ill emotion toward him. The choice was not his to make. He merely followed my direction, like a dumb, starving animal in need of nourishment."

Arwan studied Marzena, who sat stiffly, focused on their host. He had never seen Marzena express such obvious rancor. The sharpness of her stares cut into Contessa, so much so that it caught her attention.

"Ah, Marzena. I nearly forgot you were here. It has been quite some time. You look well." Contessa propped her elbows on the table and rested her chin on top her laced fingers. "You simply must share your secret with me before you leave. After all this time, you don't appear a day over ten."

Marzena's glare intensified.

"With all due respect," Renato said, "you still have not answered my questions. Where is the boy? Is he safe?"

After a brief moment of silent taunting, she dismissed Marzena and sat back in her chair. "He is ignorantly sleeping in my chamber as we speak. No harm has come to him." Tara let out a hefty sigh of relief. "Now, I was promised an opportunity. I wish to collect on it."

Renato gestured to Zanya, who sat up straighter in her chair. "Sarian stole the stone of Muuk'Ich from me. We need to get it back. We came here because we think he's hiding in the Victorian era with the stone, but we can't go back that far, even with our timebender."

Eyebrows arched and lips parted, Contessa perked up. "I was sure there was something special about the young man beside you."

The light in her chest flickered on.

Contessa's stared at it curiously and cocked her head. "So, you need my assistance in retrieving the stone?"

"No." Zanya swallowed, her heart still pounding. It was so loud, Arwan heard it thumping against his ears. "We just need your help getting to when and where Sarian's hiding. We'll take over from there."

Even Contessa's laugh was alluring. Arwan cringed back in his chair as she let out a deep sigh. "And what makes you believe you are capable of recovering it from Sarian?" Her tone turned stern as she continued. "You are a group of highly untrained, asinine adolescents with an incompetent instructor." The cups rattled when she slammed her fist on the table. "Hundreds of people over thousands of years have attempted to bring Sarian down. All of them have failed."

"I don't know if we'll be successful, but it's my job to protect the stone. It's the only part of my mother I have left. I have to get it back."

Contessa searched Zanya's face. "I was acquainted with your mother before Sarian captured her. She was just as determined as you are to save her precious stone from that pathetic miscreant I once laid with. But pathetic or not, he is cunning and powerful." She paused. "Have you given any thought as to how you are going to retrieve the stone without Sarian recognizing you?"

Zanya's eyebrows shot up, then shook her head. "Actually, no. I didn't think about that."

Anger flared behind Contessa's eyes. "You are an unprepared warrior, stumbling into a fight. Did you not think it would be necessary to veil your identity? Have you given your strategy no consideration at all?"

Zanya shifted in her seat, her cheeks flushed. "I guess I haven't."

Contessa passed her hand in front of Zanya's face. She gasped and gripped her chest.

Arwan knelt beside her, her heartbeat pounding in his ears. "You're going to make her heart explode."

"If she cannot endure a simple masking spell, she will indubitably fail at her mission, and you will all die."

"Masking spell?" Zanya wheezed.

"Yes. It will keep Sarian from seeing you for who you truly are, but only by appearances. Make no mistake that he is clever. You must remain inconspicuous."

"Deep breaths," Arwan said softly, stroking his thumb over her knuckles.

Zanya drew in slow, steady breaths until her heartbeat slowed to a safe pace. "What do you want in return for your help?" she asked.

"In return? Why, I simply wish to bask in the satisfaction of doing a good deed for a deserving friend."

Arwan's muscles coiled even tighter. From the little he had learned about Contessa, she'd do nothing for free.

"You don't want anything?" Zanya said.

She must have been thinking the same thing as him.

"That, and a lock of your lovely hair."

Zanya tucked a silky wave behind her ear. "My hair?"

Arwan returned to his chair. "No."

Contessa ignored him completely. "The choice is yours."

"No, no, that's fine." Zanya gathered a lock in her fingers. "Do you have scissors?"

"You're not going through with this," Arwan said. "We don't know what she will do—"

Contessa reached across the table, grabbed a chunk of Zanya's hair and yanked it out of her scalp. Zanya yelped and pressed her hand over the sore spot. Contessa tied the strands into a knot, and tucked them into her sleeve.

Arwan fisted his hands. After spending so much time with Drina, there was one thing he knew about a witch. Never give her blood or hair. *Never*.

Zanya rubbed her scalp. "Now that we have that

cleared up, would you mind waking up Peter?" She paused before spitting out another word. "Please."

"A deal is a deal." Contessa tapped her fingers gently on the table. Moments later, a door creaked open, and Peter stumbled out. His eyes wide open, he ran his hands along the doorframe, and then the wall.

"His vision will return soon. It is merely a side effect."

"Peter!" Tara ran to him and threw her arms around his neck.

Contessa handed Zanya a glass vial containing a multicolored liquid. "This is to be used as transport. You must throw it to the ground and shatter the vial at your feet. Stand in the mist as you hold a mental picture of the location and time in which you wish to go. Take caution not to allow your concentration to falter during the process. You must keep a clear destination in mind. You have only one, so use it wisely."

Zanya stood and slipped the vial in her jacket pocket. "Thank you, Contessa. Your generosity is really appreciated." She hesitated, then extended her hand. "I hope you consider us friends."

It was clear Zanya was being smart—keeping a valuable person in their corner in case they needed her help again in the future. That didn't stop Arwan from hating the idea of the temptress touching Zanya. Even to shake her hand.

To his relief, Contessa ignored her gesture completely. "Before you go, allow me to bestow some words of advice. Trust no one. Make no commotion to draw attention, and complete your task as hastily as possible. Every minute you spend there is another opportunity to be spotted.

"The masking spell covers only the guardian." Contessa waved her hand over the table, producing a sack of gold coins. "You may use these as currency. They are extremely valuable and should cover your needs with excess.

"Sarian will only be found living among the affluent. Do not waste your time searching the towns or villages. But most importantly." Her tone became grave. "Do not underestimate Sarian's abilities. He grows stronger by the day. His magic is far more powerful than you realize."

Contessa dolloped a clear ball of spit in the palm of her own hand, then smeared it on the table. She traced a symbol in it with her finger. "Farewell." She flicked her saliva at them, spittle speckling their cheeks.

The cozy kitchen transformed into the rainy streets of a dark Victorian town.

Arwan stood beside Zanya, who stood with rigid shoulders and wide eyes. A horse-drawn carriage bounced past them while the driver shouted, his whip clapping against the air.

Arwan grabbed Zanya's wrist and pulled her onto the sidewalk. She stared after the wooden cart as it disappeared into the fog. Her legs buckled. Arwan caught her around the waist, his own strength returning now that they weren't near Contessa anymore.

Hawa buried her fingers in her hair. "Holy. Shit."

"I second that." Jayden zipped up his sweater against the bitter cold.

Hawa searched around them. "Where are Peter and Marzena?"

Jayden glanced around. "And Tara."

Zanya spun in a circle. "How could Contessa forget them?"

"I'm not sure she forgot," Renato said. "I have a feeling she intentionally left them behind."

"Why would she do that?"

Jayden scoffed. "I don't think Contessa likes Tara very much. Her or Marzena. And Peter was still recovering from whatever she did to him."

Renato inspected their surroundings. "We need to find a place to sleep, and some more appropriate clothing."

They wandered around the unfamiliar town until Renato loitered in front of a shabby wooden building. A narrow sign swung from two rusted chains over the door. "Ah, here we are."

Arwan read the sign aloud. "Salvation Army. Four Penny Coffin House."

When Renato pushed open the door, a bell tinkled to announce their arrival. A man dressed in an officer's uniform with high leather boots and a police hat stepped directly in their path. "Will the bunch of ya need a box?"

While Renato talked to the guard, Zanya grabbed Arwan's arm. "What are we doing?"

"It's a homeless shelter."

Her grip tightened. "He wants us to sleep here— in a coffin?"

"Apparently so."

Renato waved them over. They gathered around the pile of clothes thrown in a wooden box. The stench of mildew, body odor, and liquor rose from the garments.

Zanya covered her nose. "These are rancid."

"Perhaps, but they will allow us to enter a shop in the morning to purchase some decent clothing."

"Why can't we just wear what we have on? Our clothes are cleaner than these."

"And unlike the attire of this era." Renato reached in and fumbled through some of the garments. "We'll stay here tonight, and go shopping first thing tomorrow."

Hawa lifted an article and shook it out. She winced at its condition. "I guess I'll take this."

"Well, apparently I have no choice." Zanya slipped on an oversize trench coat and tied it around her waist.

Arwan chose an old wool coat with tears and stains. He didn't want to imagine what kinds of stains they were. At least the wool would keep him warm, even if it did stink of alcohol.

Renato rubbed his hands together for warmth. Clouds of breath puffed into the air. "Get some rest. We have a long day ahead of us tomorrow."

CHAPTER TWENTY-FOUR

Zanya

Zanya examined the boxes—each wooden, damp, and disturbingly similar to a coffin. Her breath clouded the air when she blew into her hands, trying to regain sensation in her fingers.

"Well, I guess we should get some sleep." Jay stepped into a box.

Zanya walked along the crooked rows until she eventually found one that was dry and cleaner than the others. Settling in the center, she pulled her legs to her chest and pressed her face to her knees. She couldn't remember if she'd ever been so cold in her life. Even that winter at the orphanage when a bad storm blew out the electricity, at least she'd had a heavy blanket to keep her warm.

"Scoot over." Arwan lowered himself into her box and wrapped his arms around her from behind. "Come here, lie against me."

Zanya gratefully pressed her back against his chest and curled up. So she didn't have a blanket, but this was way better.

Arwan buried his nose into her neck.

She gasped and cringed away. "Your nose is freezing." His hot breath caressed her neck.

He squeezed her tight and buried his nose in her hair.

"Guard." Jayden pointed at them. "Those two are fraternizing in their box."

The guard gripped his baton. "One body per box. Don't make me tell ya twice." He jabbed the air with his thumb over his shoulder. "Or you're outta here."

Arwan slid from behind her and hopped to the neighboring box. "*Idiota celoso.*" He glared at Jayden.

Jay spread a tattered wool blanket over him like a young child tucking himself in. "There." He grinned smugly. "Now I can sleep."

"And while you sleep, Zanya will be miserable all night."

Jayden's grin vanished. "I didn't think—"

"Because you don't think!"

Sure, Arwan had a point, but if she didn't say something to quiet them down, someone would end up in a nineteenth-century prison. "It's okay." She forced a smile through her quivering lips. "Really, I'll be fine." As long as she didn't freeze to death overnight. Zanya curled up at the bottom of the box, the grooves digging into her hip. She tucked her hands under her chin. Losing fingers to frostbite wasn't an option.

A heavy wool blanket landed on top of her. She peered over the edge of the box.

Jayden gestured to his peace offering. "There. You'll be warm now."

He may be a total jerk sometimes, but he was worth every snarky comment she put up with. "Thanks." She took a second to find Hawa, and spotted her on a bench pushed up against a wall. "What? You're not going to sleep in one of these luxury pallets?" Her teeth chattered through her words.

"No." Hawa's voice was cut off from the cold.

"Seriously, it's probably warmer in here. At least the walls trap in some body heat."

Hawa stretched the sweater tighter around her shoulders. "Yeah, and make a nice house for the bedbugs and fleas. I'll take my chances with the cold."

"Bedbugs?" Zanya sat up and searched for anything crawling along the cracks of wood or folds of fabric. She'd already agreed to sleep in a coffin, but she had her limits.

"Don't worry," Arwan said. "These boxes are made of cedar. Bugs don't like cedar."

"Oh…" That gave her a little reassurance, at least against the bugs. Too bad the cold couldn't have such an easy fix. She lay back down and curled into a ball. "I don't think very many bugs would survive in this weather anyway." Hopefully she'd be more lucky.

The blanket was lifted off her, and a gust of wind shocked her body. Arwan lowered himself beside her. He wrapped his arms around her and whispered in her ear. "To hell with the guard and Jayden. I'm not going to watch you freeze all night."

Zanya sniffled and clung to him, her teeth still chattering. "My nose is freezing."

He pulled the blanket over their heads. "There." Even under the shelter of the quilt, Zanya could see his dark eyes watching her. "Now you should get warm. The blanket will trap in our body heat." He touched her cheek. "Any better?"

How was she supposed to sleep while lying beside him? He meant well, and his efforts were paying off considering she could feel the tips of her fingers again. "Much better."

His heartbeat soothed her, captivated her. She shifted, trying to escape the head of the steel nail digging into her butt. She tilted her head and unintentionally brushed her lips against her neck.

He swallowed.

Although she didn't mean to, didn't want to, tried not to even, she reacted to the shiver that crawled over her body.

"Are you still cold?"

She shook her head. "No. Not cold."

"You're shivering." He scooted closer. Her breath caught in her throat. With a delicate brush of her fingers, she pushed a silky strand of dark hair away from his face. He was stunning. Even being hungry, uncomfortable, and wrapped in musty clothes, his body heat was all she could focus on.

She curled her fingers into her palm and pulled away. *Self-control. Just…breathe.*

But she couldn't. Not with the butterflies in her stomach.

He slid his hand up to her waist, spreading his fingers over her ribs.

Self-control. Just—

"Do you want me to get out?"

Hell no she didn't want him to get out. She ran her hand down his arm and to his hand. "No, I'm just…"

Totally freaking out.

A complete coward.

She shook her head and laughed at her own lack of courage.

Still, the temptation to kiss him tingled over her lips. She tilted up her chin, giving the invitation if it was what he wanted.

He curled his hand around the back of her neck, entangling his fingers in her hair. He leaned in closer, hovering close to her lips. She closed the gap and found the warmth of his lips with hers.

His mouth was like velvet. The fire inside her grew hotter, and her fingers somehow found their way back into his silky hair. His tongue to teased the opening of her lips. Her stomach jumped.

The energy built between them was explosive. Her body pulsed with heat, mirrored by the enthusiasm of his mouth. His hands tightened on her waist. A noise escaped her, one that began in her throat and ended as a tiny whimper.

Zanya recalled her dream, hanging in his arms while his lips trailed down her neck. She wished it were real. She traced her hands along his chest and under his shirt where her fingers traced his abs. He had the body of a Greek god and the kiss of an angel, or maybe the devil, with how the taste of his mouth affected her.

***

Arwan

Arwan lay awake, watching Zanya while she slept. He'd been awake for hours—not because he wasn't tired, but because there was no telling when he would hold her again like this.

Her breathing was rhythmic. Long eyelashes were draped over the blush of her cheeks.

Dread washed over him when he imagined telling her the truth. The image of her backing away haunted him—her hands in front of her and her eyes wide with horror. He blinked, and the vision vanished.

Zanya stirred. Her arms tightened around him, then relaxed as she settled closer to his chest. He placed a kiss on her forehead, and watched as a faint smile tugged on her lips.

What he wouldn't give to put a stop to all the madness and spend another lifetime lying beside her.

"Why are you awake?" Zanya's whisper was groggy, her eyes still closed.

"Why are you awake?"

She groaned and pressed her cheek against his chest. "Because you're thinking too loud."

He paused. "I'm thinking too loud?"

"Shhh. Just go to sleep. You need to get some rest." She kissed him tenderly. He savored the warmth of her lips and the way his blood spiked with adrenalin when she touched him. He ran his fingers over the curve of her jaw until she pulled away and lay against him.

"Go back to sleep," he said. "You need your rest." At least for a few more hours, if that was all he could have. "*Que sueñes con los angelitos.*"

"Hmm?"

"I think it translates to, 'may you dream with the angels.'" It had been many, many years since he'd referred to angels.

Hours of darkness passed until the coffin house slowly filled with crisp, morning light. He was still awake when she drew in a slow, deep breath and curled into a tight ball. "Do we have to get out of this coffin?" She blinked open her eyes. "Okay, I never thought I'd say that."

He chuckled. "Unfortunately, yes." Though he'd spent the entire night wishing they didn't.

She pushed up on her elbows and peeked out of the box. Arwan followed, scanning the silent room. Everyone lay asleep.

He pulled Zanya back down and nuzzled his nose in her hair. "You always smell like vanilla and lavender."

She snorted. "Surprising, since I haven't showered since yesterday morning."

"Arwan." Renato's voice tore through the air in a sharp whisper.

Arwan threw the blanket off of them, the crisp morning air sucking the heat away from their bodies. Zanya stood, flipped up the collar of her jacket, and hugged herself.

Arwan's muscles tensed in the cold. Hawa still lay on the bench, her nose bright red and jaw clenched—obvious signs of a dreadful night's sleep.

She sat up, her blanket wrapped around her legs, and only the faded gray sweater from the box to keep her top half warm.

"I don't know why you picked that thing," Zanya said "There had to be something warmer than that."

"Maybe." Hawa slowly sat up. She rubbed her watery eyes and curled up on the bench. "It's no big deal. I've had my share of nights sleeping in the cold."

Zanya tightened the belt of her coat around her waist. "You could have frozen to death or caught pneumonia. Don't forget what era we're in. There's no IV fluids or hospitals around."

Her lips quivered over her chattering teeth. "Yeah, well, not all of us grew up with a silver spoon in our mouth, princess. At least you had a warm bed every night."

"Uh, have we met? I—" Renato grabbed Arwan's attention and signaled them to move out.

"Come on." Arwan followed Renato's lead, as did the rest of the group. Soon they were all gathered in a tight circle.

Renato rubbed his hands together and blew into them. "We should get an early start. First we shop, and then we find a suitable place to sleep." The group nodded in compliance.

They slipped out of the coffin house and into the streets of a bustling town. The city of London was bright, enchanting and frightening all at the same time.

Women sauntered beside their chaperones, holding their hands properly in front of them while they walked. Young boys ran through the streets.

They shot imaginary guns while playing cops and robbers, shouting and laughing as their leather shoes slapped against the cobblestone streets.

A gentleman crossed in front of them, his gaze turned to the ground. He tipped the rim of his top hat to cover his eyes. Arwan glanced down at his tattered wool coat. They must look like a gang of drunkards wandering the town.

Renato guided them to a small dress shop. He turned to Zanya and Hawa. "You two find some clothes. When you're finished, pay with these." He dropped several gold coins in Zanya's hand. "This should be more than enough to pay for a dress and ladies' accessories for both of you. The rest of us will go to the gentlemen's store across the street. We will meet back here in exactly one hour." Renato gestured to Arwan and Jayden. "You two, come with me."

Arwan stepped close to Renato. "Do you think they'll be safe there alone?"

"Hawa knows how to protect herself quite well, and Zanya…well, I'm not concerned."

His mentor was right. Zanya had become more powerful than ever since she bonded with the stone. Still, he couldn't ignore the need to protect her.

They arrived at the men's clothing store and were measured for suits. Jayden fumbled through the clothing and cringed away from the tailor as he measured his inseam.

Looking in the full-length mirror, Renato cocked his head. "Something is missing." He glanced at a top hat and snatched it off its rack. "There." He fit it over his head and slid his hand along his lapel.

"Much better." Renato's focus shifted in the mirror to Jayden, who stood behind him, tugging at his tie. "Stop pulling on that. You'll untie it, and I highly doubt you know how to put it back in place."

"Easy for you to say." Jayden craned his neck side to side. "It's like you live in these things."

"Perhaps, but you look like a man of class. At least try to act the part."

Jayden huffed.

Arwan buttoned up his coat and smoothed down the fabric. His shiny black dress shoes and midnight black pants fit well with the tuxedo jacket and white dress shirt. The suit maker dusted Arwan's shoulders with a wooden hand brush. Arwan handed the man a coin.

"Well," Renato said, smiling. "I would say London has done wonders for you."

Arwan smirked. "You don't look bad either, old man."

"Why don't you two get a room?" Jayden walked past them, out the door.

Arwan and Renato exchanged glances. "I still don't trust the seeker being here," Arwan said.

"We don't have a choice."

They followed the seeker out of the suit shop and onto the streets. This time, rather than averted gazes and turned down top haps, Arwan was greeted with stares of admiration. "Do you think Hawa and Zanya are finished?"

"My experience with women is not to rush them. They may take a bit longer to dress, but their beauty is worth every moment spent in waiting."

Arwan nodded, making a mental note. His

attention was stolen by a girl in a canary yellow dress and matching satin gloves loitering in front of the dress store across the street. He stepped off the sidewalk, onto the street. A laced, corseted top accentuated her waistline, and her hips were made wider by the fluffy bottom of her gown. She fiddled awkwardly with the caplet hanging over her shoulder.

She was like an angel.

Arwan nearly forgot he was standing in the middle of the street. A carriage barreled behind him. He stumbled to the other side of the road and onto the safety of the sidewalk where she stood…where Zanya stood.

Jayden was already there. "You are seriously hot in that dress."

Arwan tried not to curl his lip at the comment.

"Thanks. This dress is…" Zanya smoothed down the thick fabric. "Heavy."

Renato bowed, tipping his hat. Zanya curtsied in response. "Absolutely lovely."

"Why thank you, good sir. You're looking pretty great yourself." She turned to Jayden. "And you. I haven't seen you so sharp since the snowball dance in tenth grade."

"Yeah?" Jayden tugged at his collar "This thing is killing me."

"Stop that." She straightened out his tie. "You'll make it crooked."

He grinned and flicked a bobbing quail feather on her hat. "Nice hat."

Arwan stood patiently, admiring the shimmering crisscross patterned veil that cast a delicate shadow over her face. Her eyes were like two storm clouds peering from behind it.

"Ahem." Hawa spun a white sun umbrella shielding fair skin from the heat. Arwan's eyes grew wide at the sight of her cardinal red dress, embellished in lace around the bust and trim.

Jayden crossed his arm over his body and bowed. "Good morrow, Miss Jezebel."

"Jezebel?" Hawa gasped and stuck her nose in the air. "Don't be envious, Jayden, it's unbecoming." She stepped off the sidewalk. "Maybe I'll do some shopping before we go back to Moscow. I wouldn't mind having a few more of these dresses in my wardrobe."

Finally, Zanya's gaze found him. "Arwan." She pressed her gloved fingers over her lips. "You cut your hair!"

"Yeah." He slicked it back. "It's…different."

She walked toward him. "I like it. It suits you."

Arwan touched the butterfly bracelet fit over the outside of her satin glove. She smiled.

"It matches the dress, don't you think?"

"Absolutely." He kissed the back of her hand.

Jayden coughed. "I think we should get going."

"Agreed," Renato said.

Jayden snorted. "Apparently it was the first right thing I've said all day."

CHAPTER TWENTY-FIVE

Zanya

Renato took the hotel keys from the front desk. "Thank you."

The concierge smiled. "Have a pleasant stay at Queen Victoria's Auberge."

Renato turned and handed Zanya a heavy metal key with the number fifty-two engraved in it. "The elevator is over there." He gestured to the far end of the room.

The pudgy elevator attendant slid both sets of doors open. A Fu Manchu twitched above his lip. "Watch your step."

They were joined by a mother and her young son before the doors slid shut.

"Can you believe it, Mother?" the blond-haired boy squealed in a British accent, tugging on the woman's dress. His eyes beamed with excitement. "We are in an ascending room! I cannot wait to tell Matthew about this when we return home. He will be green with envy."

She took her son's hand. "I'm sorry. This is his first time in an elevator. All of his schoolmates have been quite stirred up over David's boasting about the matter." The boy rolled his eyes. His mother noticed, and tugged on his arm. "You mustn't boast about your advantages, David. There are many people far less fortunate than we."

His shoulders slumped forward. "Yes, Mother." The car jerked and rose upward. Zanya grabbed onto the railing with a tiny gasp. *Please don't stop working.*

The young boy leaned close. "Did you know, miss, that this elevator was installed in the honor of Prince Albert's passing, just after the one at the Grosvenor Hotel?"

"David!" His mother's scolding tone startled the boy. "We shouldn't talk about such things." She turned toward Renato. "Her Majesty was very much in love with the prince. It's a terrible misfortune he left the world so early. She has even refused to attend the ball." She sighed. "Her heartache is just too heavy a weight to bear."

Renato tipped his hat to her. "I'm sorry, madam. But what ball are you speaking of?"

"Surely you're being facetious."

"We're not local to London. Just visiting on holiday."

"Oh. I see. I assumed you were here for the ball, considering you are escorting the young ladies. It is in honor of the Princess Helena, and her recent engagement. The queen hasn't come out of seclusion, and has declined to attend. Word of the event has reached as far as New York."

The elevator joggled to a stop at the third floor.

The boy stole a glance at his mother, then shielded one side of his mouth and whispered, "My mother is rather disappointed that Her Majesty isn't going. It was a sore topic at supper last night. Mother was hoping to meet the queen."

Zanya nodded and mouthed, '*oh.*' He nodded in return, puffing his chest out as if proud of his extensive knowledge on the matter.

The elevator stopped, and the attendant slid open the set of double doors. "Watch your step."

The boy glanced over his shoulder while following his mother into the hall. He waved, and then turned the corner out of sight.

Zanya smiled. "Cute kid."

Hawa scoffed. "You'd think so."

"What? You don't like kids?"

"They're dirty and high maintenance."

"And you're not high maintenance?" Jayden said, grinning.

"Wouldn't you like to know."

The elevator stopped at the next floor, and the attendant slid open the doors. "Watch your step."

"Watch your step," Jayden echoed in a baritone voice. He tipped his head and saluted him on his way out.

Hawa rolled her eyes. "Idiot." She passed the attendant and smiled curiously. "Thank you."

Zanya followed the others into the hall. She examined her key and read the sign mounted to the wall. "I guess I'm down here." She gestured to the right.

"I'm this way," Arwan said as he stepped left.

"I'll watch after her from here." Renato tipped his hat.

Arwan nodded. "Then I'll get some rest."

Renato escorted Zanya to her room. "I ordered some food," he said. "I hope you're hungry."

She found her room and unlocked the heavy wooden door, then pushed it open. "Yeah. I'm starving."

"Good. It should be here very soon." He followed her inside and sat in a chair in the corner, removing his top hat. "We have quite a task ahead of us."

"Yeah." Zanya kicked off her shoes and wiggled her toes. She slipped the vial Contessa had given her out of her bust and placed it on the nightstand. The elixir swirled and churned, shimmering in the light that poured from the windows. "Do you think we can do this? I can't stop thinking about what Contessa said. About us being unprepared."

"She may be right, but that can't stop us from making every last effort to recover the stone. We have fought too long and too hard to give up now." There was a knock at the door. Renato stood and smoothed down his coat. "That must be the food." He opened the door and pulled the room service cart inside. "Thank you." He tipped the server, who glanced at her, and then back to Renato.

She cringed at what the server must have assumed.

Renato shut the door and pushed the cart toward the bed. "Take a seat, Zanya. Have some brunch. We didn't have dinner last night. I'm sorry if you've been hungry."

She yawned. "It's fine. Things were pretty hectic."

"Indeed. Well…enjoy." He inched toward the door, glancing back every few steps.

Zanya examined the various covered plates. "Do you want to keep me company?"

He turned with a smile. "Are you sure you wouldn't mind?"

"No, of course not." She sat at the table. "There's too much food here for me, anyway."

He sat across from her and tucked a cloth napkin into the collar of his shirt. "I usually have breakfast with Marzena at the house. I'm not used to dining alone."

"Yeah, I like the company too." He lifted the covers off of each plate, one at a time, releasing aroma into the air. "Oh. My. God." A smile spread over her lips. "This looks so good."

Eggs, bacon, sausage, beans, tomato, mushrooms and some kind of dark toast. It was like heaven.

They sat for what seemed like hours, dining on a proper English breakfast. Zanya was glad to have family to talk to, and listened eagerly while Renato told stories about his childhood and her mother.

"Oh, you've gotta be kidding." She giggled.

"No, no. On my word of honor, I'm not. And if that wasn't enough to scare him away indefinitely, when she swung the bat, it flew out of her grip and hit him straight in the gut."

Zanya laughed so hard her stomach ached. She dabbed the corners of her eyes with a napkin. "So what happened? I mean, how did they manage to fall in love after that kind of introduction?"

"Well, your mother fled the playing field and returned home. Later that evening, he came to return the bat."

She slapped her knees. "No he didn't!"

"He and your mother sat on the patio for hours. By the time Ellie returned inside, it was nearly midnight. I waited for her, peeking out at them every so often to make sure she was safe."

"Aw. You're such a good big brother."

"Ellie was my life. She and I were very close. It took me years to warm up to the idea of her wanting to be with your father."

"Really? Why?"

"It was just difficult to face that my little sister was all grown-up. It happened so fast, it seemed. One moment we were children, playing in the creek behind our parents' farmhouse, and the next..." His features saddened.

"Well, she was lucky to have you." She would have given anything to have had a brother while she was growing up.

He smiled softly. "Once your father came into her life, I realized she didn't need me anymore. He gave her everything she wanted. She was happiest when they were together. He always made her laugh."

Zanya traced her finger around the rim of her coffee mug. "What was he like?"

"Your father? Well, let's see." He removed the cloth napkin from the collar of his shirt and dropped it on the table. "He was inquisitive and smart. A very hard worker, holding two jobs for the first few years he and your mother were dating. He was saving up to buy a small house in the country, something he shared with me when he asked my blessing to marry Ellie."

"Really? He asked permission?"

"He did, and I said no, at first."

"Why did you do that?"

Renato sat back in his chair. "I suppose I was being selfish. I didn't want to lose her. Plus, a marriage between a Riyata and a human is rare, and tend to end badly. We live indefinitely, unaffected by time. Humans…" He sighed. "They age, become ill. It's not easy to watch the one you love slip away into death." He sat silently for a moment. "But he loved your mother. Anyone could see that. After he asked for my blessing the third time, I realized he was not going away."

"So then you said yes."

"No. I said no again." He laughed lightly. "But your father, he would not take no for an answer. He came back again and again, until finally he wore me down. I believe it was the fifth time he asked." Renato paused. "Or perhaps the sixth. He was an honorable man. There is no doubt he was your mother's soul mate, and I am honored to have called him my brother-in-law."

"So…what happened to him?"

He exhaled. "That is a question that has gone unanswered to this very day. We know he was captured by one of Sarian's henchmen, and by now, there is no doubt he is dead. How his life really ended, though, has never been made clear."

Zanya sat back in her chair. She picked apart her biscuit, discarding the crumbs into her plate. "Wow.

It's too bad. I would have liked to meet him. I'm sure if my mom loved him so much, I would have too."

"Indeed you would have. Indeed you would."

Zanya heard pounding coming from the hall. Renato jumped to his feet, flung the door open, and ushered Jayden into the room.

"I sought Sarian and found him. I think now that we're in the same time era, the block is gone."

Zanya stood up. "Where is he?"

"In some kind of mansion, if I had to guess."

Renato nodded. "Keep watching him, but I would bet my bottom dollar I know where he'll be."

***

An image formed in Zanya's mind. At first she thought it was a dream, but after only a few moments, it was clear it was something else. When she dreamed, her senses were heightened. She would taste, feel, and smell everything around her.

Instead, this time she was an audience member sitting in the back row. The sounds were muffled, indiscernible. She peered into the wavering picture until it finally stabilized.

Sarian mumbled. He held the stone, which was pulsing with dark shades of purple and blue.

He tapped his index finger over his tightly pressed lips. When his expression grew sinister, Zanya's heart sank. He picked up a thick book—a book Zanya recognized. Sarian scanned through the pages until he settled on one, and read aloud.

Every nerve in Zanya's body seized with

electricity. Her mind spun into a frantic state of panic. She forced herself to wake up, but when she did, the pain spiked and became nearly unbearable. A horrific scream broke out of her, one that echoed through her room and into the halls.

The door flung open and Renato sprinted inside. "Zanya!" His voice was muffled while electricity surged through her body. "It's her power. It's turned on her," Renato shouted at Arwan, Jayden, and Hawa as they scrambled in.

"Stay away from her; she'll kill you!"

"We have to do something."

She could hear their voices, but wasn't sure who was talking.

The agony intensified when another wave of electric shock seized her muscles. Her chest rose toward the ceiling, arching her back off the bed. She screamed.

"We can't just stand here. She'll die."

Renato knelt beside her. "Zanya, we cannot help. You will have to do this alone. Focus, concentrate on controlling the energy inside of you."

Even with Renato's encouragement, she was left helpless. All she could do was grind her teeth and pray the waves of electricity would soon subside.

"Focus. You are the Stone Guardian. Command your powers. Your mother trusted you with the responsibility of protecting the stone. You will not fail."

The memory of her mom cradling the stone and gazing at her with such hope brought her strength. She couldn't fail, and wouldn't. Not if there was even a chance she could succeed. She would fight until her last breath.

Zanya bore down and fought from deep inside, calling on all of her power to control the surges. She pushed the pain away and detached her mind.

Even as the sparks and currents filled her ears, she took an inner hold of her abilities. She had never brought it forward on impulse, but if she were to survive this, she would have to learn fast.

The light in her chest flickered on and soothed her burning lungs. It tamed the heat until another surge exploded through her, smothering her power before it could grow.

Something popped in her ears. At first she thought it was the electricity, until she tasted the blood and felt a corkscrew pain in her mouth from shattered teeth.

For the first time in her life, the pain motivated her to work harder. With a great inner drive, she commanded it to life. The orb in her chest returned and again tamed the electricity, absorbing the shock, and pushing it away from her skin. Before long, the sparks fizzled out, and the energy that churned with such vitality flickered out with it.

Zanya lay exhausted on the bed, tears streaming down the sides of her face. But she had done it. For the first time, she conquered something she thought she could never defeat.

Arwan gathered her in his arms. Every muscle in her body screamed at his touch. "Get some cool rags." He pressed his hand to her forehead. "She's burning up."

Zanya tried to lift her head, but with little energy to do much more than breathe, she just lay in

Arwan's arms. She still didn't know what exactly had happened, but she'd beat it. She finally controlled her light.

When the ice-cold rag draped over her forehead, she gasped, and her vision went black.

***

There was no way to tell how much time had passed before Zanya opened her eyes. Light poured in from the windows. She swallowed and winced under the pain.

Someone rested a hand on hers. "How are you feeling?" Renato's voice was soft and warm.

She slowly turned her head, her neck and back stiff and tender. "Not great." She blinked, and a tear slid down her cheek.

"You frightened us."

She braced her forearms on the mattress and scooted herself up the bed, groaning under the effort.

"Zanya, you should rest."

"There's no time." Her hands shook and her sides throbbed. She sucked in a breath and collapsed into her pillow. "Sarian did something to the stone." Her voice was still raspy, her throat tight and tender. Tears welled in her eyes. Her heart ached from the torment her stone translated— infinite loneliness and fear. "It's been suffering, and I haven't been there to protect it."

"You cannot blame yourself."

She could blame herself, and she did. Her mother had given her the stone to protect, and she didn't even go an entire day before she lost it, and now…"The stone managed to stay strong until Sarian read from a book. Then…" She shook her head. That's when it all fell apart. Whatever was written in that book tore through the obedience spell like it was rice paper. "He finally did it."

Arwan sat on the bed beside her. She hadn't even noticed he was in the room. "It could not be a simple spell book. It wouldn't be strong enough to break the stone's only protection. That spell was put on there by the shaman of the first Riyata tribe. His magic was the most powerful in history. What if it's from someone else. A Riyata gone rogue, maybe?"

"Riyata do not usually dabble in black magic. It's against our nature. If one of us has turned dark, it is by the doing of another, more powerful force that is most likely the source of the book."

Oh God, the book. She forgot to tell him about her dream. "I've seen the book before. I dreamed about it. I just didn't think anything of it at the time. I've always had nightmares. It's something I've gotten used to."

"Perhaps this book is responsible. We'll have to do more research when we have more at our disposal."

There was a knock on the door. Arwan crossed the room and opened it to let Hawa and Jayden inside. Jayden walked directly past Arwan without any acknowledgement and stood at Zanya's side. "Hey, beautiful." He rested his hand over her forehead. "No fever."

She tried to smile, but had almost no energy to pull it off in an even half-assed kind of way. "What, now you're pretending to be Peter?"

"No. I sensed you were awake, though, and wanted to come check on you."

"Sensed." She nodded ever so slightly. "As in you were seeking me."

He shrugged. "Same difference." He leaned against the wall with his arms crossed. "I couldn't help but overhear what you guys were talking about, and I think we should just find Sarian and take the stone as fast as we can. This is dangerous enough without Zanya turning into a human light bulb. The next attack could kill her. Especially now that Sarian broke through."

Arwan paused. "The question is, if he can control the stone, why is Zanya still alive?" He glanced around. "Why are any of us still alive?"

"Yeah." Hawa leaned against the wall. "The sky isn't falling. I mean, this might sound weird, but...that worries me."

"Indeed. We will press forward as soon as Zanya is recuperated."

She sat up in her bed. It was like someone had beaten the hell out of her with a bat. "If I can heal as fast as Peter, I should be fine by the end of the day." She ran her tongue over her shattered tooth, which had already seemed to heal.

Renato walked toward the door. "You've been sleeping for thirty-six hours. Let's hope your body has done much of its recuperation already." He left the room.

Arwan placed a kiss on Zanya's forehead. "I have to go talk to Renato."

Jayden lingered in her room after Arwan left. "I

should let you know I've been seeking you from my room, per Renato's instructions. He asked me to keep an eye on you in case anything else happened. Just give me a heads-up before you change or shower."

It had never occurred to her that Jayden could have looked at her during any time of the day, including when she wasn't dressed. Her eyes widened like a deer in headlights.

He laughed. "I may be a lot of things, Zanya, but I'm not a perv."

CHAPTER TWENTY-SIX

In honor of the engagement of Princess of Helena Augusta Victoria, Her Majesty the Queen Alexandrina Victoria requests your presence at the celebration ball. Mesdames and Messieurs holding invitations are invited to join. This event will be held at the Grosvenor Hotel, on the day of Our Lord, the 12th of December, year 1865.

Zanya lowered the invitation with gold script writing. "And you want us to go to this?"

"Sarian will certainly be there. This may be our only opportunity to retrieve the stone."

"Where did you get the invitation?" Jayden leaned closer to see it.

"I purchased it from a swindler on the street."

"How are you feeling?" Arwan asked. "Do you think you can go?"

"Do I think I can go to a royal ball?" She held up the invitation. "You know what this means, don't you?"

Jayden hung his head. "More shopping."

Renato took the invitation. "Not all of us will need ball attire. Arwan and Hawa will stay behind while I accompany Jayden and Zanya to the event. And before you begin—" he held up his hand to Arwan, "—I will tell you why. Sarian is less likely to recognize one of us if there are less of us there. Jayden is able to seek Sarian without succumbing to a violent episode. He is also less likely to stand out among the fair-skinned locals."

Jayden's pompous grin clearly agitated Arwan. "Sorry, man. You're just too culturally enriched."

Zanya raised her finger at Jayden. "First, shut up." She lowered her hand and turned her attention to Renato. "Second, if Sarian attacks us, all of us need to be there to fight."

"That's exactly what I was thinking," Arwan said.

"But we are less likely to be spotted and attacked if we travel inconspicuously. We do not want to increase the chances of being recognized. There will be a clash, and blood will surely be shed."

That made sense. The less danger, the better for everyone. "Fine. We'll do it your way."

Arwan looked at Renato. "I need to be there to protect her."

"I'll be there," Jayden interjected. "We don't need you."

"You're not capable of fending off Sarian if she's attacked."

"Incapable? Why don't we see who's incapable, Arnie?" He shrugged off his coat and threw it on the floor.

"Would you knock it off?" The agitation in Zanya's tone set the room quiet.

"Sorry, Zanya." Jay snatched his coat from the floor. "He started it."

Arwan jabbed his finger in the air. "He's like a child! He doesn't think before he acts—or speaks. He'll do something to jeopardize Zanya's safety."

Jayden shoved his arms in his jacket sleeves. "I would never jeopardize her safety."

"The decision has been made," Renato said sternly. Arwan stared at him for a moment before silently exiting the room.

Zanya glared at Jayden. "You don't have to get under his skin like that. You two have to learn to get along."

"I suggest you get ready," Renato said. "We have a ball gown to buy."

***

While Hawa spent the next week pouting over not attending the ball, Zanya and Jayden were tutored in the proper etiquette of the nineteenth century socialization. Arwan dutifully supervised, while Renato forced hours of prepping and pruning.

There was a way to speak, to stand, and several dance routines to be learned. Apparently there was also a specific way to greet ladies, men, elders, and royalty. Each had their own introduction procedure they were expected to follow, while still adhering to the conventional mannerisms of every proper socialite.

"Not like that," Renato instructed. "You must bow deeper."

Zanya leaned against the wall. Wherever he got her heels from, they were pinching her toes. "But last time you told me to just kind of dip."

"That was for greeting a socialite. We are currently practicing the introduction to royalty. You must bow deeply, nearly touching your bottom to the floor, while keeping your back straight. Spread your gown around you, and your arms should be bent, only slightly."

Dipping, back straight, feet throbbing and dress almost too heavy to bear, Zanya lost her balance and toppled over.

Jayden laughed, then stifled his chuckle when she glared at him. "Sorry."

Zanya picked herself up and brushed off her gown. "Why does Jay get it so easy? He's had the same introduction this whole time. And these shoes are killing my feet." Typical. Men got a break while women had to be perfect.

"Perhaps, but we must continue. You cannot be presented without knowing social etiquette. Speaking of presentation, what name would you like to be announced under?"

"What do you mean?"

"Everyone is introduced when they arrive. We must settle on the name you wish to go by."

"I was dropped off at the orphanage without any identification except name embroidered in my blanket from what my records said." She shrugged.

"I don't have a last name."

"You most certainly do." He pushed out his chest, standing tall. "You are my niece, and the descendant of the first Stone Guardian of Muuk'Ich. You are a Coreandero."

It was so odd. She'd never had family. Never even had a last name. "I've always just been patient A692."

Renato took her by her shoulders and stared into her eyes. "I promise you, Zanya. You will never be without family again. I will care for you, just as I have cared for Hawa. I will never leave you."

She smiled softly. "Thank you, Renato."

They stood silent for several moments. Renato cleared his throat, blinking away unshed tears. "Let's continue with our lesson, shall we?"

***

Hawa grudgingly assisted Zanya with lacing up the back of her gown. She slipped on her flat dress shoes, a pair she'd picked out herself to replace the heels.

Using all the practice she'd gotten with Renato, Zanya glided gracefully into the hall. Arwan waited for her by the door. He took her hand and spun her in a circle, flaring her dress like a bell.

"I wish I were accompanying you."

"Well, don't feel too bad. If I can avoid dancing, I will."

"Still, it would be an experience." He searched her face. "Promise me you'll be careful."

She wanted to make it out of this alive as much

as he did. "Yeah, of course."

He seemed satisfied with her answer. "Where's your escort?"

"Jay should almost be ready."

He frowned. "I was talking about Renato."

"Oh, right. He should be out here any minute."

Hawa came up behind her. She separated Zanya's curls and draped them over her shoulder. "Don't go messing up my masterpiece. I didn't spend two hours doing your hair with those ridiculous metal curlers for you to leave it hanging down your back like a wet mop." She slipped a shimmering hairpin into the small bunch of curls and leaned into her. "Hair accessories can be deadly." She stepped away and arched one side of her lip into a half-smile. "I'll go let Renato know you're ready."

"Can I at least escort you to the lobby?" Arwan extended his arm.

Zanya smiled and slipped her arm around his. They walked together down to the main lobby and through the front doors. People stopped in the streets, smiling and whispering to each other while they passed. Zanya held up her gown from dragging on the dusty street. The crystal jewels sparkled against the layered chiffon.

The landau carriage arrived right on time, pulled by two glorious Clydesdale horses. Their silken coats and black manes shined under the sun.

Renato was equally fashionable, in a chocolate brown swallowtail coat with matching dress slacks and shiny leather shoes. He promptly removed his top hat upon sitting in the horse-drawn carriage.

"Where to, sir?" the coachman said from his tiny

seat perched in the front of the carriage.

"The Grosvenor Hotel, please."

The coachman tapped the lead horse on its flank.

The ride was long, but Zanya didn't mind. The open carriage gave her the chance to enjoy the hillside towns. It was beautiful without skyscrapers and concrete in every direction. Jayden would— hey, wait. "Where's Jayden?"

"He will meet us there. It would be improper for him to accompany us."

That's right. He'd told her that when they were talking about social etiquette. People were strict in this era. "Tell me more about what I should expect. I'm a little nervous."

"Every person has their place, and various levels of wealth stay within their own class. This ball allows members of the aristocratic community from far and wide to come together and socialize. They make introductions, form new connections, and sometimes, scout out eligible young ladies for their unwed sons."

Zanya imagined every man in the room, probing with his eyes, searching and scrutinizing each woman for her appeal, or lack thereof. "At the ball, are you planning on introducing me to anyone?"

"I plan to introduce you to Jayden. This will be our tactic to scout for Sarian without drawing attention."

"Oh, good."

"But if a young man inquires about you, it would be rude to turn him away."

It took nearly an hour to arrive at the hotel, which was bustling with activity. Doormen assisted the guests out of their carriages. The horses snorted and threw their heads, their bits and bridles tugged on by the coachmen. Ladies chatted and fluffed each other's dresses, cooing over the latest fashions. Gentlemen lit their cigars while they stood in groups, viewing the ladies as they arrived.

Renato escorted Zanya through the Grosvenor's doors. The lobby glistened with polished floors and high ceilings, embellished with white columns with gold trim. Everyone stood in line, speaking just above a whisper.

The line moved forward. Each party handed their invitation to the doorman. He took it and nodded before the next couple offered theirs. Only those holding a golden inscribed card were granted access beyond the mahogany booth.

The golden ticket.

Zanya nudged her uncle and pointed to a flag that hung in the lobby. It displayed a family crest, matching what Marzena had taken from Tara's memory.

Renato handed the doorman their pass. The herald stood in waiting when they entered the ballroom. Renato spoke softly, and the herald cleared his throat before turning to the growing crowd.

"Ladies and gentlemen. It is with great pleasure that I introduce Sir Felipe, Duke of Toledo, and his lovely niece, Miss Camilla."

Renato smiled, and in just a few more steps, they meshed with the crowd. "Here we go."

CHAPTER TWENTY-SEVEN

Arwan

As Arwan paced the room, Hawa sat, watching him walk back and forth, his fists clenched. Renato expected him to just stand by, as if he didn't know what was at stake. Years of searching and focus had led up to this point, and he wasn't even there to face Sarian and put an end to this once and for all.

Hawa sighed. "Why don't you sit—?"

"I can't believe Renato wants us to stay here."

She sat back in her chair and inspected her nails. "Well, Uncle knows best and all that, right?"

Not this time. He had known Renato almost his entire life. Trust was something his mentor earned when Arwan was a young boy. Still, deep in his bones, this wasn't right. "Renato always tries to be cautious, but this isn't smart. We should be there. I should be there."

"Well, don't even think about taking off without me. If you're going, so am I."

He stopped pacing. Zanya needed him, and

Sarian was so close. "Do you know where we can get some weapons?"

Hawa sat up straight. "Are you serious?"

"If anything happens to her, it'll be my fault."

She held up her hand. "All right, Prince Valiant. Don't go riding in on your white horse without a plan. You'll get everyone killed."

She was right. But he couldn't just stand there and wait for them to return. He ran his fingers through his hair, then opened the door. "I do have a plan."

Hawa jumped up to her feet. "Let's hear it."

"My plan is to forget Renato's plan, and go anyway." Maybe it wasn't very solid, but if he knew Hawa, that wouldn't be a problem.

She grinned. "I'm down."

"First we get weapons." He slipped on his coat. "I have a score to settle."

Hawa and Arwan slipped out of the hotel and through the streets. She signaled to an armory, and they walked through the old wooden door. The hinges creaked when it swung shut.

"Good morrow." The short, pudgy man behind the counter was busy polishing the handle to a dark metal gun.

Hawa set her predatorial sights on the shopkeeper. "Let me handle this." With a lick of her lips, she strutted to the counter. "Good morrow. My brother and I are in need of some weapons."

"Ya came to the right place." He winked at her. "What'r ya lookin' for?"

"Well, I'm not entirely sure. Maybe you can give us a little tour of what you have available?"

"You know, it's not entirely common to sell a gun to a woman."

Hawa bent over the counter. "It's good I'm not an entirely common woman."

Arwan watched her seduce the poor man right into compliance.

"A'course, dear." He set down the gun and removed another from the display behind him. "This here would do ya just fine. It's brand-new in stock. Perfect for a lady's hands." He leaned in close to her. "And perfect for fitting in your garter, so I've heard."

Arwan whispered, "I don't know how to shoot a gun."

"Well…" She paused, waiting for his attention to leave her cleavage. She snapped her fingers. "Up here, darling." His eyes shifted up to her face. "Good boy. Now, I was thinking, maybe you have something a bit more…close contact?"

"What kinda close contact do ya think ya need, darling?" He peered at Arwan. "You sure he's your brother? Ya know, I don't look down on a workin' gal. Everyone's gotta eat."

She stood up straight and perched her hands on her hips. "I am not a hooker."

His brows knitted together. "A what, miss?"

She scoffed and turned toward Arwan. He had better rescue the poor shopkeeper before he ended up on the floor of his own store.

Arwan straightened his coat. "Do you carry any knives or swords?"

The man pointed across the store. "I have a few old blades 'n' such hangin' over there. But a gun'll do ya better, I think."

Arwan followed Hawa to the corner. Her eyes glimmered with excitement. "Jackpot."

***

Zanya

Zanya stood beside a small group of women. One of them stepped aside, a subtle invitation to join them—only after she'd scrutinized Zanya's appearance, and apparently came to the conclusion she was suitable company. The ladies clucked and giggled, whispering about the particulars of the princess's engagement.

"I heard the queen ordered the two to marry, due to the princess having affections for the former royal secretary."

"Mr. Ruland?"

"Yes, didn't you know?"

Zanya had the urge to yawn, but she pushed it down and searched for Renato. He stood on the stairs, scanning the room.

The herald's voice rose through the room once again. "*Mesdames* and *messieurs*. Please welcome Mr. James Bond."

Zanya turned to see Jayden descending the stairs, wearing a navy suit with a silver vest, his hair combed back with oil. If Zanya didn't know better, she would be fooled into thinking he was a real gentleman.

He strutted toward her and grabbed a flute of champagne from a waiter's tray, then swallowed half of the contents with one gulp. Zanya giggled. He stopped in front of her.

"May I be so bold as to say that you are the loveliest creature I have ever laid eyes on?"

The group of ladies swooned.

"Mr.…Bond, was it?"

He grinned and finished the second half of his champagne in another gulp.

Renato shook his head, obviously displeased with the attention Jayden was attracting from the women.

An older man with graying sideburns approached Renato. Jayden took Zanya's hand and pulled her onto the dance floor. She glanced back at Renato and the man talking. "Who was that guy?"

"Probably just a pretty boy asking to dance with my date."

A jolt of energy ran through Zanya's body. Her palms clammy, she fought the dizziness that washed over her. "The stone's here. I can feel it."

"Sarian must have just arrived." They continued to dance, searching in every direction. "He's here on the dance floor. If I can get you close enough, maybe you can grab the stone."

"Where?"

"Two o'clock."

Zanya spotted Sarian twirling with a young brunette in a plum-colored gown.

Renato circled the room. They passed Sarian several more times, but he flew by too quickly for her to sense anything. "I can't find the stone like this." But if she got closer to him, she may be able to get it—with the help of the masking spell. "I have an idea." She closed her eyes and communicated to Renato.

Renato's eyes narrowed, the creases of his mouth turning downward. He clearly didn't like her plan, but they had no other choice. Renato couldn't approach Sarian on his own. He would be recognized immediately. If she made enough eye contact, he'd get the hint.

Zanya stole a glance at Sarian every chance she had in the hopes of snagging his attention. Jayden swayed her side to side and spun her in a slow circle. All the while Zanya's eyes were focused on Sarian like a ballerina doing fouettées.

It seemed her efforts had finally caught his attention. Zanya leaned in closer to Jayden. "Is he looking over here?"

"He put his drink down. There's only one reason a guy does that." Jayden gripped her hand tighter. "Shit. He's coming over."

"Let him."

A moment later, Sarian reached them on the dance floor and addressed Jayden. "May I cut in?" He extended his hand to Zanya.

She curtsied to Jayden and took Sarian's hand. Her heart stomped in her chest. She hoped Contessa didn't give her a bum spell for the sake of being spiteful.

Sarian smiled and led Zanya in the dance. "I do not believe I have had the pleasure of making your acquaintance this fine evening."

She swallowed, his gaze lying pleasantly over her face. It was apparent didn't recognize her. Not yet at least. "We've had the pleasure now."

Sarian's pulled her closer. "It seems we have."

She drew in a deep breath, the corset constricting her rib cage. "It's a bit warm in here, isn't it?"

He paused and gestured to an upholstered couch against the far wall. "Perhaps you should rest."

Sarian blended in so well with the others. His polished appearance and exquisite mannerisms shielded anyone from seeing the darkness that fashioned his soul. He was like a shark lurking below its prey, hidden under the reflection of the water's surface.

Zanya heard the stone's whispers in her ears. It still recognized her, but it sounded different…confused.

"Perhaps I just need to get some air."

"Then the veranda, perhaps?"

She nodded and extended her hand, inviting him to offer his arm. "If you'll escort me."

CHAPTER TWENTY-EIGHT

There were no glaives in the weapons shop. Arwan would have done best with a tool he was familiar with. He scanned the options until the glint of a double-edged axe caught his eye. He lifted the labrys off its stand and held it in his hand, testing the weight.

"Nice." Hawa examined his choice, and then made her own. A mace. It was shaped like a king's scepter, but with spikes reaching from the steel ball at the end. She would do some serious damage with that.

Arwan walked to the counter and placed two gold coins in front of the shopkeeper—more than what all of the weapons in his shop were worth. "Thanks." He waited for Hawa while the shopkeeper bit on the coin, and then stared up at him with a widening smile.

They walked back outside. The cool night air soothed the heat pulsing through his body.

"Where to, chief?" Arwan eyed Hawa in a pair of leather pants and a tight sleeveless shirt. "You couldn't have worn something a bit more inconspicuous?"

"Like what? That frou-frou gown? It was nice to wear for about an hour, but I can't fight in that thing, and I don't have anything else."

They'd have to walk fast, sticking close to the buildings and traveling in alley ways as much as possible as not to be seen.

The night was getting colder, which meant it was getting later. If they wasted too much time walking there, he may miss his chance to face Sarian. "Go ahead. You can get there a lot faster than I can if you sprint."

"I won't be able to go inside, or even close to the entrance. They'll have guards at every corner with the princess there."

"So breeze past them. They won't be able to stop you if you're quick enough."

"Do you have any idea how much it hurts to slam into someone when I'm sprinting? And balls are crowded and people are dancing. It'd be like Russian roulette."

"Fine. Then go and try to get eyes on Zanya. If you see Renato or Jayden, get their attention if you can without anyone else seeing you. The hotel isn't far. About two miles that way." He pointed north.

"Are you sure? We don't have time to screw up."

"I checked the back of the invitation before Renato took it. Trust me. Grosvenor Hotel is that way. You can't miss it."

"Got it."

Hawa was gone in the flash of an eye. If Arwan pushed hard, he could be there in ten minutes. He ran as fast as he could over uneven cobblestone streets and past the tall arches over doorways. Dodging around people as he passed, he stumbled over a risen stone in the street and caught himself, then pushed harder to regain his speed.

His heart pounded as he grew closer. Not because he ran, but because he was moments away from finally standing face to face with the man who led his mother to her death. He may not have killed her directly, but blood was on Sarian's hands.

By the end of the night there would be blood on his hands, too.

More carriages cluttered the streets as he grew closer to the Grosvenor Hotel.

As he reached the top of a hill, the hotel came into sight. The gates were open as ball guests rode through them. If he could slip through without the guards noticing, he would be one step closer.

When he drew closer to the gates, he spotted two guards on either side, asking carriage drivers for their invitations before they were allowed to pass.

Jumping the wall was impossible without a grappling hook. Going around wasn't an option, considering the wall surrounded the hotel and the courtyard. If he tried to simply walk through, he'd be stopped for sure. With a weapon, he would be arrested on the spot. A Victorian prison was not a place he wanted to end up, and there was no telling how it would effect the ripples of events if he bent time in this era—even for a moment.

He straightened his suit and ran his fingers through his hair, slicking it back. He wiped sweat from his forehead, searching for a solution. He eyed each carriage driver, all of them dressed in a suit and top hat, perched on an elevated chair behind the main carriage.

Arwan tucked the handle of his ax under his coat and slowly fell to the back of the line. Once he'd reached the last carriage, he sneaked to the rear. He would have to do it quietly or the passengers would be alarmed, and his cover would be blown.

The carriage rolled to a stop and the horses huffed, swatting their tails in the air. Voices of the passengers were muted from inside the covered wagon. Arwan hung his ax on the railing of the coachman's chair. He positioned himself behind the driver and leaped up, wrapped his arm around the driver's throat, and dragged him to the dusty ground.

The driver struggled and kicked while Arwan choked him from the back—just enough to make him go unconscious. Once the man stopped struggling, Arwan snatched the invitation from inside the man's inner coat pocket, and then picked the driver's top hat off the ground and propped it on his head. He quickly rolled the man to the side of the road where he wouldn't be seen. At least not until he woke up.

"Move up, coachman," a voice called from inside the carriage.

Arwan spun to see the line moving. He quickly climbed the back of the carriage and took the reins. "Step." He flicked his wrist and the horses trotted forward. The passengers didn't seem to notice anything strange. Arwan exhaled, his stomach tight as they approached the gates. Just before he reached the guard, he remembered the ax hanging on the back of his chair. He rested it on his chair and sat on top of it just in time.

"Invitation." The guard held out his hand, his bushy eyebrows nearly hiding his eyes. Arwan removed it from his inner coat pocket and handed it to the guard, who took the thick paper and examined it for a moment, then handed it back. "Move on."

He flicked the reins and trotted forward, scanning the crowd for the others. They were probably already inside.

"Psst."

Arwan glanced around, searching for the sound.

"Hey!"

He turned to see Hawa crouched, walking along side his carriage. "What are you doing here? Someone's going to see you."

She shrugged. "We have to go. I spotted Zanya and Sarian on the back veranda."

***

Zanya

The outdoor entertainment area was desolate, everyone preferring the warmth and comfort of the ballroom in the frigid temperatures. Sarian positioned himself behind Zanya and placed his hands on her bare shoulders. The breeze pushed his bitter stench around her. "Such a beautiful young lady with pure intentions does not attend a ball, and watch a man from across the room while dancing with another. What exactly are your intentions with me, Camilla?"

Sarian didn't waste any time, and she would use his impatience to her advantage.

Zanya hugged her body in an attempt to keep warm. "We all fight with our carnal nature, as it battles with our bodies to overpower our minds." God, that was lame. She just hoped Sarian bought that load of crap.

He ran his fingers down her arm. She needed to get closer to him. That might require a little incentive. With a deep breath, she braced herself to get what she was about to ask for. "I'm rather cold. It would be ill-mannered of you to allow me to catch a chill."

He wrapped his arms around her and kissed her shoulder. Zanya cringed in disgust while his dry, hard lips nipped at her skin. She turned and slid her hands around his torso, searching for her stone.

The light in her chest glowed in response. She quickly snuffed it out.

Kissing her neck with more enthusiasm, he ran his teeth along her skin. She pressed her lips together in an attempt to not shout in revulsion. A second later, she gripped the stone tightly.

Sarian cradled his cheek against hers and brushed a curl over her shoulder. "I hadn't a doubt in my mind you would come to your senses, my queen."

Zanya gasped, and he clenched her wrist, staring at her with narrowed eyes. "Your light betrayed you, guardian."

So close, she wouldn't be scared away.

Not this time.

Not ever.

She tightened her fist and jerked her arm back. "Give me back my stone."

He snarled. "You forget, it has two masters now."

Renato and Jayden charged out from the ballroom. In Sarian's brief moment of distraction, Zanya slipped out the hairpin Hawa had given her and severed the pouch from its strap. She leaped back, cradling the stone against her chest.

Sarian's eyes grew dark. "That will be the last time you defy me, guardian. By the end of the night, you will be mine."

"You'll have to get through me first." A double-headed hand axe gleamed in Arwan's hand.

Hawa stepped out from the shadows. "Really?" She glanced at Arwan. "You couldn't come up with anything better than that?"

"What are you doing here?" Renato said, sounding more horrified than relieved.

Hawa pointed at Arwan with the spiked club in her hand. "Prince Charming here said he had a dragon to slay."

Arwan stepped forward. "I see you've gotten rid of your limp, old man."

Sarian squared his stance. "I find it easier to dance in this era, before I needed my cane."

"You don't have anywhere to hide this time."

The overwhelming, bitter scent hit Zanya in the face. She covered her nose with a fold of her gown.

Hawa stepped beside Zanya. "Get out of here."

"I'm not leaving you guys."

"You have the stone. Get out of here, and we'll meet up with you later."

"I can't leave." She looked at Arwan. "Not without him."

Sarian unbuttoned his coat and let it drop to the ground. "Why do we need to fight? After all, great minds think alike. Isn't that what they say? You cannot continue to deny who you are."

He stepped closer, his eyes focused intently on his target. "I am not like you."

"You are exactly like me."

With a warrior's cry, Arwan charged toward him, his axe positioned to kill. He swung at Sarian, who dodged the blade and grabbed both ends of the weapon, pulling it against Arwan's throat from behind.

"You have caused me more trouble than you are worth," Sarian grunted, struggling to choke Arwan with his own weapon.

Zanya gasped and positioned her stone. She would have to use its power to protect him—protect them all. But it was cold, distant. "Don't abandon me," she whispered. "Please. I need your help."

It didn't respond.

Footsteps strode quick and light. Before Sarian could turn, the spikes of Hawa's mace planted deep into his back. He spun and backhanded her across the face, throwing her across the veranda. She crashed into the marble pillar and her limbs went limp, knocked unconscious.

Arwan scooped up his weapon from the ground. "Why don't you stop picking on women, you coward, and face me like a man."

Sarian slowly rotated toward Arwan. "A man? But we are not men. We are something more than man could ever be." He reached over his shoulder and dislodged Hawa's weapon from his skin, tossing it to the ground.

The stench of Sarian's blood shot up his nose. "We choose who we are." Arwan traded the axe to his other hand.

"Your father won't be very happy to hear I have killed his only son."

Zanya paused. *His father?*

Arwan stepped forward, his eyes gleaming.

Sarian readied his stance. "Then you insist on fighting me?"

Arwan grinned. "I thought you'd never ask."

Sarian's muscles trembled as if he were having a seizure. Zanya watched in horror as a transformation took place.

His joints popped out of his sockets, contorting his figure. Sarian's thrashing and shouts caught the attention of the crowd inside. People gathered in the doorway. Several women screamed and fainted.

Zanya stumbled back, clenching her stone. She heard Sarian's bones crack and splinter. His clothes tore under the pressure of bulging muscles. His face deformed and pours took on a metallic shine, covering his body until he changed into something…inhuman. When it was done, a beast stood in the center of the marble patio, panting clouds of hot breath into the air.

Sarian produced a growl that fermented in his chest. With his lips curled back in a snarl, he bellowed an unearthly roar.

The partygoers screamed and shouted. "Save the princess!" a guard yelled from inside.

Zanya's heart dropped. She stood frozen, gawking at Sarian's animal-like body, his front feet armed with deadly claws. His back legs were short, with mounds of muscle packed under his wrinkled, graphite-colored skin.

"Come and fight." Sarian's voice projected at them, not from his mighty jaws, but from somewhere else. *His mind*, Zanya thought. *The mind of a demigod.*

Arwan charged again, his speed unlike anything Zanya had ever seen. He moved fast, nimble, and sometimes, she thought, inhuman.

Sarian snapped his jaws at Arwan, who rolled and planted the axe deep into the beast's thigh. It growled and swung its tail, ramming Arwan across the patio. He slammed into the side of the building, cracking the stone on impact.

Zanya took the vial from the bust of her gown and turned to Jayden. "Get everyone together."

"Yeah, I'm ready to get the hell out of here." He sprinted away.

Zanya ran to Renato's side. He watched with sadness in his eyes as Arwan and Sarian fought like two bloodthirsty animals. She grabbed his arm. "Hey, we have to go!" Renato only stood, staring. "What are you doing?"

Renato's frown deepened. "I knew this day would come. I've known since Arwan came to our side."

"What are you talking about?" Shards of sharp stone rained over them when Arwan was slammed into the building again. She screamed and covered her head. "Sarian will kill him!" She tugged on Renato in a desperate attempt to shake him out of his daze. Whatever had gotten into him, they didn't have time to waste. Contessa was right. Sarian was more powerful than they realized, and if they didn't get out of there soon, none of them would make it out alive.

Grunts and animal-like sounds mixed together while the two battled in the center of the marble arena. Arwan shouted when Sarian grabbed hold of his shoulder with his jaws. Zanya gasped, then whimpered, staring at Renato for the guidance he was always there to provide. "Help him."

Renato shook his head. "He does not need help." His eyes finally met hers, and the depth of sorrow that filled them nearly took her breath away. "Arwan is not who you think he is, Zanya."

Sarian's claws now pinned Arwan to the ground. She didn't care who he was. Arwan wouldn't die. Not here, not now. "Fine." She slipped the stone out of its pouch. "If you won't do something, I will." With the stone held in front of her, she closed her eyes and connected the invisible bond between her and her legacy. "I am Zanya Coreandero, descendant of the first Stone Guardian." The light in her chest burst to life, as did the light of the stone. When the two powers connected, a great burst of energy shot through the air and struck Sarian in the ribs. He howled and tumbled over the stone patio.

Arwan pushed himself to his feet, blood dripping down his arms.

Sarian regained his footing with a large burn

stretched over his skin. He shook off the impact like a wet dog and limped forward, focused on Zanya. As if his violet irises were his bond with the stone, it too glowed a deep purple.

Sharp pain tore up her arms. Zanya screamed and dropped the stone. She outstretched her trembling hands, raw and red with burns.

Her stone didn't recognize her. Worse, it had rejected her.

Arwan picked up his axe and hurled it at the beast. The blade sparked when it hit his armored skin.

Sarian crouched and leaped at Zanya. She dropped to the ground and covered her head. The impact of the beast's landing rocked the building. She looked up at Sarian's underbelly while he stood over her, like an animal claiming its territory.

Renato stepped forward. With a clenched fist and fury in his eyes, he struck Sarian with all his might, hurling the beast across the floor. Sarian scratched at the ground, reaching for anything he could before crashing into the stone handrail, snatching Hawa's limp body. Renato screamed as Sarian dragged her into the forest, out of sight. "Hawa!"

"We can't fight him for long," Jayden said. "He's too strong."

Renato scrambled past the rubble of marble. "I'll go get Hawa. You work on a way to get us out of here."

"I can't leave without the stone." Zanya crouched beside it. It was angry, fearful, and it didn't trust her. He must have influenced it, or it would not have lashed out like it did. Her hands were already healed, but if she tried to touch it again without its permission, it might kill her. It may take time to convince it that she wasn't the enemy, but time was something they didn't have at the moment. "Shh." She extended her hand. "I'm your guardian. You can come with me." She paused, listening to its whispers. "I know you're scared, and confused, but it's okay. I am too. But I'm here to protect you now." A tear slipped down her cheek. She hummed the same tune as when she bonded with the stone. The melody swam through her, and she closed her eyes, picturing the day she sat in her mother's bedroom with the stone. The song was even more beautiful on her violin, and she could almost hear the strings vibrate beneath her fingers as she hummed through the tune.

She opened her eyes to the stone morphing with colors of blue and white. "See. You remember me." She caressed the stone's surface. "It's okay now." She cupped it in her hands, and it reacted with a warm glow. "We're going home."

Sarian barged back onto the patio. Renato followed close behind, cradling Hawa in his arms. "Her leg is broken."

Zanya jumped to her feet. "Everyone's here. Let's go!"

Jayden, who had only a patio umbrella as a weapon, tried to hold Sarian at bay. He glanced back at Zanya, and for a split second, they locked eyes.

Sarian grabbed Jayden's torso and thrashed his head from side to side. Zanya watched in disbelief as Jayden's body was flung to the stone floor where he slid, leaving a trail of blood in his wake.

Zanya ran and collapsed beside him. He lay with his gut torn open and deep puncture wounds in his chest. He opened his eyes, sucking in shallow, labored breaths. She grabbed his hand and wrapped her fingers in his.

"You're going to be okay." She sobbed. "I'll heal you. I can do it now. I can heal you." That's when the realization hit her like ice water. What would her life be like without Jayden? He filled a gap in her heart like no one else could. Losing him would mean losing a piece of herself.

A strange silence filled the air. Jayden stared up at her blankly.

Something was wrong.

He was so still.

The gaping holes in his chest no longer leaked blood. "Jayden." Her demanding tone somehow ached with desperation. "Jayden!"

It was as if the universe had collapsed on top of her. The air became heavy, pressing on her skin and chest. Her stomach twisted, acid and bile coating her tongue.

Renato and Arwan were busy distracting Sarian, but they were out of time. "We have to go. Now!"

Even in Sarian's beastly form, his eyes churned with magic, and hunger.

Zanya jumped to her feet. Renato grabbed Sarian's back leg with one hand and screamed like an enraged madman. "I may not be the guardian, but I will tear you limb from limb before you touch my family ever again." Like an Olympic discus thrower, he swung Sarian's body and launched him into the air. The beast's heavy frame crashed into the alabaster railings, and then tumbled down a steep cliff, out of sight.

"Let's go!" She threw the vial to the floor. It shattered, and the fog rose around them.

Sarian let out an animalistic scream from the valley below. The snapping of branches and scratching footsteps grew closer.

Zanya closed her eyes, envisioning a place and time. There was only one place she wanted to go— to the only one who could help. Without the smallest hint of transition, they stood in the center of Contessa's kitchen.

"Contessa!" Her screams filled the small room. "Contessa!"

She appeared, clearly angry to see the group in her home. "Why have you come here?"

"Jayden; I think he's dead. You have to help him." She dropped to her knees and cradled his head in her lap while the temptress inspected him.

Zanya dragged her fingers through Jayden's tangled hair. Contessa would know exactly what to do. She had survived being stabbed in the heart.

With every moment of silence, her anxiety grew. What the hell was taking her so long? Why wasn't she doing anything?

Contessa reached out and closed his eyes. "His soul no longer dwells in his body. I don't smell it. I don't see it. It's gone."

"What?" Zanya's breath stalled. There was no way he could be gone. She wouldn't accept it. After lowering Jayden's head to the floor, she jumped to her feet. She didn't care if this bitch could snuff her out with a flick of her wrist; there was no way they were giving up that easily. "No. You have to help him. You have to bring him back."

Contessa shrugged. "There is nothing I can do. It is too late."

Zanya balled her fists. "There has to be something, anything. I'll do anything."

"The only one who can help you now is Houn, bearer of souls."

Renato stepped closer. "Zanya. We cannot bargain with the gods of the underworld. They are a dark kind, who reign with ruthlessness and greed for souls."

"I have to get him back." *Whatever the cost.*

"Many have fallen in the cause of protecting the stone. Jayden is one of many. I understand you are mourning the loss of a fallen friend, but this is not an option."

"This is the only option." She squared her shoulders toward her uncle. Jayden had earned his respect, and he wasn't showing even a hint of gratitude. "How can you turn your back on him after he came to help us? He deserves the same efforts I know he would make for me in a heartbeat."

"Jayden fought bravely to defend your life, and the security of the stone. Let him die with honor."

So that was how it would be. Fine. She didn't need his help. Not with this. Zanya ignored Renato and twirled to Contessa. "How do I get to Houn?"

"The soul bearer lingers at the gateway of the underworld. You must first travel through the caves of Naj Tunich. One of its tunnels leads to a lake where you can pass to the gate of the dark realm. When you reach the cave, you must gain access before you descend.

"How long do I have?"

"Houn will hold his soul for three days before deciding his fate."

"I will not allow this," Renato shouted. "You have no heir to pass your legacy to. If you die, the stone will not only obey Sarian, but whatever hands possess it. Do you have any idea how many lives you are endangering if you pursue this insane plan?"

"I won't let Jayden die."

"It is already done."

Zanya stared down at his lifeless body, his skin a sick gray.

Renato recollected himself. "This is counterproductive to our mission."

"I have the stone. My only mission now is to get Jayden back."

"Just because you have the stone does not mean your job is done. You need to continue to protect it. If you die now, Jayden's death will have been in vain."

Zanya swallowed. This was such bullshit. "If you won't help me, I'll go alone."

"You won't go alone." Arwan's voice clawed its way out of his throat. "I'll go with you." He limped beside her.

"Very well," Contessa said.

Zanya gave her uncle one last chance. "You won't come?"

He paused for a moment, then pinched the bridge

of his nose, and exhaled. "I'll be damned if you are not an exact replica of my sister. She never listened to me."

"What do you have arranged for the empty vessel of your pupil? It cannot stay here."

"We have nowhere else to keep him," Renato said. "If we can leave him here for just a few days—"

"Absolutely not. He will begin to bloat and stink. Treat your fallen warrior with respect. Keep his body preserved if you wish to reunite it with his soul."

Renato's gaze darted from Jayden's body to Hawa, who lay moaning in pain. "I'll figure something out. Perhaps Marzena will have an idea since our welcome here is clearly overstayed."

It was going to be dangerous. They were about to venture to a place only spoken of in myth and legend. A place where the dead dwelled, trapped beneath the roots of the tree of life. Nevertheless, if she had to face the gates of hell, she would. She had to, for Jay.

EPILOGUE

Sarian

He paced while his dogs sat on either side of him, holding so still Sarian would have thought they were statues if he didn't know better. One of the hounds growled.

Sarian watched carefully, his eyes focused intently on the king, who was quiet. Even though he would never admit it openly, his silence was frightening. Shouting orders, demanding the hellhounds to tear another underworlder to shreds; he was used to that. He had seen many unfortunate dwellers of the ninth realm torn limb from limb.

Sarian cleared his throat. "I will get it—"

"You fool," he bellowed, his eyes dark with wrath.

Sarian stood from his general's chair and straightened his coat. He had led the underworld army for thousands of years with great success. He had spent so many years of loyal service to the ancient king, and had earned his place as heir. Now if he could only convince the king. "I seized the stone before; I will do it again. You need not be concerned."

"You allowed the guardian to recover the stone, you inept halfling! You cannot even prevail over a group of inexperienced Riyata."

The largest dog cocked its head and released a threatening bark. The king stroked the hound between its ears and it submitted, as everything in the underworld did at his command.

The king looked at Sarian in disgust. "You are no match for the true heir of the throne. My son…" He turned his head sharply. "Does he still refuse his rightful place?"

Rage simmered in Sarian's bones. His breath quickened while he stood there, outwardly calm, but inside him churned a furious storm of wounded pride and provoked scorn.

"That boy is no more an heir to your throne than you are human."

The king stared at Sarian with such hate in his eyes, they lit up like burning coals, glowing a mixture of red and black.

While the lord of the underworld strode across the room, for a fleeting moment Sarian wondered if he'd said too much. The dogs followed closely at the king's side. The train to his royal cape dragged behind him, leaving molten lava on the ground where it touched. "You are running out of options, General." His tone was low and ominous. Sarian swallowed. "As you continue to fumble with the book, I grow weary of your doltishness. If you do not soon succeed at your task, I will be forced to take control of the situation."

One of the hounds barked ferociously.

Sarian startled, then composed himself. His gaze averted, he bowed.

As he returned to his seat, his fury and humiliation calmed. Another emotion took over—gratification.

The king did not know he had already broken the obedience spell, and had other plans for the middleworld.

It was the guardian he wanted.

He wanted her so badly the tips of his fingers tingled at the mere thought of her. When his mind lingered for too long, his lips burned with the taste of her skin.

Sarian's stomach tightened, remembering how she tasted as he ran his mouth along her neck and shoulders. Oh, how he wanted to consume her. He'd shown such restraint; restraint he did not have when he captured the last guardian. But he'd learned since then. He was willing to wait, to plot, and to be patient for the right moment to strike.

Sarian touched his chest, where a crescent-shaped scar sat hidden under his clothes. The wound was his fault, really. He didn't notice the pain until she nearly took a chunk out of his muscle.

She fought so vivaciously, and like a wild stallion being tamed, he enjoyed the process of breaking her. It was the thrill he lived for, which made his chest stir with exhilaration.

This guardian was so much like her mother. He sighed. It was unfortunate the last guardian was not more submissive. She would have made an equally suitable queen.

So powerful. So beautiful.

Just like her daughter was now.

While he taunted her in her dreams, it was difficult not to reach through her subconscious and take what he wanted. But like a fine wine that becomes more decadent with age, his patience would someday pay off.

Soon she would rule by his side, and he would take her as he pleased. She would complement him with her beauty, cower in his shadow, and then perform at his will.

Sarian opened his eyes and peered across the room. The king, with his hounds faithfully beside him, now also stood completely still. Not a word, nor a gesture. Not even the hint of a breath passing out of his lungs.

In one quick motion, the king locked eyes with him. "If you do not leave now, I will release the guards." The dogs stood at full attention, yelping and growling in anticipation.

Sarian stood and pressed down the creases in his clothes. After retrieving his cane from its spot propped against the wall, he limped across the room.

He would possess the guardian, and then be in control of the great powers of the middle and underworld. The stone, the guardian, and the book. When he did, he would overthrow this kingdom, slaughter the king, and have complete, absolute power over all.

Sneak Peek

Interlude

Book Two of the Stone Legacy Series

CHAPTER ONE

Tara

Tara rested her head on Peter's chest while they lay in his bed, watching TV. She kicked the blanket off of her, and then sighed. She should be happy. She finally had a family of sorts—a boyfriend who would do anything for her, and a best friend who was more like a sister. But she wasn't happy, and she couldn't tell anyone.

Peter's bed was somehow more comfortable than hers, and he seemed to want her there. That didn't stop her from feeling terrible over waking him up—for the third time that week. Her plush bed looked inviting, but it was home to her horrible nightmares. At least she wished they were nightmares…

She used to find solace in Zanya, back in the orphanage, when they were all each other had. Funny how life had changed so much, so fast. Best friends, they spent their entire lives dreaming of a future outside of the orphanage's walls, only to be sucked into a reality that surpassed even *their* idea of insane.

Back then it was Zanya whose dreams were filled with terror.

They'd been taken from the orphanage to Renato's estate in Belize, where they'd experienced so much, and discovered Zanya's dreams were real. Then they traveled to Moscow. That's when things had gone from bad to terrible for Tara.

Her throat tightened. She curled her fingers around Peter's T-shirt. Half asleep and with the TV on, he didn't seem to notice.

She fought to stay awake out of fear of reliving her time spent with Sarian, the underworld general. The nightly reminders hadn't gone away. In fact, they had only gotten worse.

It was just like when she was a kid, before she was taken from her mother by child protective services. Then, the fear of another encounter with her mother's "boyfriends" had coiled around her in a paralyzing way, stalking her day and night.

Her eyelids grew heavy, and her muscles ached for just a few hours of sleep. Being close to Peter somehow made it all better, for the moment. He chased away her demons and made her forget.

Peter pushed one of her curls aside and placed a soft kiss behind her ear. "How are you feeling?" he said in a groggy whisper.

She shrugged. He nudged her shoulder with his chin and rested his lips on the curve of her neck. His breath teased her skin.

She smiled and cringed away. "Knock it off. You know I'm ticklish."

"Mmm." He trailed kisses down to her shoulder.

The tickling subsided, and Tara's eyes fluttered closed. Her lips parted, fingers tightening around the blankets underneath her.

The smell of fresh rain filled the air. God, she loved his scent. The first time Peter had stepped close to her at Renato's house, it had washed over her like a wave of relief. After that, she just couldn't stay away.

"You think you can get some sleep?" he whispered. "You need it."

Tara composed herself and nodded. Even though he didn't push the issue, a tiny piece of her wished he'd keep kissing her neck to see where it went—see if she felt comfortable, without committing to anything from the beginning. After all, it was *she* who didn't want to take the next step in their relationship. Peter, however, would never put her into a situation she didn't ask for. He loved her too much. It was the first time she had experienced that kind of commitment from anyone. There was no way she'd risk ruining it with sex.

Tara sat up, rubbing the tight muscles in her neck. Every nightmare threw her body into a more tense and agitated state. Her appetite was all but gone, her sense of humor dimmed, and since the flashbacks had become more vivid, she'd nearly lost the ability to smile.

Peter's hands replaced hers and worked around her shoulders, massaging the knots into submission. Warmth radiated from his fingertips and spread through her body, soothing the tension. His healing ability had come in handy more than once over the last few weeks.

She exhaled and melted into him. "Thanks." She glanced at the digital clock. It was almost four in the morning. Guilt tore at her. "I really have to stop coming in here every time a memory breaks through. I'm not five."

"No, what you really have to do is tell Marzena that you're remembering more."

Marzena, the group's dreamwalker, had helped Tara unlock the hidden door in her mind, allowing them to find the memories to locate Sarian. If only she could go back in time and block that door with concrete and chains to seal the memories inside...

"I won't do that," Tara said. "Not yet anyway. It's not that bad." Only bad enough to wake her in a cold sweat with her stomach knotted and muscles so tender she was achy for days. "Besides, she isn't even in Moscow, so it's not like she could do anything about it."

"She would come back if you needed her."

"Well, I don't." Not if that meant putting her issues on display. "She already reached into my head once. I don't need her doing it again."

Peter leaned forward and wrapped his arms around her. "Even if it'll help?" He kissed her temple. "Come on, Tara. You know you can't keep doing this."

He was right, but she couldn't admit it aloud. She had been so selfish, staggering to his bedroom, shaking like a leaf. Not exactly a romantic midnight rendezvous. "I'm sorry I keep dragging you into this."

If she could just leave him alone, at least one of them would get some rest and not feel like a zombie.

With her stomach in knots, she scooted to the side of the mattress and stared blankly at the wall. Lights from the TV danced, casting shadows over the room.

"Whatever you're dealing with, I'm here for you." His voice was soft and comforting.

She swallowed down the urge to cry.

Zanya was still working to counter Sarian by travelling decades into the past with Renato, Arwan, Hawa, and Jayden, leaving Marzena, Tara, and Peter behind. Tara had tried to curb her bitterness about that, especially since she had nobody to channel it toward. It wasn't Zanya's choice to leave them. That's what she kept telling herself, anyway.

Tara rubbed her throbbing eyes. It was probably good that Marzena had gone back to Belize to manage the workers while they patched up the damage to Renato's house. It needed to be done before they all went back—if they went back. Renato's house had already become her home. Her heart ached at the memory of it under attack. And with Marzena gone, no one had to know Tara was steadily losing her mind. Again.

Peter grabbed the remote and flipped through the channels. "There's nothing on that's not in Russian."

She glanced at the screen. Had the actors been speaking Russian? Showed how much she'd been paying attention. He stopped on a news station with a woman speaking English in a heavy Russian accent. Behind her, emergency lights from police cars and ambulances flashed. Tara sighed and slumped her shoulders forward. "The news?"

"There's nothing else on." He lifted the remote. "You want me to just turn it off?"

She shook her head. "Nah. Leave it. At least it's in English." She tuned in for the first time.

"Officers responded to a call of a suspected gang clash outside of the Moscow Academy of Science. Authorities say a confrontation occurred between a student and an alleged gang member when the student's younger sister was forced into a gang-marked vehicle. The victim, who was wounded at the scene, was a freshman. Sadly, he died before the ambulance could respond, while the alleged attacker, who was also wounded, is now being treated at the Yakimanka Hospital where he is in critical condition."

Tara pushed the power button on the remote and the screen winked off. "I changed my mind. Even if it is in English, that's just depressing."

"Yeah. Seriously."

"Poor guy," she whispered, imagining the look of terror on the brother's face while his little sister was being dragged away. "I hope they get her back."

Peter moved to the far side of the bed. "Get who back?"

"The girl who was kidnapped."

"Yeah." His yawn deepened her guilt. "Come on." He patted the mattress. "Lie down next to me."

It was still dark out. If she left now, he could catch at least a few hours of sleep before the morning. She stood up and walked toward the door.

"Where are you going?"

She paused with her fingers wrapped around the handle. "I'm letting you get some rest. I'll be fine until morning."

Whether that would prove true or not, only time would tell.

ACKNOWLEDGMENTS

I seriously couldn't have written this series without my mother, Winnie Donat, who cooked many dinners and lead endless craft projects for my three beautiful children so I had time to work.

Also, a big thanks to Susan Walsh, who critiqued my work and helped fuel the evolution of my career.

ABOUT THE AUTHOR

A long-time enthusiast of things that go bump in the night, Theresa began her writing career as a journalism intern—possibly the least creative writing field out there. After her first semester at a local newspaper, she washed her hands of press releases and features articles to delve into the whimsical world of young adult paranormal romance.

Since then, Theresa has gotten married, had three terrific kids, moved to central Ohio, and was repeatedly guilt tripped into adopting a menagerie of animals that are now members of the family. But don't be fooled by her domesticated appearance. Her greatest love is travel. Having stepped foot on over a dozen countries, and traveled to sixteen U.S. states—including an extended seven-year stay in Kodiak, Alaska—she is anything but settled down.

Wherever life brings her, she will continue to weave tales of adventure and love with the hope her stories will bring joy and inspiration to her readers.

Facebook:
https://www.Facebook.com/theresa.dalayne

Twitter:
https://www.twitter.com/theresadalayne

Goodreads:
https://www.goodreads.com/author/show/7847410.
Theresa_DaLayne

Website:
http://TheresaDaLayne.com/

Instagram:
http://www.instagram.com/authortheresadalayne